BEEFCAKE & Mistakes

JUDI FENNELL

Published by Judi Fennell

Cover and interior design by www.formatting4U.com

Please contact the author at JudiFennell@JudiFennell.com.

For more information on the author and her works, please see www.JudiFennell.com

This book is also available in electronic formats at online retailers.

10 9 8 7 6 5 4 3 2 1

To my children

This is for you. Always.

Chapter One

He had a son.

Bryan Lassiter stood at the end of the grocery store aisle and stared at the little boy three feet in front of him.

The curly black hair was the same, including the identical cowlick above the right eye that drooped a little lower than the left, and the same dimple in his right cheek. The eyes, too, were the same. Those damned, cursed violet eyes that Bryan had hated ever since Julie Richardson had called them pretty in first grade. Him and Elizabeth Taylor.

And now this boy.

And if *those* weren't enough, it was the birthmark on the kid's arm that sealed the deal. Bry had the same one, shaped like a five-pointed star with a rounded tip on the bottom right spoke. Bryan had eventually had a tattoo put on top of it—in the shape of a star—but it was the same.

He had a son.

"Trevor? Where are you?" A pretty brunette rushed around the end cap, worry etched across her face. It softened when she saw the boy—the exact opposite of Bryan's reaction.

He didn't know her.

Oh, he'd slept with a lot of women in his life, but he did pride himself on remembering what they'd looked like, no matter how drunk he'd been—

No. That wasn't entirely true. Brad's bachelor party had passed by in one drunken haze and there could have been a stripper involved…

Considering Brad's party had been four years ago, and the kid looked to be about three or so… Yeah, it looked like it was more than possible, though he'd never been so drunk he hadn't worn a condom.

Which have been known to break.

Hell. Given that the kid looked like every one of his baby pictures, one night of debauchery and bad luck *could* have led to him having a son.

"Sweetheart, I told you never to run away from Mommy. This isn't the place to play hide-n-seek."

Bryan's eyes flew to "Mommy." About five-six, with curly brown, chin-length hair that she kept tucking behind her ears but which wouldn't stay, high cheekbones, and wide eyes—blue or gray, he couldn't be sure. Graceful movements of a dancer that would be lost in a strip joint, but the legs that went on forever definitely wouldn't be.

Had they been wrapped around him? Bryan felt himself grow hard just thinking about it.

But then he looked at Trevor and his whole *body* got hard. If that little boy was his, she'd kept him from him.

Did she even *know* who the father was?

"I sowwy, Mommy." Trevor stuck his thumb in his mouth and Bryan was even more convinced the boy was his.

Lots of kids sucked their thumb, but it was the way Trevor played with his cowlick—just like Bryan had. Until his finger had gotten caught in the tangles and his older brother Kyle had laughed at him. Mom had had to cut his finger free and that spike of hair at the front of his head had been one more thing for Kyle to tease him about. It'd been the last time Bryan had sucked his thumb.

"Yes, well, you scared me, honey. I don't want anyone to take you from me, okay? You have to stay with me." *Mommy* knelt down and hugged Trevor, the action tugging her figure-hugging tan pants low in the back.

No tramp stamp, so at least he'd had some taste in women when he was drunk. Even strippers.

Bryan shook his head. He of all people shouldn't judge her. He'd done some stripping in his day and now owned an exotic dance revue, BeefCake, Inc. But he and his partner Gage ran a classy business and No Fraternization was *the* top rule of the house. Too bad she hadn't prescribed to the same rule.

"Why would someone take me, Mommy?" Trevor stopped twirling his hair with a lock swirled around his finger.

Mommy smoothed a ring-less left hand over Trevor's hair, disengaging the tangled finger, then slid her palm down to cup his cheek. "Because you're a very special boy, Trevor. That's why I love you so much. So you need to stay with me at all times and not run away, okay? Even if you're playing."

Trevor nodded and Bryan felt as if he were looking in a mirror. "But *why* am I vewy special?"

She pulled him against her and kissed his cheek. "Because you're my little guy."

Bryan's vantage point gave him the perfect view of the fierceness of her expression when she said it, the quick tightening of her bicep beneath the short sleeve of her t-shirt as she hugged him. She loved the kid. But obviously not enough to give him the father he deserved.

Bryan had half a mind to tell her that, but supermarket aisles weren't exactly the best place for airing dirty laundry. He checked the time on his cell. An hour and a half until the meeting with Gage.

He slid his sunglasses on and pulled the baseball cap rim lower. He could hang around for a while. Follow her to see where she lived—and then plan when *would* be the best time to show up and discuss his fatherly rights.

***

Jenna Corrigan hugged her son and tried to will her heart to stop thundering. God, she'd thought she'd lost him.

Three years since he'd become hers, and she still hadn't gotten over the feeling that somehow, some way, he'd be taken from her. And she didn't mean by a stranger.

What if the father came back? What if he wanted his son?

Jenna squeezed her eyes tighter, hugged Trevor closer until he started to squirm and she had to let him go. Ah, to be so carefree.

That's what she had to focus on, not the fact that the guy who'd impregnated her sister and then skipped out might want to take on the responsibility he'd run from. Besides, she and Mindy had gone to a lawyer before her sister's cancer had progressed to the terminal stage and they'd done the paperwork so that when the end had inevitably come, there'd been no glitch making Trevor hers.

"Can I have some ice cweam?" Trevor slurped around his thumb.

Jenna smiled. If only all of life's ills could be made better with ice cream. "Sure, honey. What flavor?"

"Wocky Woad. It's my favowite."

This week. Last week it'd been peppermint stick.

Jenna released him from her hug, her body instantly craving his closeness again. She hadn't carried him inside her, but she might as well have. She'd slept with him every night for the first three months after Mindy's death—more for her comfort than his.

She stood up and put all thoughts of *that* from her mind. This was her life now. *Trevor* was her life. She had to go on. She *would* go on.

She reached out her hand. "Let's go pick some out then, kiddo."

"Okay, Mommy." Wet fingers slid into her palm and Jenna wouldn't have it any other way.

They headed down the aisle and Jenna caught the smile on a man's face as he averted his head, the rim of the baseball cap obscuring his eyes. He'd been listening in. Probably a father himself, if that wry grin was anything to go by. Knew the relief she'd felt at realizing her child wasn't gone.

As always, the thud in her stomach hit with excruciating pain and Jenna paused for half a step behind the man. Would that feeling ever go away?

"Can I have chocwate, too?" Trevor, as always, pulled her back to the present. A place that was so much better to be than their past.

"There's chocolate in Rocky Road, Trev. Bits and pieces."

"Oh. Okay." His thumb went back into his mouth and he switched to her other side, the fingers that normally swirled his hair now gripping her hand. She should probably work on getting him to quit the thumb-sucking, but giving up a comfort thing went against the grain with her. She knew, first hand, how important comfort things were.

Especially when life could be a little too tough without them.

Chapter Two

"Come on, Trevor, it's time for your nap." Jenna pulled the stuffed sock monkey from between the sofa and the chair, thanking St. Anthony and whoever else was responsible for her finding it. Naptime did not go well without Mr. Monkey.

"I don't wanna."

Didn't look like naptime was going to go well now, regardless. Jenna sighed. Naps were getting tricky these days; Trevor wasn't into wanting them and Jenna wasn't into wanting to stop them. She needed these precious two hours for work. Single parenthood wasn't conducive to establishing a career, but Jenna had been lucky when she'd moved back to not only find her teaching position, but also have it be at a school that had daycare. But that daycare wasn't free, so her summer tutoring sessions had to make up the difference. For the past two years, she'd scheduled the sessions during Trevor's nap, but next year she was going to have to come up with something else, which would involve paying a babysitter, money she didn't necessarily want—or have—to spend. She couldn't rely on her friend Cathy's help *all* the time.

"Come on, Trevor. You can have some ice cream when you wake up." She hated resorting to bribery. If only she could ask her mother—

No. That option was out. *Ellen* had given her enough grief about having Trevor to begin with. Jenna hadn't told her mother the truth about Trevor's parentage because Mindy was actually her *half*-sister, the result of the affair that had ended her parents' marriage. Ellen, as she preferred Jenna to call her—and as Jenna preferred to call her—would have relished the idea that Mindy had had an out-of-wedlock child and been more than happy to tell anyone who'd listen what a tramp the girl had been. So Jenna hadn't told her.

"Trevor, come on." She and Mr. Monkey headed into the kitchen to remove a recalcitrant little boy from behind the trashcan and into his "big boy" bed where he belonged. Now if he'd only stay.

She hunkered down by his hiding spot. "Mommy needs you to be a big boy and take your nap. And Mr. Monkey is tired." She waggled the toy in front of him, but Trevor wasn't taking the bait.

"Big boys don't take naps," he grumped, wedging himself tighter against the wall. "Only babies take naps. Michael says so."

Jenna bit back her retort. Michael was an authority on anything and everything according to her son. Of course, Michael was only four, but that didn't matter to Trevor. Jenna got the "Michael Report" every day when she picked her son up from daycare. "Michael did this," and "Michael did that." Nine times out of ten, however, it was more along the lines of "Michael kicked the teacher," or "Michael broke Rebecca's crayon," instead of any great revelation from the learned, four-year-old sage. Michael sounded like he needed a lot of therapy.

"Michael is wrong, Trevor."

Oops, wrong tactic. As far as Trevor was concerned, Michael was God.

"I don't wanna." He stuck his thumb in his mouth and started slurping.

Jenna glanced at the clock. Fifteen minutes until Jason got here. If it were any of the other students, Jenna could maybe try to settle Trevor in front of television to keep him occupied, but the little boy idolized Jason. He always barraged the teen with a hundred questions about his "cool" truck. The orange-and-red-striped clunker wasn't much in the way of mechanical ability, but to a three-and-a-half-year-old truck nut, it was "cool." Jason was a good sport about it, but he had to take the SATs in the fall, and they really needed to focus today before football camp started.

"Trevor, you have to take a nap. It's your job, remember? Just like Mommy has a job, you have a job, too."

"Wike Michael's daddy? He wears a tie. Can I wear a tie?"

So Michael was good for something. His daddy.

Jenna couldn't ignore that twinge of pain now any more than she'd been able to the earlier. But she couldn't think about Carl. He obviously hadn't been the man she'd thought when he'd dumped her for adopting a baby.

Trevor didn't need men like him in his life. And neither did she.

Still, the guilt that, somewhere, Trevor did have a daddy wouldn't go away. Mindy just hadn't known who that daddy was. A big, cold INFORMATION NOT RECORDED graced that line of Trevor's birth certificate.

Would the father care about Trevor? Want him, maybe?

And what if he did? What if he came back and took her to court? Would a judge recognize her rights?

It was a question Jenna never wanted to have to answer.

She got Trevor into bed with the promise of buying him *and* Mr. Monkey ties when they woke up, then hurried down to the dining room she'd converted into an office-slash-classroom. A far cry from the house she and Carl had been looking at, complete with its own playroom for their kids, before Carl had called off their engagement. Fiancé, big home, now her living room… she'd sacrificed a lot for the good of the toys.

And, yet, when she looked around at the primary-colored chaos, she wasn't sorry in the least. Well, that she'd had to sacrifice the living room. Carl, on the other hand…

She was sorry he hadn't been the man she'd thought he was.

The doorbell rang and Jenna winced. Jason knew not to ring the bell.

She listened at the bottom of the stairs, but there wasn't a peep out of Trevor. Thank goodness.

She hurried to the door and opened it, fully prepared to remind Jason exactly why he shouldn't ring the bell, but Jason wasn't standing there.

A man was. Or rather, *the* man was. The one from the grocery store. She would recognize that build, and that delicious aroma of soap and him, anywhere. And the baseball cap, too.

"Can I help you?"

The man gave her the once-over. Not that she could tell since his eyes were covered by his sunglasses, but it was more of a feeling. Every part of her tingled as he perused her.

That was ridiculous. She couldn't see his eyes, so how did she know when they reached which part of her body?

And what was she doing even thinking about it in the first place?

And, more importantly, what was he doing looking?

"Is there something you need? I've got a student coming over in less than ten minutes, so you're going to have to make this quick."

"You give lessons? That's a twist." His voice hovered somewhere above bass but below tenor—and vibrated along her spine like an orchestra. He didn't need to stare at her to get her attention.

And the way he filled out his t-shirt *kept* her attention.

Oh, for Pete's sake. She wasn't sixteen anymore. She was a mom and she had a client coming over, so Mr. Tall, Dark, and Gorgeous needed to hurry up and leave. "I'm sorry—what did you say?"

"What's your going rate?"

He wanted her to tutor his kid? Kind of a rude way to go about asking. But she could use the money so beggars couldn't be choosers. Not in this house.

"Forty dollars an hour." Competitive, but not unaffordable.

"*How* much?" Obviously he didn't agree. "Are you kidding me? Forty bucks?" He shook his head. "Lady, you need to have some standards."

"Look… Sir. I do have all the standards the state requires. I can't guarantee results, but my clients have recommended me to their friends, so I must be doing something right." Jason's truck pulled up at the curb. "Look, I have to go." She grabbed one of her cards from the key shelf next to the door. "Here. Take this, think it over, and call me. We can work something out."

"Hey, Ms. C. You doin' okay?" Jason gave the requisite chin nod to Tall, Dark, and Gloomy as he climbed the stairs to her porch, the weathered oak creaking under the muscle of a seventeen-year-old who wasn't banking his future on getting a football scholarship but was definitely working toward that goal.

"Everything's fine, Jason. Ready for your session?" She stepped back to let Jason in, then gave the man a smile. "I look forward to speaking with you." She started to close the door.

The guy slammed a hand against it, effectively halting its momentum, and his other hand grabbed her arm. "What are you doing? That kid's not even eighteen!"

Half her senses registered the anger in his voice; the other half registered something entirely different.

Her skin… *sizzled* where it met his. Sizzled. She was

surprised she couldn't hear the spit and fizz or smell smoke, but that was most definitely fire between them.

"Look—" He glanced at the card he held in his hand on the door. "Ms. Corrigan. You can't just invite a minor into your home without anyone knowing."

Jenna shook her head, trying to regain focus. She didn't need to be attracted to this guy, especially not with his erratic behavior. She yanked her arm free and he almost lurched into the house. "His parents know where he is. Why wouldn't they? They're footing the bill."

Jason stuck his head out of the office. "Is there a problem, Ms. C.?"

Jenna arched an eyebrow at the visitor. "No, there's no problem, Jason. I'll be right in. Why don't you get everything set up? This gentleman was just leaving."

And she made sure he would by firmly shutting the door in that gorgeous face.

Bryan thought nothing could hit him harder than seeing a little boy who could possibly be his son in the grocery store aisle in his hometown.

Boy, was he wrong.

She, this Jenna Corrigan, was taking clients—underage ones!—into her home. Where his son was. And there was no way anyone was going to convince him that that *client* was there to do anything other than make time with the instructor—he'd seen the interest in the kid's eyes. All male, carnal lust. That kid was here for one reason and one reason only and yeah, it had to do with stripping. But not as a career choice.

What was she thinking? What were the kid's *parents* thinking?

Bryan knew what the *kid* was thinking. Hell, if he could have gotten a shot at someone who looked like her when he'd been seventeen—

What the hell was wrong with him? She was a high-priced hooker—or, at forty bucks an hour, a rather low-priced one.

And she Thought It Was Okay.

Bryan looked at her card. *Jenna Corrigan, By Private Instruction.* Jesus, she didn't even *bother* trying to hide what she was doing.

He had to go to the police. He had to. He was an honest citizen. A concerned one. He'd heard about suburban housewives who turned tricks in their picket-fenced homes; he'd just never actually believed it.

And with underage boys? And no one raising a fuss? The kid's parents actually *paying* for it? What was this world coming to?

Bryan somehow managed to make it off the porch without breaking his neck, but he was still flabbergasted when he reached his truck. Sure, the economy had been tough on everyone and maybe a baby had done a number on her stripper figure—though from what he'd seen, not much—but prostitution? And with her child in the house? *His* child?

Bryan pulled away from the curb, memorizing the truck's license plate. If the kid's parents weren't going to do anything about it—no, scratch that, because they *were* doing something about it, but not anything he'd ever heard of—he had to turn her in and save that little boy from being raised in that kind of environment.

If Trevor *was* his son, it'd make getting custody easier.

Chapter Three

"Hey, Ms. C?" Jason did a bongo-type drum roll on her office wall. "You coming?"

"Um, yeah." Jenna stopped staring after the man who'd turned her world upside down with one touch of his hand.

She shook her head. *Get a grip*. She had a job to do, a child to care for, and bills to pay. Daydreaming about a gorgeous guy with major attitude problems was not conducive to any of them. Besides, there was the distinct possibility she'd see him again.

Next time she'd check for a ring.

Jenna closed the door, double-checking the lock again. Sometimes she and Jason got so engrossed in their work that she didn't want to take a chance Trevor would wake up from his nap and try to go outside without her knowing. Not that he ever had, but she'd heard stories from friends whose kids had wandered off to play with their best friend and were too young to remember to tell their parents. That wasn't a scare she wanted to live through. Today's was enough. She'd turned her back for one second and he'd been gone around an end cap.

Jason stood up when she walked into the office. "Who was that guy, Ms. C.?"

Jenna shrugged. "I have no idea. He needs a tutor though, so I guess I'll find out."

"Was he bothering you? I could, you know." Jason

cracked his knuckles. "Have a talk with him for you."

Jenna hid her amusement. Jason had never been so overt with his crush before. "I don't know who he is, but I'm fine. No need for brutality. I guess he just wasn't aware of how much extra help costs. Not like you, right?"

She had to hand it to the teenager. Dyslexia made schoolwork that much harder, and he could have skated by on his football laurels, but Jason had dreams. Big ones. Enough to promise his parents that he'd pay them back every cent of what they were paying her if he didn't do well enough on the SATs to qualify for early decision.

No pressure or anything. For both of them.

"I think I finally got the hang of the math problems, Ms. C." Jason waited for her to sit. Chivalrous, but she hoped his crush wouldn't become an issue. Mr. Tall, Dark, and Gorgeous' visit had opened some pheromone floodgates that hadn't been oiled in a long time.

"Great, Jason. The last hurdle done for our last session. I'm sure you'll do fine on the SATs."

"Yeah, well, except for the essays. I don't think I'm gonna pull that part off."

And there went the pheromones to be replaced with Seeds of Doubt. She'd heard that same sentiment from so many kids. The ones who came to her were usually close to failing, if not already doing so. So far behind, catching up didn't seem feasible.

Mindy had been like that.

Jenna shook her head. She couldn't think about Mindy. She'd loved her kid sister, but she was more than aware of the wrong decisions Mindy had made in her life. It's why she now had a three-and-a-half-year-old asleep upstairs.

Not that Trevor was a bad decision. Matter of fact, the best decision Mindy had ever made was to keep the baby. The second best was to sign him over to her when the inevitable had begun.

Mindy had tried to make up for all her mistakes. Flighty and irresponsible, bad choices… still, she'd had a good heart.

If only Jenna could have made her mother see that she'd at least have one family member—and sadly, the only one she had left—on her side, but the subject of Trevor always brought up the subject of Jenna's own "mistake" when she'd been seventeen.

She caressed her stomach, remembering what it'd felt like for those three months before Nature and a drunk driver had made Ellen's disgrace go away. That pain was still raw. Sure, getting pregnant in high school hadn't been the best idea, but that didn't mean she didn't mourn the loss. Then and now.

"… the essays. Right?"

Jenna shook her head. "I'm sorry, Jason, what did you say?"

She had to focus. Jason was paying her for her time, not for her painful memories.

"I said, too bad there aren't any numbers in the essays."

Jenna caught herself before she squeezed his hand. Insecure and worried he might be, but Jason was on the brink of manhood. No sense courting disaster. She settled for a quick tap with the eraser end of her pencil on the table. "True. But you can do it. Just use the strategies we've worked on. Look how well you've done in English Comp that way. You'll get through the essay part of the test."

Jason smiled, a lazy, I've-got-the-world-by-the-horns smile that, twelve years ago, would have had her teenage heart going pitter-pat. Had, actually, thanks to Dave Miller. And *no thanks* to Dave Miller that same heart had been broken that horrible morning when he and life had one-two-punched her, destroying her hopes, her heart, and most of her family. Her own smiles had gone on hiatus until Trevor had come into her life.

Jenna reached for Jason's notebook where they'd practiced the writing exercises. Having Trevor made all of it worthwhile. It's why she hadn't given him up for Carl. Why she wasn't giving him up for anyone. The next man in her life would have to love both her *and* her son.

Or he wouldn't be the man for her.

***

The police sergeant wouldn't stop laughing. Neither would the deputy, the two guys on desk jobs in the corner, and the dispatcher. Even the lunchtime pizza delivery guy contributed a couple of chuckles.

But Bryan didn't find any of it funny.

"So you think Jenna Corrigan is running a house of prostitution in her home?" Sergeant Benton let out a loud "whoa!" and doubled over in laughter.

"Look, Sergeant, I know what I saw." Bryan tried to his voice steady. "She even told me how much she's charging."

That stopped the laughter. Benton's eyes narrowed. "You propositioned her?"

"Yes—no. Of course not. She just started telling me what she did and I was like you; I couldn't believe it. I had to ask what she charged. It just sort of slipped out."

"I'll tell you what's slipped, Lassiter." The sergeant slid his chair closer to the desk, rested his elbow on it and jabbed a finger toward Bryan's head. "Your brain. You got hit one too many times on the head playing college ball. Good thing you never played pro. I knew Jenna's dad my entire life. That girl isn't hooking."

Bryan reined in his temper. Sam Benton's son, Matt, had played backup QB all four years of high school when Bryan had been the starter; there was a lot of resentment there. Always had been. He should have known he wouldn't get anywhere with Sam. And he hadn't even *mentioned* Trevor yet.

"And you might want to think this whole pot-kettle thing. After all, we *know* you're peddling smut. You're not one to talk."

More temper-reining. He was *not* peddling smut. The dancers were well trained. Sexy without veering toward lewd. The club had standards—including not putting four-year-olds in the line of sexual fire.

Speaking of which… Bryan checked his cell. He was going to be late for that meeting with Gage and the guy who owned the property next to the club if he didn't hurry. Gage's fiancée had come up with the idea of having both male and female dancers, which had not only put the kibosh on some townspeople's claims of sexism, it'd doubled the club's demographic. Now they had couples showing up for date nights, and the money was really starting to come in, so they needed more space.

Maybe *he* should hire Jenna. Keep her off the streets, so to speak. At least, then, he could keep an eye on her.

And maybe a hand or two, just to remember what she'd felt like that night—

Yeah, so not going to happen.

"So you're telling me you don't believe me?"

The sergeant leaned back in his chair and stretched the waistband of his no-descript uniform pants. "Damn right, son. You might be a genius on the football field, but when it comes to Jenna Corrigan, you're dumber than a chicken in a foxhole. Jenna's no more hooking than I am."

With the sergeant's beer gut preceding the rest of him by a good foot and a half, that statement was met with more laughter.

Bryan did not like being laughed at.

He stood, knowing his size was intimidating, and he stabbed a finger onto the desk in front of the sergeant for good measure. "Look, Sergeant, I'm a concerned citizen. I know what I saw and heard, and I reported it. You have to investigate."

The sergeant raised an eyebrow at him. "I don't tell you how to do your job, Lassiter, don't tell me how to do mine. I'll follow procedure, just like always. But I don't have to be thrilled to let Jenna know there's a nut job on the loose in this town."

Let's see how much of a nut job the sergeant thought he was after interviewing the kid who was at Jenna's right this very minute.

An image of that young kid, all sweaty and horny, leering at Jenna, tied Bryan's stomach in knots. Jesus. He was *not* jealous of a high school kid.

Of course not; he was worried about Trevor. That's what this was about. His son. His possible son.

No. Trevor *was* his. He knew it; he just didn't know *how* Trevor was his son. He would have remembered sleeping with Jenna. She was exactly the type of woman he liked—well, except for the stripper part. Yeah, it was double standard, but Bryan didn't share. Never had. Never needed to. He'd always gotten women, and just because he'd had his choice didn't mean he'd gorged himself to the point of not being able to remember something as intimate as making love with them.

Now *there* was an image. Jenna, beneath him, all hot and sweaty and writhing and—

Shit. Bryan shoved his hands into his pockets to hide his growing hard-on. He needed to get out of the police station or Benton would think *he* was the one who needed to be investigated.

Chapter Four

"Hey, Jenna!" Sergeant Benton grabbed the railing as he hit the third step to her porch. An improvement. Usually he grabbed it on the first. His diet must be working.

Jenna lowered the watering can. The Mellors' elm kept most of the sun's damage off the impatiens. The flowers could wait a little longer.

"Hi, Sarge." He'd been "Sarge" ever since Trevor had started speaking. It was the closest he'd been able to manage and Sarge had been fine with it. "What can I do for you? I've set out yogurt and apples for Trevor. Would you like some?" The ruse was her contribution to his diet whenever he stopped by—which, in the time since she'd moved back, was pretty frequent and directly attributable to Trevor. She'd often wondered if one of Sarge's sons could be Trevor's father.

But she hadn't asked. Didn't want to know.

"Is he up?"

"Not yet. I had a hard time getting him down, so I didn't think he was this tired. But I guess you never know with kids."

"Not just kids."

"What?"

Sarge shook his head. "Nothing. I will take a little snack, if you don't mind."

Jenna held the screen door open and swept her hand inside. "My pleasure."

Sarge, however, was old school. His hand did a bigger sweep than hers, one involving his entire arm. “After you.”

How could she resist? Jenna led him into her kitchen, the room she was most proud of in the house. The place had barely been habitable when she’d bought it—the main reason she’d been able to afford it. A rental for twelve years, the house had been begging for love and attention—two things Jenna had had plenty of.

Good thing, because many times they’d had to go further than her bank account.

“Iced tea or lemonade?” She tugged on the heavy door of the antique Philco refrigerator. It’d been too heavy to move when she’d bought the place. She’d never seen one before, so when the guy who’d come to take it off her hands told her how much it was worth, she’d hired him to fix it instead. It’d been her first monetary investment in the house other than the house itself, and had set the tone of the kitchen.

Now a bright red, it was the perfect complement to the black-and-white checkerboard tile floor she’d laid and the white cabinets and appliances beneath the wall of windows she’d scraped, sanded, re-glazed, and painted. A chrome retro table and chairs set she’d picked up at a yard sale and scoured with steel wool butted up to the interior wall. The red vinyl on the seats matched the gingham valance over the windows. Shelves full of milk glass bottles and vases that had decorated the countertops until Trevor started to walk now filled the shelf that ringed the top of the nine-foot walls.

“Iced tea’s fine.” Sarge sat at the head of the table—the best spot to see Trevor’s face when he came through the doorway. Sarge and his wife, Beverly, had two grown sons, but neither had any kids. Because of the Benton’s friendship with her (and Mindy’s) father, they were the closest things to grandparents Trevor had since Mindy’s mother had died, and he the closest thing to a grandchild for them.

"Yogurt?" She yanked again and the heavy door opened.

"You have any with blueberries? Strawberry seeds stick in my teeth."

Jenna sorted through the towers Trevor liked to make with his favorite snack on the bottom shelf. No rhyme or reason as to why he made his asymmetrical stacks the way he did, but there'd be time enough for organization later on in life.

"No blueberry. I have plain vanilla, though. I can add some banana slices if you like."

The sergeant waved the yogurt cup over. "Don't go to the trouble. I'll take it as is. Here, have a seat." He slid the chair next to him out with his foot.

"Thanks, but I have to get dinner started. Trevor wants ravioli tonight and I should thaw out the ground beef for the meatballs."

"Jenna, please. Sit."

Sarge hadn't used that tone with her since that awful afternoon in the hospital when she'd come out of surgery—and her father hadn't.

She groped for the back of the chair closest to her. Trevor's. But she didn't care. She didn't think her legs would carry her to the other side of the table. "Wh… What is it?"

Oh, God. What was it? Beverly? Sarge?

"I had a complaint, today. At the station."

"A complaint?"

He nodded. "About you."

"Me?" Now that really didn't make any sense. Who could complain about her? After the scandal she'd created in high school, bringing attention to herself was the *last* thing she did these days.

"Yes. Someone thinks you're, um…" Sarge rubbed the back of his neck. It, and the rest of his face, turned redder than any strawberry.

"Thinks I'm what?"

He smacked his lips, glanced at her, then folded his hands on the table and stared intently at them. "Someone thinks you're running a… bordello. Here. Out of your house."

That was one she hadn't seen coming. A bordello? A house of— "Someone thinks I'm a hooker?"

Sarge was shaking his head. "I know. I can't believe it either."

"That's why you're here? To find out if I am? Really? You didn't just tell the nosy busybody to mind her own business?"

Or did Sarge really think—

Hell. One mistake in her past and even Sarge was willing to think *that* of her?

She should never have come back. She should have just stayed where she was and built their life there, never hoping for anything from her mother because the woman wasn't capable of it anyway.

"Who was it?"

Sarge looked at her sheepishly. "I can't tell you that."

"Oh really? Yet someone with more time than sense can accuse me of that and you have to come disrupt my day? I don't believe this."

She slammed her palms on the table and stood. God, when would it be over? Hadn't she paid for that one mistake enough? Bad enough Dave had dropped her—and accused her of sleeping with someone else—but then to lose her baby the same day *and* her father… And now this.

Jenna walked to the sink and leaned her hands on the cool porcelain edge. She stared out the window—right into the Mellors' screened-in porch. Had *they* accused her? They had the perfect vantage point to see all the teenagers going in and out of her house, but those were *kids* for Pete's sake.

She hung her head. God, what a mess. And now Trevor would grow up with the insinuation—

"If it helps," Sarge said, "it's not one of the neighbors. And he's not really one to talk. But I had to do my job. You understand."

Oh she understood.

He.

The guy who'd been on her porch two hours ago when Jason had shown up—

Oh no. *Forty dollars an hour.*

And Jason's parents paying her—

Jenna's shoulders started to shake. Forty bucks. No wonder he'd told her she should have some standards.

"Jen? Honey? Don't cry. I told him he was nuts. But I had to do something since he came to the station—"

She whirled around. "Other people know about this?" A funny mistake was one thing, but gossip and public ridicule was something else entirely.

"Everyone else told him it was a crock, too. Don't you worry. We've got your back." Sarge reached for something in his pocket, the chair leg scuffing the tile as he shoved away from the table. "But for the record, I do need to ask you to state what you're doing here."

He flipped open the spiral notebook and licked the tip of his pencil.

She thought only dime-store novel detectives nibbled their pencil tips, but apparently there was something to be said for small towns and their old ways.

Sadly, there wasn't nearly as much to be said for small town gossip mills. Whether or not she was guilty of Mr. Tall, Dark, and Idiotic's assertions, the fact that he'd made them—and Sarge had had to "investigate"—was going to toss her name through all the mahjong and bridge clubs until the next scandal.

She took a deep breath. *This too shall pass.* She had to stay here for Trevor. She couldn't run like she had before.

This was the only home he knew. She had a good job where she could have him on campus with her and be able to afford their home. Her childhood friends, the ones who hadn't left, were here, and, most importantly, memories of her father and sister.

"Okay, Sarge, for the record, no, I am not running a house of ill repute out of my home. I have a tutoring business. Everything is above board. I pay my taxes, have a special permit from the township, advertise, and get paid for helping kids improve their grades. I can provide testimonials if you need them."

Sarge dotted an *i* in his notebook then flipped it closed. He slid it and the pencil stub into his breast pocket. "That won't be necessary, Jenna. We're good. I just have to file the official report and we can all forget about this."

Easy for him to say. She wasn't going to forget about it—

Nor the man who'd put her back on the town's gossip radar.

Chapter Five

Bryan drove by her house again on the way to his meeting with Gage. Yeah, it was out of the way, but he couldn't, in good conscience, leave that kid in his son's home.

Luckily, the battered pick-up was gone. Good. The last thing he needed was a hormonal punk trying to out-testosterone him.

He pulled against the opposite curb two houses down. It was a nice street. Homey. Victorian houses, picket fences, big old trees, perfect for climbing or fort-making. His dad had made the perfect hideaway for him and Kyle before he'd died. Bryan had been planning to do the same for his kids someday.

No time like the present.

He opened his door, about to step into the street when *she* appeared on the front porch.

Jenna Corrigan. Bryan pulled the door closed and turned in his seat. Resting his right forearm on the steering wheel, he fingered her business card. Beige with brown lettering. *All your instructional needs*. As innocuous as could be. Gave nothing away. Perfect for vetting the clientele before taking on any unwanted assignments.

How in God's name had that muscle-bound kid passed muster?

Bryan snorted. Did he really need to ask? She was late twenties/early thirties; the kid was just coming into his sexual prime. Bryan was no math scholar, but the equation was easy enough to solve.

It was the parents' involvement that stumped him. The kid's parents were actually *paying* for it? God! His dad had died when he'd been fourteen, and, while Henry Lassiter had been a great father, he couldn't see Dad being *quite* so progressive.

Jenna dead-headed a few flowers from one of the hanging baskets and her shirt slipped free of her waistband. Tanned, toned skin peeked at him.

Of course it would be. All that dancing and other, er, aerobics would keep her in shape. Maybe not stripper shape, but—

Who the hell was he kidding? That *was* a stripper's shape. The woman was perfectly proportioned—emphasis on *perfect*.

Bryan pinched the bridge of his nose. It didn't matter how perfect she was in the body arena; it only made her more unfit to raise his child.

He reached for the handle again and had the door halfway open when Sergeant Benton joined her on the porch.

Good. The cop was doing his job.

Bryan squinted, trying to see her face, bracing himself against the tears he'd probably see. It was her own fault. If she weren't doing something illegal, she'd have no reason to…

…be smiling at Sergeant Benton.

Nor should she be *hugging* the guy.

Shit. Was *that* how it was? No wonder the cop didn't want anyone reporting her.

Hell. This had just gotten more complicated.

Bryan put on his sunglasses and hit the pavement the minute the sergeant's car turned the corner. He sprinted across the street, taking the four porch steps in two.

The smile she'd had for Benton disappeared when she

spun around and saw him, but only briefly. Then she pasted on a new one, but it didn't quite reach her eyes.

Of course, he wasn't paying her or giving her kickbacks or looking the other way or whatever it was ol' Sarge gave her in return for one of those smiles—and maybe a whole lot more.

Bryan allowed himself to give her a quick once-over.

"You're back." The frost in her voice when she answered told him she wasn't overjoyed at the fact. "Is there something I can do for you?"

If she only knew. "As a matter of fact, yes. There is." He held up her business card between his first two fingers. "This. I'd like to hire you."

She arched a delicate eyebrow. "You do."

Not a question. As if she'd expected it. But if Benton had told her what he'd accused her of, she wouldn't have been smiling when the cop left.

Unless the two of them were cooking something up.

Bryan cleared his throat. Conspiracy theories? First, he was seeing previously-unknown sons, and now this. He was getting paranoid. She'd given him her card; of course it wasn't a surprise he was back. Sarge was a professional; he wouldn't have spilled what he was there to investigate and he sure as hell wouldn't have told her who'd accused her.

"Yeah, I do want to hire you." First time in his life he'd ever hired a hooker. He raked a hand through his hair. Even though he was hiring her, it wasn't for what she thought—not for what anyone would think. The *last* thing he'd do is take advantage of what he was paying for. Not if he wanted the charges against her to stand up in a court of law—without getting his ass thrown in jail.

"Are you sure my *standards* are up to yours? I mean, since I have such low ones." She reached down for the watering can, giving him a quick peek down her shirt.

On purpose? Maybe that was how she bargained. Give the customers a little sample, let them see what they'd be getting—

"How much for the rest of the summer?"

She rose slowly, the watering can still on the porch. Her eyes narrowed.

Was she calculating her hourly rate? Forty hours at forty bucks per—not a bad weekly amount for a normal job. But for hers?

Hey, Bryan liked sex as much as the next guy—some said even more—but he'd want a lot more than forty bucks an hour to do it full time.

He didn't even think he *could* do it full time.

But then she cocked her hip and looked at him from under her lashes, making him re-think that last thought. His body was definitely up for giving it a go.

Pity he didn't remember being with her. That night had been one big vodka-infused blur.

"I don't work full time in the summer. I have a son to take care of."

"I'll pay you to be available twenty-four seven. What's that worth to you?"

This time he did see wheels churning in her head and dollar signs in her eyes as if her face was a slot machine. A pretty slot machine, but one nonetheless.

"You can't afford it."

"You let me be the judge of that." He crossed his arms. "How much?"

"If we go by my hourly rate—"

"How much?"

She nibbled her lip."Ten thousand."

"Done." It'd take up the majority of the ROI he'd just received from BeefCake, Inc., but he would've paid twice that. Getting her to stop hooking was worth ten grand; her taking the money and him using it against her in a custody battle? Priceless.

"I want cash."

Of course she did. And he'd demand a receipt. "Fine."

"All of it. Up front."

At least she was a savvy businesswoman. He should be happy her contribution to his son's DNA was more than just good looks.

"Not a problem. I'll be back tomorrow." He stuck out his hand. This was, after all, a business deal.

But the touch of her skin on his felt as far from business as you could get. Almost made him wish he *was* going to get his money's worth.

She tugged, but Bryan didn't let go. Matter of fact, he held her hand tighter. Tugged *her* closer. So close he could smell the scent of the flowers clinging to her hair and see her eyes—blue, not gray—widen. So close he thought about getting even closer and running his tongue over that cute Cupid's bow mouth of hers.

How many others already had?

Right.

Bryan leaned back, just enough to break the hold those lips had over him. "And let's get something straight. From now on, you work for me, so no more Jasons. Got it?"

Jenna tossed her head back and the smile she gave him was definitely real. Went all the way through those beautiful blue eyes. But it wasn't exactly friendly.

This time, *she* took a step closer. Until her knuckles were touching his abs, and his, hers. "*I* get it. But *you* need to get something. I don't work *for* you. I work for myself and my son. I am *employed* by you. There's a difference and it's a big one." She nudged him in the gut. "Don't *you* forget *that*."

Oh he wouldn't. Just as he couldn't forget that he'd offered—and she'd agreed to—money for sex. And, ya know? Even if he wasn't planning on collecting, she owed him.

A kiss ought to do the trick.

One second Jenna had been gloating about pulling one over on this guy, and the next she was in so far over her head she couldn't see daylight.

Who kissed like this?

He was built like a professional athlete, all hard, ripped muscle, and he towered over her with leashed intensity. Strong fingers threaded through her curls, his big hands cradling her head. Lips that felt like heaven on hers. Just a tiny nip. Fluttery, even. But they sent a straight shot right to her core, fire burning along every nerve ending she possessed.

He changed the angle of her head slightly, but, oh, it was enough to turn that fire up a few thousand degrees. His lips pressed more firmly against hers and she knew, in the far… back… dim recesses of her brain that this wasn't a good idea, but for the life of her she couldn't stop him.

Not that she was trying very hard.

It'd been a long time since Carl had walked out. Longer still since Carl had kissed her like this—actually, Carl had *never* kissed her like this.

Mr. Gorgeous pressed her back against the porch railing, changing the angle and the pressure and the softness and the whatever-it-was that zinged through her, and Jenna realized *no one* had kissed her like this. Ever.

When he kissed her yet again, a little more pressure, a little more insistent, Jenna realized she didn't even know his name.

Then he flicked his tongue along the seam of her lips, and she realized her own name was becoming a distant memory.

And when he moved his hand along her back, then wrapped his arm around her waist, hiking her into the *perfect* position to feel that, hey, he wasn't kidding here, she stopped realizing anything, and her body went on autopilot.

A more-than-welcome involuntary gasp when his

fingertips danced across the top of her backside gave him the perfect opportunity to slip his tongue inside and taste her. Which gave her the perfect opportunity to return the favor, and, man, did he taste good.

She leaned in to him and that was good, too. More than good. She slid her hands around him, feeling his obliques clench, his back muscles contract, and his legs bracket hers. It'd been so long since she'd felt this. This desire. Carnal and hot and utterly unexpected.

From a guy who thought she was a hooker.

When his lips moved along her jaw to the hollow beneath her ear, Jenna let herself fume for a bit on what he thought she was. What she was letting him think she was.

Dammit. So, okay, he didn't know her, but a hooker? Really? What was it about her that made him think so?

His breath might be the right temperature of *hot* against her throat, but that thought was better than a dousing of frigid water to put things in perspective, and Jenna shoved against him to get away.

But his arm only tightened, his lips became more insistent, and the rod against her abdomen jerked. The guy was presuming *a lot.*

Ten grand pays for a lot of presumptions.

His lips moved lower, and Jenna didn't care what ten grand paid for. She didn't need any more neighborhood gossip ruining her reputation and costing her her job.

Anger overrode her libido—thank God—and Jenna wrenched herself free.

"What? You want the money first?" Sarcasm not surprise—which quickly changed when she slapped his chiseled cheek with a resounding *smack!*

A sparrow chirped from a tree limb by the porch, the only other sound. Well, other than their heavy breathing, passion—lust, attraction, whatever—still coursing through their veins.

Jenna spun around and ran inside, slamming the door

behind her and resting against it.

Great. The noise had probably woken Trevor. Another sin she was laying at that guy's feet.

She peeked out the sidelight. He was still standing there, one hand rubbing his cheek, the other on the pillar that supported the porch roof. He looked at the door and Jenna jerked back out of view. She wasn't up for confrontation right now.

That would come tomorrow.

The man had agreed to pay her ten thousand dollars for her services. She was so going to enjoy enlightening him as to exactly what those services were. *After* she took his money, of course.

She'd give it all back. No need to get sued for fraud or whatever he'd trump up against her when he learned the truth, but this was going to be worth keeping up the ruse for the next twelve hours or so. Call her a hooker and report her to the cops without even asking her? Self-righteous bastard; served him right.

"Mommy, can I come down now?" Right on cue, Trevor called her with the name that made her even happier than imagining the look on Gorgeous' face when she tossed his money in it tomorrow.

"Sure thing, Trev. I'll be right there." She glanced out the window as her new "employer" headed toward the curb.

Tomorrow was going to be full of surprises.

Chapter Six

"So you let him think you're a hooker?" Cathy, Jenna's best friend, grabbed her arm and dragged her even farther from the picnic table where their boys were playing with modeling clay. The park was a much easier place to clean up, keep the boys busy, and give them a dose of vitamin D than either of their homes for their weekly play date.

Jenna tapped the brim of Cathy's straw hat that her friend had worn every second of every day in the five years since she'd had that melanoma removed. Cathy's safety blanket, but one more reminder to Jenna of the fleeting nature of life. She'd lost too many people. "Yep. I let him think that. And I can't wait to toss it in his face."

"Ten grand." Cathy shook her head. "What I wouldn't pay to see that."

"I'm sure it'd make me some kind of hooker's hooker in his mind if I took money from you for that."

"Or make you a madam," Cathy joked.

They chuckled over it, but, really, it wasn't funny. "*Why* does he think I'm a hooker, Cath? I keep replaying the conversation we had and all I can come up with is he must be nuts. Jason *was* at the house, but he's a kid."

"A hot kid who's got the hots for you."

Cathy had watched their sons in Jenna's backyard on days Jenna had had to schedule sessions at non-nap times. Whenever the need arose, Jenna tried to schedule those sessions during Trevor's play dates, knowing Cathy had the time off from work. Otherwise, it was always a juggling act to keep Trevor busy while she worked with her students. More often than not, she'd had to discount the session, so Cathy's help was invaluable. As was her perspective now.

"But I didn't give any indication that anything else was going on. And Jason kept calling me Ms. C, so it wasn't like he was being overly familiar."

"Oh? So Jason has called you Jenna before?"

Jenna sighed. "No. Will you knock it off? Jason's always been respectful. Has never crossed the line. He even offered to 'have words' with the guy."

"Uh oh."

"Uh oh, what?"

"When does Jason turn eighteen?"

"Next month."

Cathy shook her head. "Don't you get it? Once he's eighteen, he'll be legal. And you're single. And now he's getting all caveman-protective. Come on, Jen, do the math."

"You're being ridiculous. Jason has a crush, but that's it. I'm older than he is and I have a child. He's not going to want to go there."

"He wants to go somewhere, all right, and apparently he's recognizing the same thing in your Tall, Dark, and Gorgeous crazy rich guy. What is Stud's name by the way?"

"I forgot to ask."

"You *forgot*?"

"It's not the first thing on my mind when he's standing there tossing ten grand at my feet simply to sleep with him." Or kissing her senseless on her front porch—a little factoid she'd neglected to share with her friend.

"If he's as gorgeous as you've described, I'm thinking you might want to pay *him* ten grand. Or, at the very least, take his. So what if you're not a hooker? Anyone could be if the price is right. Ten g's sounds right to me."

"He accused me of not having standards. Me!"

"Sweetie, let's not lose focus. Ten grand, a hot guy, and sex. None of which you had prior to yesterday. I'm thinking it's a win-win situation."

"Except for the part where everyone in town is now going to be looking at my house as a brothel. Memories are long in this town." She sighed and tucked her frizzy hair behind her ears for the tenth time. And for the tenth time, it wouldn't stay.

Cathy tapped her foot.

"What?"Jenna asked. "You're saying I ought to consider it?"

Cathy shrugged. "What you do with your own love life, or lack thereof, is no business of mine."

Since when? "Cathy, he *propositioned* me. Treated me like a hooker." Although if he kissed all hookers like he'd kissed her, Cathy was right; those ladies should be paying him.

"So? If you *were* one, you'd expect him to. I mean, those chicks aren't exactly looking for soft lights and flowers. It's business, through and through."

"But *why* does he think I'm a hooker? That's the part that's bugging me. What did I ever do? I mean, I met him in the grocery store, and even then, I didn't *meet* meet him. He was just in the aisle."

"How'd he find out where you live?"

Jenna shrugged. "Who knows? Maybe he asked someone at the store. It's not like it's a big secret. Someone could have pointed out the flyers that I have on the bulletin board there, advertising my services."

"Nah, he would have known you were a tutor if he'd seen that. You list every subject you're qualified to teach. He certainly couldn't make that mistake."

"Yet he did."

"Yeah, but that's the thing. Why does he need a

hooker? If he's a rich, gorgeous lust-magnet, what's up with that? And, hey—does he have a brother?"

Jenna rolled her eyes. Some things never changed. "You're married."

"Doesn't mean I'm dead. I can still look." Cathy let out a low whistle. "And, oh, mama, am I looking now." She nodded behind Jenna. "Tell me that's your Stud."

Jenna blew out an exasperated breath and looked over her shoulder. "He's not my—"

Oh hell yes he was. Especially if her hormones had anything to say about it.

"Stud" was circling the track around the park in nothing but running shorts, sneakers, and a shirt crumpled in his fist. And sunglasses.

Sweat glistened on him. So not fair, when sweat always made her look like a drowning poodle. Not an ounce of flab jostled with any footfall; no, on him, muscles moved as nature had intended, flexing, contracting all over the place in all sorts of mouth-watering ways. And she wasn't the only one who noticed.

Mrs. Parker, who'd just had a hip replaced last month swiveled with her walker so fast, she might end up needing a second surgery if the guy got any closer or his smile grew any more devastating. Megan and Mallory, the sixteen-year-old Baxter twins, were definitely salivating, and, sadly, Jenna could find nothing wrong with that. The guy was an equal-opportunity lust magnet.

"He's heading over here." Cathy gulped. Even happily married pregnant women weren't safe from his pull.

Jenna shook her head. The guy could be as gorgeous as he wanted, but he still thought she was a hooker. And worse, had treated her like one.

Though that kiss had been nothing to sneeze at…

He rounded the bend, his chest expanding with each breath, abs tightening. Not that she was looking, but it was kind of hard *not* to when it was right there on display.

She also wasn't drooling, but she tucked her chin down and headed toward Trevor just in case. Hormones or innuendoes—or repeat kisses—she was up for none of them.

"Jenna?"

But when he said her name like that—out of breath and husky, which she knew was because of his run but her hormones weren't getting that message—Jenna had to face him.

And cursed herself for doing so. And then him even more.

No one should look as good as he did—covered in sweat or otherwise. Which begged the question of why he was interested in hiring a hooker in the first place. Maybe if she could get beyond that, she could forgive him for going to the police—

No. That wasn't happening.

He jogged over and ran the t-shirt over the back of his neck. "You're out early."

"Oh? You think I should be sleeping in?" She wanted to bite her tongue. Her hormones needed no mention of anything remotely having to do with bed around him. The memory of the kiss was enough to keep them hopping. "That my late nights keep me up? I told you, I have a son." She waved her hand toward the picnic table. "Three-and-half-year-olds don't sleep in. I hear that doesn't happen 'til they're teenagers."

"When does his dad get him?"

She'd like to see his eyes, but he had the reflective sunglasses on again. Hmm, come to think of it, he'd had them on whenever she'd seen him. Maybe he had a problem with his eyes. Maybe that's why he needed a hooker—no one else would—

She didn't allow herself to finish that thought because there was no way that was the reason. The guy could get anyone from senior citizens to jailbait and all ages in between as proven by the looks he was still getting as he spoke to her; vision problems wouldn't matter. Besides, he'd recognized her easily enough.

Or maybe buying someone's body put an automatic homing device between them.

He's not really *buying your body. Remember that.*

Duh. Jenna shook her head. "Trevor's dad is… out of the picture. Trevor stays with me."

Mr. Gorgeous ran a hand over his jaw—which just drew attention to the square perfection of it. Was there *nothing* wrong with this guy?

Oh, yeah. He hired hookers.

"What's your name?" she asked. "If we're going to be, um—"this ought to be good; how to phrase this?—"*working* together, I should have something to call you."

The grin he gave her only highlighted those lips that had been on hers yesterday with all sorts of good vibes and bad consequences. "It's Bryan."

"So, Bryan, what do you do that lets you go jogging instead of clocking in early and still be able to blow ten grand on me?"

That question hung between them with all its interpretive nuances, sparking embers that hadn't really burned out from that kiss on her porch yesterday.

"I work for myself."

"What do you do?"

"Electrical and some construction. Getting ready to start a big project next week."

Yes, he looked like a construction worker—the kind they used as fantasy heroes on the covers of the romance novels she used to read before life had kicked the belief in happily-ever-afters out of her.

"Ahem." Cathy cleared her throat louder than seasonal allergies would require as she approached—and Cathy didn't have seasonal allergies.

But Jenna welcomed the distraction from imagining

what that six-pack would do when Bryan hefted a couple of two-by-fours.

"Cathy, this is Bryan. Bryan, Cathy Mayfield. Best friend extraordinaire and happily married mother of soon-to-be-number-two." No sense lumping Cath in the same hooker boat she was in.

Bryan adjusted his glasses, but he didn't remove them. "Nice to meet you."

Cathy tittered like some blushing virgin, which Jenna knew hadn't been the case since tenth grade.

"So, are you in town for long, or are you just passing through?" Cath asked with a hand on her cocked hip.

What was this? The Wild West?

"I have to check on the boys." Jenna excused herself and headed back to the table. Men were tough enough to figure out, let alone ones who were deliberately being obtuse. Toss in a lust-struck best friend, and Jenna wanted out. Trevor was easier. When he cried, he was either hurt or tired. When he was cranky, he was either hungry or tired. And when he smiled, he was pure joy to be around. She could use some pure joy in her life right now.

"Hey, kiddo. Whatcha makin'?" She ruffled his hair.

"A felefant." Trevor held up the gray blob. This brand of modeling clay didn't come in gray, which meant the clean-up job of separating their creations back into the correctly-colored canister was now a non-issue.

"An elephant? That's great! Look how long his trunk is."

"No, Mommy. That's his tail. This is his twunk."

Jenna hid her smile. She'd thought that was a leg. Ah, well, *sculptor* probably wasn't high on Trevor's list of What I Want To Be When I Grow Up. Right now it was a policeman, a fireman, or a football player. Jenna didn't like any of those—too dangerous for her baby.

"You're doing a great job, Trev."

"Look at mine, Jenna." Cathy's son, Bobby, held up

his glop of gray and peered out from under his baseball cap. "I made a hippamouse."

"You guys have your own zoo."

The two three-year-olds' eyes lit up and more gray clay got pulled apart as they dug in and started working on "rhinosaurs" and "moo cows."

"He's pretty talented," Bryan said over her shoulder.

Jenna stiffened. Not because he was standing so close, but because he was stepping into her world. Her real world, not his make-believe hooker one.

She had half a mind to turn around right now and ask him what kind of mother he thought she was that she'd turn tricks with a three-year-old in the house. She'd also like to ask him what kind of guy propositioned suburban moms. And kissed them on their front porch as if the world were ending tomorrow.

"Does he play any sports?"

Jenna was just about to push him away, but, unfortunately, Trevor heard that question and squinted up at him.

"I pway soccer and t-ball. Mommy says maybe I can pway football when I get big and stwong like you. I wike football. Do you?"

"Yeah, I do." Bryan adjusted his sunglasses. "Who's your favorite team?"

"Michael's. He's the cutie and makes all the points."

And squashed kids with nasty elbows to the face if they tried to take the ball from him. Even his own teammates. No way was she letting Trevor play with that bruiser. Not until he was big enough to defend himself.

She bet Bryan could defend himself.

Jenna blinked. Now where had that come from?

Then Bryan shifted his weight and his arm brushed hers, sending the little hairs there to full attention, with the skin and nerves beneath needing no urging to follow suit, and she knew. *God*. It was as if he'd bathed in pheromones.

The sweat probably had a lot to do with it. As did those abs.

"QB's a good position. Have you ever played it?"

Trevor shook his head, but Bobby bounced to his feet on the picnic table bench, waving his baseball cap in the air like a rodeo cowboy. "I do. With my daddy all the time. I get to throw the ball to him and we make touchdowns and Mommy cheers."

Jenna didn't glance away fast enough to miss the wistfulness on Trevor's face that she was sure matched hers. If only Carl had wanted to be a family. Oh, he'd wanted *a* family—his own. Not some "whore's bastard," as he'd called Mindy and Trevor.

As if anyone could call Trevor anything other than what he was: sweet and loving and a wonderful little boy. She didn't know who Mindy had created this child with—sadly, Mindy didn't either—but whoever the mystery DNA donor was, he had great genes.

"You want to play football with me some time, Trevor? I'm a good catcher, too."

It was all Jenna could do not to kick Bryan's shin. This was *her* son. He might have bought her for ten grand, but he hadn't bought Trevor. And she was going to make sure he knew it the moment they were alone.

"How about I come over this afternoon and we play? I'll even bring lunch so your mom doesn't have to make any. What do you think? Would that be okay?"

Jealousy twinged in Jenna's gut. Bryan was relating to her son in a testosterone-way she never could, and the hope-filled look Trevor gave her killed any excuse she would've made.

Two sets of expectant eyes—well, one set and one pair of sunglasses—turned her way.

As if she could say no now. "Sure," she said through gritted teeth, but ended up lightening her tone when Trevor smiled. "That's a great idea. Right, Trev?"

Trevor was so happy he could only nod. There might even be a tear in his eye. Which put more than a few in hers.

Jenna turned away. Trevor had started asking more questions lately. Wanting to know why he didn't have a daddy and if Jenna could get him one. She'd love to, she really would, but her dating pool was severely limited now that she'd gone through her friends' single friends. Those dates had pretty much fizzled out when they found out she had a child. And she didn't do the bar scene. Other than the Universe dropping a man on her front porch she didn't—

Oh no. No way. Just because Bryan had shown up on her porch and liked kids didn't mean—

He'd propositioned her! He paid for hookers! What kind of man would that be to bring into Trevor's life?

Although, as she caught a glimpse of his smile, square jaw and that hard, trim body, she had to admit he was a fine specimen of manhood. And one hell of a kisser.

The hiring hookers part, however, put him out of the running.

Even if she hadn't exactly turned him down.

Chapter Seven

Jenna had never seen Trevor as excited as he was during the three hours he waited for Bryan to show up. He kept wanting to open the front door to check for Bryan's truck so often that she ended up leaving it unlocked while she tried to let the magazine in her hands keep her attention.

When she read the recipe for broccoli mashed potatoes to the point that she had it memorized, she admitted it wasn't working.

"Is he here yet?" Trevor asked for the umpteenth time.

"Not yet." Jenna set the magazine on the end table. She didn't know when she'd ever been so nervous. Even when she'd had to tell her parents about her pregnancy she'd known what to expect: disappointment from her mother and the unflagging support from her father. That, she'd been prepared for. This?

She was in over her head with this. With Bryan. Her mind was saying one thing, her body the exact opposite. And with Trevor's reaction, her heart was siding with the body part of her.

"Come on, Trev, let's go potty one more time before Bryan gets here. That way you won't miss any of the game."

"Okay, Mommy. Will you put cereal in the water? I wanna hit them."

He was well beyond the aim-for-the-holes-in-the-cereal stage, but it'd keep his mind off Bryan.

Cereal wouldn't exactly cut it for her.

While she helped Trevor take care of business, Jenna wondered if she should stop this farce before Bryan arrived. Trevor was already developing hero-worship simply because the guy wanted to throw a ball. She'd tossed a few to him when they got back from the play date, but Trevor said she didn't do it right. That wasn't true—she had a good arm. *For a girl*, he'd said, a phrase that was sure to have originated in the know-it-all mouth of Michael.

But what Trevor had meant was that she wasn't a guy. And, more specifically, she wasn't his dad.

He *couldn't* see Bryan in that role. They'd just met him.

Which begged the question of what she was doing letting him play football with her son, but luckily, Trevor's target practice precluded her from having to answer.

"Wook, Mommy, I hit all of them!"

"You sure did. Now let's get you ready for your game." She helped him straighten his shorts, checked the temperature of the water before he washed his hands, all the while only half-listening to his chatter about touchdowns and "feed goals."

"What do goals eat, Mommy?" earned him one of her smiles—and a masculine chuckle from outside the bathroom.

Jenna froze.

Bryan wouldn't just walk in—

His gorgeous face appeared around the doorframe. "Hey, Sport, you ready?"

Apparently he would. *Ten grand's worth of presumptions.*

"Front door was open," was his explanation when her eyes met his sunglasses in the mirror over the sink. What was with the sunglasses? Did he think he was a movie star or something?

He certainly thought he was *some*one, obviously, by the way he'd just waltzed in here as if he owned the place. Owned *her*, yes. At least in his mind. But her home? No way in hell. She needed to nip this in the bud right now.

And she would have if Trevor hadn't shouted, "Bwyan!" and flown out the door into the man's legs, wrapping his arms around them as if he were hugging a tree.

Jenna couldn't speak over the lump in her throat. Why this guy? Why now?

"Trevor, honey, let's let Bryan walk, okay?" She steered Trevor over to the front door by his shoulders. Bryan had come to play catch, not join the family.

And she wasn't asking him to...

"We have to get your sneakers tied so you don't trip."

She knelt at her son's feet, wishing her hair was long enough to cover her face so Bryan didn't have a bird's eye view of her every emotion—which he was taking full advantage of. Probably checking out the merchandise.

Did she measure up?

"Huwwy, Mommy! I wanna make a touchdown!"

Thank God for Trevor. "You have to settle down, you little jumping bean, or I'm not going to be able to get this other shoe on you."

Trevor stopped hopping, but he didn't stop fidgeting. And with Bryan staring at her, Jenna was fidgeting, too.

Her fingers fumbled with the laces, but the bow was good enough. "There you go." She patted Trevor's leg. "Go get 'em, tiger."

"Tiger Twevor to the wescue!" Trevor yanked the doorknob. "Come on, Bwyan!"

"I'll be right there. Get the ball out of the bag on the porch, okay?"

Trevor beamed as if he'd just won the Super Bowl.

Jenna gathered her thoughts before standing. She had to come clean now. Before Trevor got hurt.

"Look, Bryan—"

"I'm sorry about walking in, but I heard you two talking and, well, the door was open."

"That doesn't give you an open invitation—"

"You're right. And I'm sorry. Truce?" He held out his hand, and oh the temptation to touch him again…

It took a lot of fortitude, but she refrained. "That's not important right now. I have to talk to you about our deal. About the money."

"Yeah, about that. I haven't had a chance to go to the bank yet. Can we do this later?"

"No, we really can't. I need to talk to you—"

"Mommy?" Trevor yanked the door open, then stomped his foot when he saw the two of them standing there. "Come *on*! I wanna pway football!"

Bryan touched her arm. "We don't want to disappoint Trevor, do we?"

Jenna sighed. She didn't. "Fine." She pasted a smile on her face for Trevor and scooted through the door. "Okay, Trevor, let's go. I'll snap the ball."

She had a feeling, though, that Trevor wasn't going to be the one who was disappointed.

Chapter Eight

Bryan didn't get it. He couldn't see Jenna in the role of the happy hooker.

She didn't wear a lick of make-up, her nails weren't manicured, her hair was a disaster on the women-who-care-about-their-appearance scale, though *he* liked the jumbled, just-out-of-bed mess curling around her head, and she got rough-and-tumble dirty with her son and was a little ungainly doing so. How could she dance seductively if she kept tripping over her own (really long shapely) legs like a baby giraffe?

There was nothing childlike about Jenna.

Although, grace wasn't exactly a job requirement when it came to stripper poles, merely the ability to wrap herself around it. And any man who would pay the right price?

He caught the ball Trevor tossed his way and it hit him in the gut like sucker-punch. Why'd she have to be a hooker? Why'd she have to have given birth to his son—*and* kept him from him?

He had no doubt that Trevor was his. The kid had the same mannerisms, the same lispy *r,* the same habit of sticking his tongue out to the left when he was throwing that Bryan had gotten rid of in his first pee-wee game after the guy who'd tackled him had called him a wuss. He hadn't known what it meant at the time, but he'd known he didn't want to be one. That was going to be something he'd help Trevor with.

But first, he had to get the chance to see him. To be in his life. The ten grand would help with that, but why couldn't Jenna be just some local high school teacher he could consider spending the rest of his life with?

"Catch, Bwyan!" Trevor lobbed a wobbly throw.

He lunged for the ball. Trevor had a good arm for his age; he just needed some instruction and practice. Bryan was going to make sure he got them.

"Good toss, Trevor!" Jenna ran over to the boy and ruffled his hair. The scowl that appeared on Trevor's face was like looking into a thirty-year-old mirror.

How ironic that Jenna didn't remember him or realize her son was the spitting image of him. 'Course, if he took off his sunglasses, she just might.

"It's a pass, Mommy, not a toss." Trevor rolled his eyes, giving Bryan the quintessential "Women!" look that guys were born knowing how to do.

"Well it was a good pass."

Jenna shoved her hands into the front pockets of her shorts, which dragged the waistband down, revealing an inch of toned, flat stomach that Bryan had a hard time peeling his eyes off of. The sunglasses served two purposes.

"Let's do one more, Trev, then it's time for your nap," she said, which just made Bryan think of going to bed. With her.

Why didn't he remember her? What it'd been like between them. He was an idiot for getting drunk enough not to remember, but then, bachelor parties weren't known as genius pits. It wasn't as if he'd been *planning* to get drunk and screw a stripper. Not one of his finer moments in life.

Trevor groaned."Awww! I don't wanna take a nap today."

No, actually, that night had been a good one; it'd

made Trevor. His son. The *finest* thing in his life.

"Sweetheart, you have to. I have to work this afternoon."

"Can't I pway with Bwyan while you work?"

Great. Trevor knew about her job. Not the particulars, surely, but what did the kid think about men coming and going in his house? And did he equate Bryan with the rest of the, er, clientele?

"I don't mind, Jenna." It'd keep him around so he could see her next client. Chaperone, maybe.

He shook his head. This was crazy. Stupid, even, that he didn't want her to be with anyone else. Just because the condom broke didn't mean he had rights where she was concerned. But when it affected his child…

If only he'd had the chance to go to the bank, but the inspector had had a cancellation first thing this morning and since Gage had been out on one of his own projects, Bryan had had to go. Turned out that the new space had some structural issues he and Gage would need to address, and the appointment had taken longer than he'd thought.

He checked his phone. He didn't have any emergency clients today and he'd cleared his afternoon so he could spend it with Trevor. There was still time to make it to the bank. Then Jenna would be his and any other client could kiss her goodbye.

Well, no. If anyone was going to be kissing Jenna, it'd be him.

The memory of doing just that flared in front of him like a roaring flame—and just as hot.

It was no wonder they'd created a baby together if this attraction had raged through them that night. Toss in some alcohol and the bachelor-party mood, and yeah, it wasn't hard to imagine how any of it had happened.

He just wished he could *remember* it. Especially the broken condom part.

God, the one time that'd happened and he found

himself in this position.

Wonder what position they'd been in when they'd made Trevor.

Bryan shook his head. Not going there or he wouldn't be able to walk upright.

"All right. You can stay up today."

Trevor fist-pumped a, "Yes!" then he hugged his mother's legs.

The mother of his child. Bryan had always expected he'd call his wife that, not some woman he'd had too many rum and cokes with.

"Thwow it back, Bryan!" Trevor let go of Jenna and, with his little legs working so fast Bryan was afraid they'd get tangled in each other, ran to the far side of the yard, one arm outstretched for the Hail Mary of front yard football passes.

"Go long, Trevor!" Bryan pumped the football toward the end zone they'd marked with two lawn chairs, and the little boy curved to the right as naturally as if they'd practiced it.

Oh yeah. Trevor was definitely his.

He let the ball fly, putting a little spin on it since Trevor thought that was cool, and watched it land right where it was supposed to. The kid was a natural.

"Touchdown!" Jenna ran into the end zone and swung Trevor up in her arms, his little legs fanning out behind him, his smile matching hers so much it made Bryan's heart hurt.

Yes, Trevor was his—but he was also Jenna's.

What did that mean for all three of them?

***

"Can Bwyan stay for dinner, Mommy?"

Jenna tossed the ball toward the bag on the porch. And missed. She'd known that question was going to pop up. She also knew there was no way in hell she was keeping Bryan around longer than necessary.

"Thanks for asking, Trevor, but I can't tonight." Bryan beat her to the punch of disappointing her son and she'd love to thank him for that, but he'd probably consider it an advance against payment for services rendered.

"Aw, why not?"

"I have things to do." Bryan packed the ball in his duffel.

"Work?"

"Something like that."

"Michael's daddy only works in the day. He wears a tie. Do you wear a tie?"

"Sometimes."

"I think ties are cool. Mommy is going to buy me and Mister Monkey one."

"You and Mr. Monkey are very lucky to have your mommy."

"I know. Sarge says so all the time."

Jenna winced. She didn't want Bryan to make the connection between her and Sarge too quickly. While she wasn't exactly going to relish tossing his money back in his face now—not after the way he'd been with Trevor today—she didn't want him making any assumptions. Well, any more about her. Not that any other assumption could be worse than what he already assumed—

"Trevor, what do you say to Bryan for playing with you today?"

Trevor gnawed on his lip and squinted up at their guest. "Can you pway tomowow?"

She should have known a simple *Thank You* wouldn't cut it.

"Sweetheart, Bryan has things to do. He can't spend all his time playing with you—"

"Actually, I do have free time tomorrow morning. Around ten?"

She should say no. Although, after what she was going to say to him, it'd be a non-issue. Let him be the bad guy.

"Trevor, why don't you go inside and wash your hands. Bryan and I have a few grownup things to talk about." Like not playing the Little Boy card to get to her. Trevor was *not* a pawn and she wouldn't allow him to be used like one. As far as Bryan was concerned, he'd bought *her*, not Trevor.

And he *hadn't* bought her yet, so he could just forget his "I'll come by tomorrow" entitlement.

With a *blech*, Trevor headed inside. Grownup things were on par with a sick Santa Clause at Christmas to him.

"Look, Bryan—"

"Tomorrow's not a problem. I have a few hours to spare."

"About that." Jenna tucked her hair behind her ears. She could only imagine what it looked like—brillo head central. "There's been a mistake."

"A mistake? *That's* what you call it?"

She wasn't prepared for the anger. "Well… yeah. Wouldn't you?"

A muscle ticked in his jaw. And another. He opened his mouth to say something, then shut it. Then he scratched his chin, the slight rasp of the beginnings of a five-o'clock shadow interrupting the silence. He exhaled. "Okay. Fine. A mistake. Are you saying I can't see Trevor tomorrow? I mean, I did—"

"Pay for the privilege," Jenna purposely chose that wording to keep it open to interpretation. Who knew what Trevor was overhearing? "I know. But the thing is, Trevor wasn't part of our bargain."

"No kidding."

If he agreed with her, why the argument? "Okay. Good. I'm glad you see things my way."

"Actually, I don't. And I don't see how you'd think I

would."

She was just about to lay into him why she thought—no, *knew*—he should see things her way when Trevor's face appeared at the living room window.

"Pwease, Mommy? Pwease can Bryan stay? Wittle Bear's having 'tato salad. I wike 'tato salad and I bet Bwyan does, too. You make the best 'tato salad, Mommy."

Trevor was going to break hearts left and right when he grew up, the little charmer. If only Bryan were as charming…

Actually, that was the problem. Bryan *was* that charming. His assumptions weren't. Nor was his holier-than-thou, you-owe-me attitude. He hadn't even paid her to be at his sexual beck and call yet; why did he think he was entitled to anything having to do with the rest of her life? And now he'd put her in the rotten position of having to be the bad guy when he should have that title all sewn up.

"Actually, Trevor, I'm going to take your mommy out to dinner if that's all right with you?"

Low. Very low, using a kid like that.

"On a date?" Trevor's eyes lit up like a strobe light.

She could already see the one-plus-one-equals-three equation in her son's head. This was getting more complicated by the minute. She was going to have to lay down the law and Bryan had handed her the perfect opportunity.

"No, he doesn't mean a date, Trevor. Bryan and I have to have a grownup talk so I'm going to see if Cathy will let you play with Bobby tonight."

"Can I sweep over?"

She felt Bryan stiffen beside her. Great. This was so not a position she wanted to be in. Trevor and Bobby loved sleeping over each others' houses, and, frankly, so did the parents. Some much needed parental time off. But the last thing she wanted Bryan to know was that she had the house to herself tonight. No need to encourage the guy. Of course, that'd be moot once she told him what he could do with his ten grand.

"We'll see, honey. I have to talk to Cathy."

"Okay, but I'm gonna get Mister Monkey just in case."

How nice it must be to have your focus changed so easily. Bryan's focus was boring into her back.

She turned around. "Fine. If Cathy can watch Trevor, we'll do dinner."

"Okay. Seven o'clock at Tosco's."

It wasn't a question. Insufferable. He hadn't even paid her and already he was dictating where and how she spent her time.

Jenna shook her head. She had to remember that she really *wasn't* at his beck and call. That she *wasn't* accepting his money for anything. And public humiliation in Tosco's would tell him so in no uncertain terms.

"Fine. Seven o'clock. I'll be there."

He adjusted his glasses. "We'll settle up then."

"Darn right," she muttered.

She was so going to enjoy flinging his money back in his face. Let the town gossips do with *that* what they would. At least she'd have made her point that she wasn't what he'd claimed and would clear her name in the process.

And maybe blacken his.

Chapter Nine

Bryan couldn't believe she was actually going to take the money. Seeing her with her son—*their* son—he just couldn't reconcile the two images: the stripper who slept with guys she didn't remember, and the woman who was so loving and protective of her child that the kid didn't have a clue what went on under their roof. If not for the fact that she wanted to settle up tonight he'd be questioning having reported her because Trevor was so well adjusted. He almost wished she'd flung his offer in his face.

He patted his pocket where the ten-K rested. Such a large amount of money ought to weigh more.

He opened the door to the restaurant and his mouth started to water from the aroma of buttery garlic bread, roasted peppers, Veal Sorrento… *not* because he'd soon be seeing Jenna.

"Table for one?" The hostess gave him a long, slow once-over, but Bryan wasn't interested. She looked like she was right out of high school and he was going to have to be the one to set a good moral example for Trevor since his mother wasn't.

"Two. Secluded, if you wouldn't mind." Let her make of that what she wanted; he wanted to make sure he and Jenna weren't interrupted as well as keep his eyes in the shadows. He'd play his hand *after* she took the money.

The girl sighed and straightened. "This way." She led him through the linen-covered tables, the soft *chink* of silverware and chafing dishes tinkling beneath vintage Sinatra.

Bryan felt the stares. He'd been used to them in high school because the state championship had been a big deal, but the ones he'd gotten when he and Gage had applied for a permit for BeefCake, Inc… notsomuch. Narrow-minded prejudice and incorrect assumptions had almost cost them the planning commission's approval. Only Gage's fiancee's contact and the viability of their proposition to create jobs and revitalize a blighted building had saved them. But people still knew who he was and clung to their opinions.

"Here you go." The girl stepped aside next to his chair. *Slightly*. Far enough that he could pull the chair out, but close enough that her breasts were within brushing-up against distance. Had she attended Jenna's "classes"?

Not the mindset he should be in to have this conversation.

Bryan took his seat, managing to keep his body parts exactly where they should be, then slid his napkin to his thigh. "I'm waiting for Jenna Corrigan. Do you know her?"

She gaped at him. "Ms. Corrigan? Sure, I know her. Everyone does."

Bryan was afraid of that.

"I'll send her over as soon as she gets here." The gaping mouth was replaced with a smile and yet another perusal, though this one wasn't the blatantly suggestive one she'd given him earlier. If pressed, he would have said it was more questioning.

Probably wondering why he had to pay for it.

Who else did? Were some of the guys here clients of hers?

Was the sergeant?

Bryan had to scrub that image out of his head, praying that kickbacks were all Benton was getting from Jenna.

The waiter approached. Another kid. Was he one of Jenna's students, too?

"Hi. I'm Richie and I'll be your server tonight. Can I get you something to drink?"

The stiffest drink in the house probably wasn't a smart thing to order given what they were going to be discussing.

"I'll take a cola."

"Very good." The waiter turned but then spun around. "By the way, Coach just showed the tape of the state game. That last play you called was awesome right before you... well, you know."

Bryan smiled thinly. Yeah he knew. Right before he'd blown out his Achilles, his ACL, and his college dreams. "What position do you play?"

"Tight end. Got a few schools looking at me."

"Hey, good luck."

"Thanks. I'll be right back with that soda."

Schools looking at him. Bryan had had that experience. Had gotten a couple of offers and been trying to decide between them when the sack had taken the decision out of his hands. Surgery and rehab hadn't been worth it to the scouts. The offers had been pulled before he'd even come out of anesthesia.

So he'd fallen back on becoming an electrician like his father, and if it wasn't as exciting as football, at least it was a steady job and he could run his own business. He wasn't getting rich—he was hoping BeefCake, Inc. could help out in that area—but he'd been able to come up with ten grand when he'd needed to.

He and Jenna needed to come to some kind of understanding. She couldn't carry on with this profession anymore. She had to see it wasn't a good life for Trevor—hell, it wasn't a good life for *her*. Hopefully, she had other skills she could fall back on, but if not, he'd find some way to pay for her to go back to school.

As long as *he* got to raise Trevor.

***

Jenna took a deep breath before opening the heavy glass door to Tosco's, praying for the mental fortitude to do this. Everyone in town had to know what he'd accused her of by now. What he thought of her. Tongues would be wagging the moment she sat at his table. Memories would be dredged up, the whispers starting again.

Her teenage heartbreak had been a big scandal; the straight-A, class president was the last person who should have committed the sin of premarital sex, let alone gotten pregnant because of it. Her stellar resume and professional references had earned her the job at the high school; she didn't need any new scandal undoing all the work she'd done for her reputation.

"Ms. Corrigan?" Sheila Brady opened the front door. Jenna had forgotten she worked here.

"Hi, Sheila."

"There's a guy waiting for you in the far corner." All the awe of extreme puppy love accompanied those words.

Though, actually, Sheila was nineteen. Not exactly jailbait any longer, and if Bryan found her attractive —

Jenna shook herself. She was stalling.

"Thanks, Sheila." Jenna straightened her shoulders and entered the restaurant.

"He's really hot," Sheila whispered more to herself than Jenna.

But Jenna heard. And, yeah, he was.

She had a few seconds to study him as she approached the table where he was studying the menu. Those black curls that'd been mussed during the game today were slicked back as if still damp from a shower, and the navy golf shirt he'd changed into was stretched just right across broad shoulders and the sculpted chest she hadn't been able to forget from his run this morning. He was a big man, but not hulking. Good-looking. Was good with Trevor. It was a royal shame she hadn't met him under better circumstances.

Her steps faltered. Maybe… Maybe they could start

over. Maybe she could come clean tonight—not out him publicly and open him up to ridicule. They could laugh about the misunderstanding. He liked Trevor enough to offer to play football with him again tomorrow. Maybe they could—

No. He thought she was a hooker. And he'd *hired* her *because* he thought she was a hooker. The man hired *hookers*.

She had no clue why, but it didn't matter how gorgeous he was on the outside, the inside didn't reach *her* standards. And how funny was it that that word should come up again in relation to him?

No, Bryan wasn't the man for her.

Then he looked up and Jenna's breath caught. No sunglasses and that, plus the slow smile that spread across his face, made him even more gorgeous. She needed to have a serious discussion with her hormones.

He stood and met her at the chair opposite his, a mix of soap and Bryan that sent those damn hormones into Snoopy-dance mode. It was the first time she'd seen him without the glasses. His eyes were… gray? Light blue? It was hard to tell with the muted lighting of the Tiffany sconces and tea lights flickering on the table, but they didn't seem to have any problems she could see that would necessitate sunglasses. Maybe he was sensitive to light.

Which was a shame. His eyes were as gorgeous as the rest of him. And they stared at her as if they could see through her.

Or her clothing…

He held out her chair. "You look beautiful."

Jenna ran a hand down the mocha dress she wore, waiting for some comment about the tricks of her trade. Or just her tricks.

When he didn't make it, she muttered a self-conscious, "Thank you," and sat in the chair he held for her. He wasn't behaving like a man with a hooker—not that she'd ever really considered the *whats* and *wherefores* such an interaction entailed, but she would've thought that pleasantries and dinners at nice restaurants weren't part of the normal arrangement.

The waiter approached. Another of her past students. "Hey, Ms. C."

"Hi, Richie. How are you?"

"Good. Going to check out a couple of colleges next week."

"More scholarships?"

He couldn't hide his grin and she didn't blame him. "Yeah."

"I told you you could do it."

"I know. But you gave me the confidence."

"You have the ability."

She could feel Bryan's eyes on her. Maybe he ought to put the glasses back on because his staring was a little disconcerting. So was the thought that he was probably *trying* to figure out if Richie was one of her clients as well.

Good lord. Richie and Jason were underage. Bryan really didn't have a high opinion of her at all. More like the lowest anyone could have about another person.

She was so going to enjoy flinging it in his face.

"Thanks. So, um." Richie put a basket of warm bread on the table. "Do you know what you want for dinner?"

Bryan cleared his throat. "Maybe she'd like something to drink first?"

Yup, very low. And he was transferring it to Richie.

"Actually, Richie, I'd love the veal parmigiana, a house salad, and I'll take a glass of pinot with it." She picked up the menu she hadn't had the need to touch. Dad had loved Tosco's. He'd brought her here on his custody nights.

"Okay. And Bryan? What can I get you?"

Bryan arched an eyebrow. Hmmm, with those glasses on she hadn't known he could do that—or how devastating it made him look. Jeez. Was there nothing bad about this man?

Well, other than the fact that he hired hookers.

"I'll take linguini with scallops, a salad, and another soda." He handed Richie the menu without looking at him.

"Really, Bryan," she said when Richie left, "you should give him a break. It's his first job."

"We're not here to talk about Richie. We're here to talk about Trevor."

"Actually, we're not. But I do need to talk—"

"Hi, Jenna." Cal Mullins stopped by her table. "Don't want to intrude, but I wanted to thank you for your help. My girlfriend and I are in a much better place thanks to you."

She'd helped them fill out the apartment application. "It's my pleasure, Cal. I'm glad I could be of service."

"I've given your name to a few of our friends. Hope that's okay. I know we weren't your usual clientele, but, like I said, you really helped us."

"That'd be great. Most of my business is referrals so thank you for mentioning me."

Cal looked over at Bryan. "Treat her right, man. The woman's a gem."

Jenna tried not to choke on the look that crossed Bryan's face. She was going to have to come clean to him soon because if anyone else stopped by they could blow her cover and she wanted her pound of flesh.

Though Cal's conversation could be taken a lot of different ways.

"You cater to *couples*?" Bryan asked once Cal had left.

Yup, he'd gone down the wrong one.

"Uh, yes. A lot of people need my services, and sometimes couples do, too." Because Cal and Julie had met in an adult literacy class, but Bryan didn't need to know that. She'd helped them with the apartment, some job applications, and even coached them for interviews.

"Is there anything else I ought to know before—"

"Before you pay me?" She plunked her elbow on the table and tapped her lips. "Let's see. I could give you references if you want. Pretty much all of the football team, a few guys on the soccer team. Coach Leland hired me at one point, and then there's the town council. At least half of them have used my services. Oh, and I have a standing arrangement with the local relocation service. They're always referring new people to me."

Because many of the kids moving into the area couldn't meet the local school district's stringent testing standards. She was usually extremely busy the entire month of June getting new kids ready for testing at the end of July.

Bryan slammed his soda onto the table. "I'm starting to think this isn't the best place to have this conversation."

"But we've already ordered."

He pulled his credit card out of his wallet. "We need to move this discussion somewhere else. I have a feeling we're not going to see eye-to-eye on this and I'd rather not cause a scene."

She just couldn't resist. "Fine by me. My place or yours?"

"Neither!"

People at several of the nearby tables turned around when Bryan practically yelled it.

"Uh, Bryan? Looks like a scene to me."

Richie rushed over. "Is everything okay? Can I get you anything else?"

Jenna nodded at Bryan. Let him do his own dirty work. He hadn't had any trouble doing it when it came to her.

"Bryan?"

Bryan looked at her, then at Riche.

He sighed. "We're fine. Everything's good. If you could get our meals, that'd be great."

"Sure thing. Right away."

Poor Richie ran off looking like a dog with his tail stuck between his legs.

"You know, that really wasn't nice. It's not Richie's fault—"

"Jenna, can we talk about something else? I really can't take any more of your client stories."

She bit back a smile. "Okay, then. What do you want to talk about?"

"Tell me about Trevor."

Her smile disappeared. "I'd rather not."

"Why?"

"Because he's none of your business."

"You can't honestly think that." Bryan set an envelope on the table between them. "This kind of money makes him my business."

She touched it. Ten thousand dollars. Not a fortune, but it'd go a long way to alleviating some of her stress and if she invested it right, could cover Trevor's college.

But it didn't give him any rights when it came to Trevor. She set her fork down and cleared her throat. "Actually, your offer didn't include my son."

"*Your* son? Doesn't his father have *any* say in whether he's in his son's life or not?"

Yeah, he'd probably said, "Do me, baby," or something equally as crude, but that didn't give him any right to be in Trevor's life.

If she could just find a man to be that father figure Trevor so desperately wanted and needed. Someone she could build a life with to give him the stability of a two-parent home, it might make the truth a little more palatable when she eventually told him.

Bryan stacked the butter patties on the plate in front of him, then did the same thing with the artisan bread slices, reminding her of Trevor. He'd been so good with Trevor today, and Trevor... He'd lit up like it'd been Christmas morning.

She owed Bryan for that. “Okay, fine. What did you want to talk about regarding Trevor?”

He set the last piece of bread squarely on top of the pile. “What… what does he like to do? Play with? Does he have a lot of friends?”

Strange questions to be coming from the man who’d hired a hooker. Maybe he was trying to come up with things for Trevor to do while they—

“He’s into building blocks. You know, those plastic ones that interlock? He likes trucks, too.” Though since his “tr”s came out sounding like “f”s, it could get a bit embarrassing when he saw one. She’d had to correct his pronunciation many times in public.

She answered Bryan’s questions about pre-school—probably trying to figure out when her son was out of the house so they could be alone.

A shiver raced up her spine. If she actually took him up on his offer like Cathy had suggested, they’d need more than the two and a half hours Trevor was in class.

Not thinking about that…

She told him about the Michael Report, grasping at anything to get that image out of her head. Turned out, Bryan had had a kid like that in his class—who’d been named Brian, also.

“You can’t imagine the phone calls my mom had to field over that. I got in so much trouble for things I’d never done until I wizened up and told her about him.”

“Trevor hero-worships this kid. Thinks because everyone’s afraid of him that he’s someone to be looked up to.”

“That’s where a dad comes in, Jenna. We can explain this whole testosterone thing in a way women can’t.”

Again with the dad thing. If she knew who the guy was, didn’t he think she would’ve tracked him down by now? Trevor did need a man in his life and she was working on that. But she wasn't about to jump on the first guy without an aversion to kids to come along just to give Trevor a father. She wanted to fall in love. Be a real family.

"I could have a talk with the teacher if you'd like."

She dropped her fork. Seriously, no amount of money would give Bryan that right when it came to *her* son. "Thanks, but I think I can handle it."

"You just admitted you can't."

Nothing burned her up more than someone questioning her parenting skills. "You know, you're right. Maybe this isn't the best place to have this discussion." Because right now she not only wanted to toss all that money in his face, she wanted to rip it to shreds too and toss it in with his damn linguini—

That Richie was just bringing out.

Great. Her window of leaving opportunity just closed.

"Here you go." Richie took their plates from the serving tray, the clink of the dishware the only sound at their table. "Will there be anything else?" he asked, looking at Bryan.

Bryan scowled.

Oh, right. He thought she'd slept with Richie so Richie wasn't one of his favorite people at the moment. "Thanks Richie. I think we're good."

"Okay, well if you need anything you know how to reach me."

Another sentence Bryan took out of context.

This would be fun if he hadn't shouted it from the rooftops in the police station. If no one knew, she could let it go on for a little longer.

But they did and she didn't owe Bryan whatever-his-name-was anything.

She cut a slice of her veal. "What's your last name, by the way? I think I ought to at least know that."

"I'm surprised you care."

Ouch. Callous. "I do like to know who I'm doing

business with." Ball was back in his court. Too bad he didn't realize they were playing a game.

He twirled some linguini on his fork. "It's Lassiter."

The veal got stuck in her throat. She reached for her water glass, but Bryan was out of his chair and patting her back before she could get it to her lips.

His lips were right beside her.

Bryan *Lassiter's* lips.

"Jenna? You okay?"

No she wasn't. She so really really wasn't. But she waved him off, wanting him to *back* off so she could figure out what the hell she was going to do.

Bryan Lassiter had been four years ahead of her in school. She hadn't known him personally, but she'd heard about him. *Every*one had heard about Bryan Lassiter.

Because Bryan Lassiter had been not only the star quarterback, homecoming king, and class president, but he'd been the town's resident dreamboat. Who'd been known for one thing in particular.

And right then, Jenna knew. She *knew.*

Bryan Lassiter had been known for his eyes—his *violet* eyes.

Just like Trevor.

Chapter Ten

Jenna had tossed her napkin on the table, discarding the thought of forking over her maxed-out credit card for her portion of the meal because Mr. Dreamboat could pay for the dinner that would never have been necessary if he hadn't made his asinine assumption in the first place, and half-ran out of the restaurant, the patrons' stares and conversations trailing after her. The rest of the trip home, however, was a blur.

Bryan thought *he* was Trevor's father.

She locked her front door behind her and dashed up to her bedroom, trailing her clothing all the way up the stairs, wanting to shed tonight like a lizard shed its skin because she was feeling just as slimy.

He couldn't be Trevor's father. Mindy would have remembered *him*. *Any*one would have remembered Bryan. He'd been the stuff of every girl's fantasy. No wonder he'd worn the sunglasses. It made sense now.

But what hadn't made sense was that Mindy hadn't been living—or stripping—in town four years ago. She'd been fifty miles away so the possibility of running into him was remote at best.

Yes, that was it. That was what she'd do to prove to him that he wasn't Trevor's father. Hell, part of the reason they'd moved back here was so that they she wouldn't run into the guy who could be Trevor's father and have to fight for custody. She and Mindy had decided that right after the cancer diagnosis had come in.

Okay, so how did she go about proving he wasn't the father?

The bachelor party. All Mindy had known was that the groom-to-be's name was Brad and he was getting married the next day, so all Jenna needed to do was google weddings on that day within her old town that had a groom named Brad.

It took her less than five minutes.

It only took thirty seconds after that find a picture from the reception and learn that one of the groomsmen was named Bryan Lassiter.

Oh shit. Bryan really *could* be Trevor's father.

Panic set in. What if he wanted custody? What if he challenged her right to be Trevor's parent? What if he took Trevor from her?

No. That couldn't happen. She'd do whatever it took to keep Trevor with her.

He wanted to know Trevor though. That much was obvious. All the questions made sense now. Wanting to teach Trevor to throw a ball, Trevor's ability to throw a ball, offering to talk to the teacher on Trevor's behalf about Michael…

He thought she was the woman he'd slept with; that's why he'd been so quick to label her a hooker. Stripper, hooker, they could be interchangeable in his mind if he'd slept with her—with Mindy.

Bryan thought *she* was Mindy.

What would he do when he found out she wasn't?

Her bloodless fingers slid from the mouse. No. That wasn't happening. He *had* to think she was the woman he'd slept with. *Had* to. It was the only chance she had of keeping him from delving too deeply into Trevor's birth. Thank God only Cathy knew the truth.

When had Bryan guessed? At the supermarket or had this been planned all along? Had he somehow found out about Trevor and tracked her down?

Jenna studied Bryan's face on the screen and morphed it one of her mental images of Trevor. Same hair and curls. Same facial structure.

Same eyes.

Oh, God. He *was* the father. She knew it. And, worse, *he* knew it.

The question was, what did he plan to do about it?

***

Bryan tossed his keys onto his desk at BeefCake, Inc. Tonight definitely hadn't gone as planned.

"Yo, Bry, everything okay?" Gage walked into his office.

Bryan swiped a hand over his face. He hadn't told Gage anything about Trevor or Jenna yet. His partner had enough to deal with with his nephew's surgeries and his day job, plus running this place, handling their expansion, and helping Lara, his fiancée, with their upcoming wedding plans. Bryan didn't need to add one more mess to the ones Gage was already dealing with.

Plus, this was *his* mess. "It's been a rough night."

"Yeah, well you ought to see the crowd out here. Talk about rough. Not so sure we should stay open every night of the week. Maybe go to four days. Keep them interested and hungry for the days we *are* open."

"And lose out on the dinner traffic? I don't think so."

"Well then, we need to hire some help. Between managing the show, the paperwork, and the expansion, I barely have enough time for my projects and Lara. And guess which one I care most about?"

Bryan didn't have to guess. Ever since Gage had met "the cupcake lady," he'd been all about sampling the goods.

Bryan couldn't blame him. He wanted the opportunity to sample Jenna's goods, but she'd run out of the restaurant without touching the money.

He pulled the envelope out and fanned the bills with his thumb. He'd worked really hard for this money. A lot of long hours and a lot of dancing. He and Gage had been the only act when they'd started out. Now look at them. Big place, dinner crowds, a dozen employees… The place was growing. Gage was right; they did need help.

Jenna.

He'd hire Jenna. She must have been a halfway decent stripper if he'd ended up with her that night. And if she needed practice or different moves, well, he could work on that with her. He and Gage did, after all, work with the dancers on the routines.

Uh huh.

Bryan tucked the envelope back into his jacket pocket. He still didn't know why she'd run out on him, and if it hadn't taken Richie such a long time to run his charge card, he would have gone after her. Had thought about doing it, but realized by then that they were too strung out to continue their conversation with any sense of rationality. They needed time to cool down.

He didn't know if he'd ever cool down around Jenna, though. She'd looked gorgeous in that dress and every guy in Tosco's had noticed.

How many of them had sampled *her* goods?

He scrubbed his face. God, he was going to drive himself nuts thinking like this. But, seriously, how could she do it? How could she let any man into her body for money? Didn't she have any self-respect? Any sense of responsibility to her son—*their* son?

Or maybe that sense of responsibility was exactly why she was doing it. It wasn't as if he was helping out with the bills.

"Bry, any chance you can cover the rest of tonight? I want to get home in time to see Connor before he goes to bed. His surgery is tomorrow."

Now Bryan felt like a double ass. He'd known when Connor's surgery was; he should have volunteered to cover for Gage tonight instead of chasing down an underpriced hooker who'd borne his son.

God, his life was spiraling down the tubes faster than it had when he'd destroyed his ankle in that last championship game.

"Yes. Go. Give my love to Lara."

"I'll give *my* love to Lara and thank you to find your own woman." Gage flipped one of their signature bow tie key chains at him. "Don't forget to lock up."

Bryan waved him off, envying him. Why couldn't Jenna be a baker? A teacher? Hell, even if she worked at a fast food restaurant, he'd be thrilled. Something other than what she was.

Tanner poked his head in. "Intermission's over. You want to do the announcement?"

"Nah, you go ahead. Consider it a promotion."

Tanner grinned. "Good. I expect a pay raise."

"You get something raising out there and I'll consider it. Go. Give the guests a show."

"We always do."

Bryan sat back in his chair. Tanner and the guys—and now the women—they did put on a good show. He and Gage prided themselves on that. That this wasn't a sleazy joint like the town council had been worried about. But not every revue was like BeefCake, Inc. He and Gage had worked for one in college before they, entrepreneurs that they were, struck out on their own. They'd made twice the amount of money and got three times as many chicks. Back in the day, it'd been all about bragging rights.

But they were adults now. Were focused on making a business so people like Tanner and Markus and Carlos had a good place to work and the clientele got a high-class show.

Maybe that was all Jenna needed. The chance to make

some real money without having to resort to selling herself. And she could work nights when Trevor had gone to sleep. Hell, he'd sit at her house himself and babysit. He could do paperwork anywhere.

Speaking of which… Bryan picked up the stack of invoices and P.O.s and new hire paperwork. He really hated this part of the job. So did Gage, but since he was doing the renovation, Bryan had taken this nightmare on.

Maybe he'd hire Jenna to handle that. It'd be worth ten grand to him just to not have to do it.

He exhaled and started sorting. Whatever he decided to do about Jenna, he better do it soon if he wanted to enjoy some of his son's childhood. Trevor wasn't getting any younger.

Chapter Eleven

The next morning, Jenna handed Cathy a bottle of water in her kitchen after regaling her with the whole nightmarish mess. "What am I going to do, Cath?"

Cathy tapped the bottle against her lips and leaned against the back door, her turn to keep watch on the boys who were playing Dinosaur Wars on the kiddie table in the backyard. "You're going to have to sleep with him."

"I'm going to have to *what*? *This* is what you come up with?" Jenna continued pacing across her kitchen floor as she had during the last ten hours. Ten sleep-deprived hours.

"At the very least, you're going to have to pretend you're Mindy."

"I know, but how? I don't look a thing like her and she was younger than me."

"Jen, if he doesn't remember her well enough to know that you aren't her, he's not going to remember her age. Or anything else about her. Which can only work to your favor. I mean, lord knows what she did with him that night."

"And neither do I."

"So it's not a problem. You can make up whatever you want. He won't deny it if he doesn't remember it. And if he does… put it down to the alcohol. People black out all the time."

Yeah, there was an image she wanted Bryan to have of her. "There has to be some other way. I mean, I do have the adoption papers."

Cathy shook her head. "He's the biological parent who never terminated his rights, and if he's got an extra ten grand hanging around to give you to sleep with him, you can bet he's got more where that came from. He does have that club, you know. No, you have to pretend to be Mindy. At least Trevor looks like you."

The power of genetics, thank God. "But I didn't take the money."

"Why not?"

"Because…" Jenna had berated herself all night for not snatching up that envelope. Legal battles cost oodles of money. "Because I don't know if I can do this."

"What other options do you have?"

Not a one if Bryan decided to push it. She could deny his paternity all she wanted but one cotton swab with a home test kit and that'd be it.

Cathy pointed the water bottle at her. "See? You have to do it. Or you're going to lose Trevor."

That was the problem. There wasn't anything she *could* do. Even if she took the money, he'd already reported her for being a hooker; taking the money would only give credence to his argument.

"I'll just tell him it's all a misunderstanding. That I thought he wanted a tutor, not a hooker."

Cathy sipped the water, her gaze back in the yard. "That ought to fly."

"Why won't it? It's the truth. Sort of. I didn't know that he thought anything different 'til Sarge told me about the report."

"Okay, fine. You tell him you're a teacher not a hooker and he's going to start investigating you. It's not going to take too much digging to find out that you've never stripped in your life so you can't be the woman he slept with, and he'll go after Trevor." She looked at Jenna again. "Is that really what you want? I thought you'd do anything for that little boy?"

"That's not fair."

"All's fair in love and war. And child custody. What do you want, Jen? Fairness or Trevor?"

There was no question.

Cathy opened the back door. "Are you okay, guys?"

"Yes. Trevor just knocked my dinosaur into the tar pits."

"Does he need a bandage?"

"Nah. He's tough. Like me and Daddy."

Jenna couldn't hide the slice of pain that word evoked.

Cathy caught it. "Take his money, Jen. You need a good attorney. Ten grand will go a long way toward getting one. Besides, then you'll have him on the hook. He'll have hired a hooker."

"Not if I don't have sex with him."

"Now that'd be a damn shame. You might as well get the perks of his big misunderstanding. And having gotten a look at him, I bet that's not the only thing that's big."

Jenna rolled her eyes. "Seriously, Cathy, do you never *not* think about sex?"

Her friend rubbed her belly. "You can ask that when I'm pooching out like a cantaloupe? How do you think I got in this condition?"

"I am *not* sleeping with him."

Cathy shrugged. "Suit yourself, but he's already reported you to the police, so there's a record. And then you were seen out with him." She untwisted the cap to her water bottle. "And there is… you know. Past history. Mindy's, I mean, which he thinks is yours." She raised the water bottle to her lips. "Plus 'you' never told him about Trevor."

"I didn't know—"

"Which isn't really a good recommendation for custody. Let's face it, unless you work with him, you're going to get screwed."

"Well what you're suggesting will get me screwed, too."

"Yeah, but that's the good kind."

Jenna sat at the table. Part of her had to admit that she wouldn't mind the physical part—if it were anything other than a subterfuge. As for the other part—

"I'm not a hooker, Cath, and I can't pretend to be one."

Cathy took a swig of her water. "You've done okay so far."

"Yeah, but that's because I haven't had to sleep with him."

"Would that *really* be a hardship?"

Problem was, it wouldn't. And she didn't need any more complications in her life.

The front doorbell rang.

Speak of the devil… "Cath, what am I going to do?"

Cathy re-capped her water bottle. "I wish I had the answers, Jen. You really need to talk to a lawyer. Until then, string him along." She stood up. "I'll take the boys for the morning."

"I'd love that, but Trevor's counting on Bryan playing with him again. He's not going to want to go with you."

"So tell him Bryan couldn't make it." She shook her head. "I can't believe it. *The* Bryan Lassiter. Father of your child and the bearer of ten grand for sex. Be still my heart."

"He's just a man, Cath."

"Uh huh. You keep telling yourself that, Jen. I met him. Sans shirt. He's more than just any man." She opened the back door. "Bobby! Trevor! Pack up the T-rexes. We're going to the park!" She looked back at Jenna. "You've got about two hours to work this out before I have to drop Bobby at the sitter's and Trevor back here. You can figure something out."

The question was, what?

Chapter Twelve

Once Cathy had the kids safely out of earshot, Jenna took a big breath and opened the door. "Bryan. Come in."

"Is Trevor here?"

Those violet eyes of his mocked her, standing out in stark relief by the chest-hugging black t-shirt that only made the violet brighter. "I thought it best if Cathy took him while we finish what we didn't start last night."

Bryan ditched the duffel inside the door and slid past her into her home. "You didn't take the money."

"And I'm not going to."

He spun around. Hmm, she'd surprised him. Score one for her.

"But you need it."

"I've done fine without your money before and I'll do fine again."

"But how will you support yourself? Trevor?"

"Bryan, you seem to be under the impression that I'm in dire straits. I'm not. I'll support us the same way I always have."

"But I don't want you to, Jenna."

"Oh? And what gives you the right to dictate my life?"

"Trevor."

"I'm doing this *for* Trevor."

"Yeah, he's going to thank you for that when he grows up and figures it out."

"Trevor knows what I do."

Bryan's mouth fell open. "Please tell me you don't let him watch."

Oh for Pete's sake. Did he *really* think she'd expose a child to the world's oldest profession? If she were doing what he thought she was doing, that is. What kind of brainless twit did he take her for?

Ignoring the fact that her argument was based on a misunderstanding perpetuated by a lie, Jenna made up her mind. She couldn't, in good conscience, let him think she was a hooker, but letting him think she was Mindy might be the only way to prevent him from taking Trevor. Or, as Cathy had said, at least give her time to find out where she stood in this mess.

Didn't mean she couldn't toss something back in the suspicious, hardheaded idiot's face. "Sometimes, yes, Trevor does watch. He likes to."

His hang-dog expression was beyond priceless. Worth way more than ten grand.

"And sometimes I let him help."

Now he was gaping like a fish and she was trying not to laugh.

"But most of the time when I'm working, he's sleeping. I can't really do my job if I have to watch him. Plus, my students find it distracting."

Bryan surged to his feet and paced across her living room, kicking colored wooden blocks out of his way. Trevor wasn't going to like that. That structure, lopsided though it'd been, was his football stadium. Where he and Bryan were going to play football sometime.

Her heart tightened at the thought. For Trevor's sake she had to find some way to allow Bryan into his life.

But Bryan never had to know she wasn't Trevor's *biological* mother. She was his mother in every other way because, like a mother—lion, bear or human—she'd do whatever necessary to protect him. And keep him.

"I can't believe this." Bryan raked his hand through his hair and turned to face her. "You actually let him *watch*? Why hasn't child protective services been out here? Or do you keep all your 'students' so happy no one complains?"

He'd actually finger-quoted *students*. Jenna wanted to laugh. Where did he come off being so self-righteous and deciding he knew what was best for *any*one? He was the one who'd slept with a stripper in the first place. My, how pride did go before the fall.

"I've never had a complaint from any of my students. Most of them are more than satisfied with my performance." She was actually enjoying dripping the innuendoes all over the place.

"That's it." Bryan shoved both hands to his hips. "I'm sorry, Jenna, but I can't let this continue. If you don't stop, I'll *make* you."

And now for the *coup de grâce*. "You're going to stop me from teaching? Why? What do you have against high school English?"

"How can you even ask that? It's not like it's a subject in schoo—" His hands fell to his sides. "What? What did you say?"

She bit her lip to stop the laughter. "I asked what you have against high school English. Shakespeare not do it for you? Or did *The Scarlet Letter* scar you for life?"

"I—" And now he was back to gaping. She'd bet it wasn't a common occurrence for him. "*English*?"

"Yes. You know, the language you're butchering so badly right now?"

Bryan looked at her as if she were speaking a foreign one.

She took pity on him and patted the sofa. "Bryan, sit down."

When he did—speechless now, and she'd bet that was new for him, too—she explained. "Sarge told me what you thought of me. That you'd reported me for prostitution."

"You knew?"

"Of course I did. And I bet all of Tosco's clientele knew, too. The secretarial pool at the police station isn't known as a big keeper of secrets."

"But… you're not? What about your clients? The kid's parents paying for it? Accepting my offer?"

This time she had to smile. The truth would set her free. Well, in this aspect of their relationship anyway. "I tutor kids in the summer. Jason is taking the SATs in the fall and needed help to improve his scores."

"Richie, too?"

"Richie has trouble with reading. Sheila with math. I'm certified to teach both. History, too."

"Cal and his girlfriend?"

"We met in an adult literacy course I was speaking at."

"So then why did you quote me that astronomical sum?"

She ducked her head, not overly proud of herself, but she had to remember what he'd done. Accusing her of prostitution. In her home with a child about, no less. He'd deserved it.

"I wasn't going to take your money, not after I found out what you thought. I really did think you wanted a tutor for your child but you were being awfully obnoxious about it, so I tossed out an obnoxious amount, hoping you'd go away. Imagine my surprise when you didn't. And, hey, if you were willing to pay that much, the least I could do was agree to take it." She took a deep breath. "But once Sarge told me, well, you ticked me off. I kept up the pretense just so I could fling the money back in your face. I was really looking forward to doing that."

He rubbed his jaw. "You must think I'm a total ass."

"Um, yeah. Kinda."

He blew out a half-breath/half-laugh. "I guess I

deserved that."

"Mmhmm."

He stood up and paced, this time avoiding the blocks. Even nudged some of them back into a pile. "I… I'm sorry, Jenna. But that doesn't seem to cut it, does it?"

No, but what would be the point. "What's done is done. We just have to move forward."

"Is there anything I can do to make it up to you?"

Kiss me senseless would be a good start.

Okay, not her brightest moment. *Leave town* would be a better wish, but, again, not something she could say without going into explanations she wasn't prepared to give.

So she opted for something innocuous. "You wouldn't happen to have brought that ten grand would you? Flinging it back in your face would be so satisfying."

"As a matter of fact…" Bryan walked over to the satchel and picked it up. He handed it to her. "Do your damnedest."

Jenna slid the zipper back. There, inside, were a bunch of hundred dollar bills, all wrapped neatly with a paper band around them.

She pulled one out. "You really have ten thousand dollars in here?"

"It was our agreed upon price, why wouldn't I?"

She'd never held this much cash in her hand at once.

Jenna broke the seal and fanned the bills in her hand. Ten hundred dollar bills.

She brought out another stack. And another. Ten in all.

She broke the seals on each one, piled all the bills together then stared at it. This is what he'd thought would buy her off.

Suddenly, the laughter was replaced by anger. He really didn't have a high opinion of her. Okay, so he thought she was a stripper, but some people—women *and* men—danced for a reason. As he should well know. And for some, like Mindy, it was all they had.

And he ran a freakin' *strip joint.* He could call it whatever he wanted, but clothing came off when people danced on that stage. What high-and-mighty respectable leg did he have to stand on?

"Well? You going to do it? Or did you change your mind?" He sat down on the far end of the sofa, one elbow braced on a knee.

Change her mind? As in, she was now going to take it and give in to his demands? Why, of all the smug, self-centered, manipulative—

Jenna threw the pile at him. Bills fluttered all over the place and she had to say, it was a very satisfying feeling.

"Feel better?" Bryan spit out one of the bills that was stuck to his bottom lip.

"Actually, yes. I do." She tucked her hair behind her ears, then flicked a pair of hundreds off her lap. Stepped on them. *That* was satisfying.

Bryan scraped a couple of bills off the sofa and stacked them on the table amid a sea of green and white Ben Franklins. "I swear, you are unlike any woman I've ever met."

That's because they'd never met, but she couldn't tell him that.

"That's right, I am. And don't you forget it."

As if Bryan *could* forget it.

He slid several hundreds from beneath the table with his running shoe, still trying to process this series of events.

She wasn't a hooker; she was a teacher. And, yes, he did think of his wish yesterday: *Why couldn't she be a teacher he could consider settling down and raising a family with?*

Looked like that one had come true. Well, the family part. The settle down part? *Could* they settle down?

Together?

Bryan studied her as she gathered the money. She was undeniably pretty in an unconventional sort of way. Jean shorts, a baggy t-shirt, not a lick of makeup, and that wildly curly mussed up hair that refused to stay nicely tucked behind her ears. Jenna was real. No pretense at all.

The mother of his child.

The words reverberated in his brain. He hadn't exactly chosen her for the role, but he had to admit he'd made a good choice in his drunken stupor.

He wanted to find out about that night. Why she hadn't sought him out when she'd learned she was pregnant. What her pregnancy had been like. Had she ever thought of ending it? Giving Trevor up for adoption?

Bryan closed his eyes as the pain stabbed him. Jesus. Thirty-four years old; he'd like to be over it by now. But it was always there, hovering in the background. Making him wonder if he'd ever be good enough.

He'd been adopted. Knew what it was like not to be wanted by the woman who'd borne him.

Oh, sure, he knew all the statistics. Had heard all the stories. Better to be raised in a loving home by a couple who wanted children than in some drug-motel by a crack-whore mother.

The thing was, he never knew if that'd been his case. Had his mother been a junkie? Had she been a runaway? Was he the product of incest? Rape? Had she been trying to manipulate someone into marrying her? Had he been a one-night stand? Or had she been a teenager who hadn't thought pregnancy could happen to her? Had she believed her boyfriend was using a condom? Had it broken?

The scenarios swirled in his head as they'd done for every one of the last thirty years. His adoptive parents had never hidden it from him; had been sure to let him and Kyle know that they'd been picked out especially because of who they were. Reassurances, Bryan recognized, from loving parents to insecure children.

He knew all that. Knew all the psychoanalysis mumbo-jumbo, but the fact remained that he knew no one in this world to whom he was biologically related.

Until Trevor.

No way was he going to walk away now.

"We have something else to discuss, Jenna."

Jenna shot to her feet, wrapped her arms around her waist—where she'd carried their child—and walked over to the front window. "Bryan, I… I can't. Not now. I need some time."

"You've had enough time, Jenna. Now it's my turn." He dropped the money inside his duffel bag, then walked up behind her and put his hands on her shoulders. "I'd like to spend some time with my son."

Chapter Thirteen

His son.

Trevor was *her* son. Hers!

"Jenna, I know Trevor's mine."

Bryan wasn't going to go away any more than she would. And, honestly, for Trevor's sake, she should be happy about that.

Unfortunately, *happy* was not what she was feeling at the moment.

She swallowed and looked at him in the window's reflection. Definitely not happy.

"I get why you didn't tell me before. We hadn't exactly exchanged phone numbers."

True. Body fluids, yes; simple means of communication? Apparently not.

But it was *Mindy* who'd exchanged fluids with Bryan. It was important to remember that—and never let on.

"But now… I know. And you know. If you hadn't before, you had to the minute you saw my eyes."

She looked at them now. Violet with a sparkle of blue around the pupil. Just like the ones she'd looked at every day for the past three and a half years.

"Yes." One word, such an impact. On not only her, but on Bryan *and* Trevor. Three letters, three lives.

Bryan removed his hands from her shoulders to rake them through his hair. "So, the question is, what are we going to do?"

That *was* the question. She turned around. "What do *you* want to do?"

"I'd like to get some answers if you wouldn't mind."

It wouldn't matter if she did. He was entitled to them. But only up to a point. Anything having to do with Trevor's biological mother was getting the spin treatment.

She turned back around to the window. Outside, everything was exactly as it'd always been. Mr. Heiner was edging his sidewalk, Mrs. Heiner hanging the laundry. The Tolofsons next door were playing baseball with their twins. Tyler Hepburn ambled from mailbox to mailbox delivering the mail. Life à la Rockwell, yet her insides felt like a Picasso, disjointed and out of whack.

"I…" She took a deep breath. "I didn't know whose baby he was." She heard his quick intake of breath and winced along with him. "One of the girls… she was jealous. Decided to get back by poking pin holes in the box of condoms." All of it, so far, true. Except this was Mindy's story to tell.

"Couldn't you find out who I was somehow? Weren't there records? I hired the strip—your company personally for Brad's party. Couldn't you retrace your… steps?"

The euphemisms for such an intimate act struck Jenna as particularly funny in a situation that was far from humorous.

"There were a lot of… parties." Though Mindy had assured her there weren't a lot of men, but still, enough that tracking them down had required a lot of work, and most guys weren't into giving up that they'd slept with a stripper. "Besides, I figured I'd get the run-around once the guy found out why I'd tracked him down. Who would want to claim a baby?"

Bryan was close enough behind her that she could feel his warm breath on her neck. Feel the electricity between them. Hear the catch in his voice as he answered, "I would've."

Pain, raw and jagged-edged, rolled over her. She rode the wave, and waited for the next one just because it would come. Like the tide, she knew it would come. “But I didn’t know that. For all I knew you were a married man and the baby would be a huge issue.”

“He’s my son, Jenna.” His stood right behind her and stared at her in the reflection on the window. “I want to be part of his life.”

Part of his life was a lot different than *he’s mine and I want him.*

“You do?”

He nodded. “I was adopted. My brother and I were. I know what it’s like not knowing who your biological parents are. I don’t want to do that to Trevor. I *can’t* do that to him.”

She ought to be thrilled. This man was Trevor’s father. Her son could finally have the dad he wanted. The dad he deserved.

So why did she want to scoop him up and bundle him off to the farthest corner of the world and keep him for herself?

Jenna moved back to the sofa and sank down onto the arm. She couldn’t do that any more than she could deny Trevor the *right* to his father. Or Bryan the right to his son.

Maybe there could be a compromise. “O…kay.”

“You’re not going to fight me?”

She wrapped her arms around herself again, nerves making her cold. “What would be the point? Anyone can see he’s yours.”

The smile that lit Bryan’s face took Jenna’s breath away. Both because it made him even more gorgeous and because it was just like Trevor’s.

“I want to take him camping. Go fishing. Take him to a game. Every sport. Build a tree fort with him. Teach him to drive, answer his questions about girls… All the things a father and son do. Maybe someday, he’ll even call me dad.”

Her heart broke over that, as much for Bryan as for Trevor. Bryan's adoption meant that he had no biological relations anywhere except for Trevor. And neither did Trevor. She owed it to both of them to let this happen.

But where did that leave her? Now, more than ever, Bryan could not know about Mindy.

"How are we going to tell him? How are we going to tell anyone?"

Bryan grimaced. "I'm afraid both of us can't come off in a good light if the truth gets out."

Especially if the truth got out; she'd be labeled a liar. She crossed her arms. "True."

"I'm willing to manufacture one if you are."

"How? I've lived here for over three years and you've been here all along. No one will believe we didn't know the other was living in the same town."

"Why not? That much is the truth."

"No one will buy it."

Bryan sat down next to her. "Does it matter? We know the truth, who cares what others say?"

"Trevor will when he starts getting teased."

"No one's going to tease my son."

She rolled her eyes. "Spoken like a true father. Who forgets what junior high was like."

"Junior high was great, what are you talking about?"

For him, it probably had been. For the rest of the tween-er crowd it was three years of acne, greasy hair, body odor, bad hair cuts, braces, and trying to fit in.

She got to her feet. It was her turn to pace. "We have to have a story, Bryan. Preferably one that doesn't make me look like a who—a woman with loose morals. After all, I'm a teacher. I have a reputation to uphold for my contract."

"I'll take the fall."

"What?"

He shrugged, then pushed off his thighs and stood. "I'll say it was me. That you came to me and told me about the baby, but I didn't believe he was mine. We had a fight and you never spoke to me again."

"But then you look like the jerk."

"I've been called worse."

It was such a sweet gesture she ran her hand down his arm before she thought about it.

And, nope, it wasn't a good idea. Her fingers wanted to stay there.

She retrieved her tempted little digits and tucked them into the crook of her arm. "Not that it's not sweet of you, but Trevor can't grow up with that story. We need to find one that's going to make *both* of us look as good as possible given the circumstances. Remember, this is what he's going to know about his conception and how he'll think about us."

"So we stick as close to the truth as possible."

Jenna was going to put a big fat veto on that one. She wasn't bringing Mindy into the equation.

Bryan ran a hand over his mouth. "We'll say we met at a party, had a good time, but by the time you realized you were pregnant, we were through, and I was gone, and you didn't know how to get in touch with me."

She headed back to the sofa. All these lies were making her head hurt. "Except the internet makes it easy to find almost anyone."

"*Almost* being the operative word. I'm not on any of the social networking sites, the only website I have is for the club and I didn't have that back then, and my cell phone's unlisted. I never told you where I was from, so you wouldn't have been able to track me that way."

"What about the other people at the party?"

Bryan dropped into the chair opposite her. "You came with a friend of a friend and the party was at a rental property. No formal guest list; we both crashed it and ended up hooking up."

"So we had a one night stand that resulted in a baby

and could never find each other again?" It wasn't the best story, but given her own past, one people would believe.

Unfortunately.

"We didn't have a reason to find each other again."

"*You* didn't. I was stuck with a baby."

Bryan turned those violet eyes her way and they were startling—both for the intensity of them and the fact that they were exactly like Trevor's. "We *are* still talking about our cover story, right? Because you sound a little angry for something I had no idea was going on."

She licked her lips. "No, you're right. I'm sorry. I could have kept looking, I guess. It's just that it was such a shock."

All of which was true. Mindy's pregnancy, trying to figure out what to do and how to support another mouth, then the cancer diagnosis and his birth and only six months until Mindy was gone. There'd been the lawyer to see, the funeral to arrange, the last-minute videos Mindy had wanted to make for her child that Jenna had stored away for the day Trevor was old enough to see them… There hadn't been any time to track down the guys at the parties and figure out which one could be Trevor's father.

"Did you ever… that is, had you ever considered getting rid of it? Him?"

"Abortion? No. That was never an option." Mindy had been adamant about it and Jenna had been glad. No matter how much raising him on her own entailed, having lost a child, Jenna was blessed to have him in her life.

"So now when do we tell Trevor?"

And now she had to share him.

Jenna took in a shaky, shallow breath. "Do we have to? I mean, right off the bat? Can't we let him get to know you, ease into it?"

Bryan shook his head. "Jenna, Trevor's my son; I will be in his life. I'd like things to be amicable between you and I, with what's best for him at the center of everything we do, but I *will* be his father. He *will* know me."

The words she'd wanted Carl to say. To feel. Not this stranger who'd suddenly laid claim to everything she held dear.

And had more right to that claim than she did.

"Okay. But let's give it a few days. Let him get used to you being around, have other people get used to seeing you here."

"How long do you think that's going to last? You'd heard what I'd said about you in under an hour. How long do you think it's going to take for this news to get around town—and back to Trevor? His 'buddy' Michael is going to *relish* sharing this little tidbit."

Michael was a jerk like that. So were his parents. The kid came by it naturally.

Jenna blew out a breath trying to settle the butterflies in her stomach. This was it, the irrevocable step. Once she gave in, there was no going back.

But part of being a parent was doing what was best for your child, even if it meant something that wasn't good for you. "Okay, Bryan, we'll tell him when he gets home later."

"Good. That's settled." He pulled the cash out of his pocket. "Now, as to the money—"

"I told you, I'm not taking it."

"Jenna, it was never for sex. I was never going to demand that from you."

So much for Cathy's suggestion.

Jenna was appalled to find out she was disappointed.

"I wanted you to have it so you wouldn't have to, well, do what I thought you were doing. But now, I want you to take it. It's the least I can do to help out. You've had four years of doing it all by yourself. You don't have to anymore."

She refused to touch the money and it had nothing to do with his mistaken assumptions. This had to do with her.

Who she was. "Let's get one thing straight, Bryan. I can provide for my son."

"Our son."

"Fine. Our son. But *I* can do it. If you want to contribute, put the money aside for college. "

"Nice gesture, but we're sharing him, Jenna. Fifty-fifty. And that includes the cost of raising him. I'll put the ten grand in a college fund, but from here on out, I'm paying half of everything."

"I'm not comfortable taking money from you."

"Jenna—"

"No, seriously. Listen. I didn't come after you for money when he was born and I'm not asking for any now. We're not getting married, Bryan, we're raising our son."

"Then work for me. *Earn* the money. Surely, you can use some extra cash."

The extra cash would be nice, but… "You want me to *strip* for you?"

Good thing she was sitting down because her knees got more than a little wobbly at that image: her and Bryan in her bedroom, seductive music playing in the background, shimmying her shorts down her legs, pulling her top over her head—

She didn't even know how to strip seductively and doing so would out her in a minute. No way would she have been hired by any dance company anywhere.

"Dance? No. But there's a mountain of paperwork in the office, however, that I'd love for you to make sense of. Invoices, purchase orders, new hire paperwork… I can dance and I can manage dancers and I can bring patrons in; what I don't want to do is figure out invoice numbers and net billing and escrow accounts and stuff like that. I'll gladly turn all of that over to you so you can earn your paycheck. Work around Trevor's schedule. What do you say?"

"Just office work? Paperwork and things like that?"

"Just paperwork."

"No dancing?"

"No." Not even if she wanted to. The dancers made great tips, but she was *not* going to show off her body for anyone.

Except him.

Bryan wanted to laugh, but it actually wasn't funny. The only way he'd get to see Jenna's body was in his dreams.

If only he could remember that night.

"Why?" Jenna was staring at him with her beautiful blue eyes. They'd sparkled in the candlelight last night and he'd fallen a little under their spell. It was happening again here.

"Why?" He dragged his gaze off of hers. He needed to keep his wits about him right now; what they defined would affect Trevor for who-knew-how-long. Momentary lust had no place in this discussion.

And then she inhaled and her breasts moved under her t-shirt, two soft mounds that he'd obviously had in his hands and probably his mouth four years ago.

Shit. There was *nothing* momentary about what he was feeling for her.

"Yes, why? Why are you so hell-bent on me working for you? You don't even know me."

But he did: in the biblical sense. Didn't matter if he didn't remember; Trevor was proof. This was not what he'd expected when he'd come here this morning. At most he'd been worried about changing her job description. Now, he had to convince her to take the legit job he was offering. "You're a single mom. I was given up for adoption by my birth mother; I always wondered if she'd had help if she would have kept me. You need help, I can provide it. It's a win-win situation for both of us."

"For all three of us, you mean."

Yeah, all *three* of them.

Chapter Fourteen

"You're sure the kid's yours, right?" Gage pointed to one of the down lights on the stage that'd been knocked out of whack.

"He's mine." Bryan checked the wiring and adjusted the light. Some patron always had a little too much to drink and leaned over it to grab the dancers. Male, female, it didn't matter; the drunks were equal opportunity grabbers. He was going to have to re-think the lighting design before someone got hurt either by having to be pulled off the stage or fried to a crisp by touching the bulb.

"How can you be sure? I mean, you don't remember what she looked like. You sure she's not after your money? This place?"

Yeah, Gage had the right to be worried. His future was tied up in BeefCake, Inc. as much as Bryan's was.

"When you meet Trevor, you'll see. There's no question. But what are you doing here? I thought Connor's surgery was today?"

Gage winced, a look Bryan was all too familiar with on his partner's face. The hit-and-run that had injured Connor had knocked his whole family down and the pressure all rested on Gage's shoulders. Bryan had never been happier for his friend than when he'd found Lara. For the first time in a long time, he'd seen Gage really happy.

"He woke up with a sinus infection. They don't want to put him under anesthesia until that clears up, so we've had to postpone."

"Ah, man, Gage, I'm sorry. I know how much you were looking forward to getting it over with."

"Yeah, seven down, two to go. We just want them to be done."

Bryan could relate on a different level. No, he wasn't facing surgeries for Trevor—that he knew about anyway; he'd have to make a mental note to remember to ask Jenna about that later—but the worry and the love and the thoughts of what the kid's future would be like... Bryan suddenly got all of those. The parental feelings had been creeping up on him ever since he'd left Jenna's house. What was his son doing right now? Who was he playing with? Or was he drawing? Taking a nap? Was Michael telling him a bunch of inappropriate things... Most people got nine months to adjust; he'd had about nine hours.

"Do they know when?"

Gage shrugged and adjusted the centerpiece on the table. "He's got at least two weeks with the antibiotics. They want to make sure it's knocked out of him before we go back."

"Makes sense. Doesn't help your stress level, but you want what's best for Connor."

Gage turned one of the chairs around and straddled it at the table. "So. A son. You have a son."

A goofy smile showed up on Bryan's face and he couldn't wipe it off. Not that he wanted to. He had a son. "I know, right? I feel like I should be handing out cigars or something. Buying blue stuff."

"Four's a little old for that sort of thing."

The smiled disappeared. "Yeah. Four. I missed a lot."

"You mad?"

Bryan had to think about that. "No, I can't say that I am. She had tough decisions to make and I have no right to question them. I wasn't there, I don't know what she went through or her situation. It was just a one-night thing and she's right; for all she knew I could have been married and the baby would have been trouble. She didn't know me."

"And you didn't know her. Yet now you want her to work here?"

"I'll pay her out of my take."

"The money's not the problem. I'm worried about you. You don't know anything about this woman."

"She's an English teacher at the high school and has lived here for three years. Sarge thinks she's great, all of her students that I've met love her, and Trevor seems to be pretty well adjusted. I think she's trustworthy."

"But the circumstances of how you met—"

"Watch it, Gage. You're talking about the mother of my child." Bryan hadn't realized the caveman attitude was lurking in his psyche, but, yeah, it was. Maybe that'd be his costume the next time he had to cover for one of the dancers instead of his cop persona. "I certainly wasn't winning any Respectable Citizen awards that night either. I'm just as much to blame as she is."

Words he had to remember. No double standards when it came to hook-up sex and broken condoms.

"Okay, as long as you know what you're doing. I just don't want you blinded by the white picket fence image and not see the weeds."

There were no weeds. He'd been the weed by making the assumption he had about her.

"So when are you turning over the reins? We've had a couple calls come in from vendors looking for their payments. I know we've got the money on the books, so I figured it was just a matter of paperwork."

"Yeah, you know me; I'd rather be doing anything than pushing papers. That's why I'm hiring Jenna."

Gage stood up and repositioned the chair. "Good. Now maybe all our female dancers will stop mooning over you."

"You're just jealous that it's not you—which it would

have been if we'd hired them before you met Lara."

"Yeah, but since the female dancers were Lara's idea, they wouldn't be here." Gage got that goofy smile Bryan had grown accustomed to seeing in the last year. One year and so much had changed for his friend. "And besides, I'm perfectly happy with only Lara mooning over me."

A couple more seconds of that goofy smile, but then Gage got serious. As Bryan knew he would. They'd been friends forever. They goofed around, teased each other, gave each other shit, but they were there for each other. "So other than hire her, what else are you going to do about Trevor's mother? Is there anything else between you?"

Bryan had been asking himself that same thing. He walked to the window and looked out at the lunchtime traffic. A young mother was pushing a baby carriage down the sidewalk towards a man who enveloped her in a hug. He gave her a sweet peck on the cheek before picking a rattle out of the carriage and shaking it for the baby. Pudgy little arms and legs waved beneath a blur of pink.

Had Jenna taken Trevor for walks? Had anyone hugged her or played with a rattle for Trevor?

He wished he had. Wanted to now.

Maybe in the future…

"Hell, Gage. I don't know have a clue." He gathered the book and invoices and the rest of the hated paperwork. "I have to get back. We're going to tell Trevor when he wakes up from his nap today."

"Don't you think you should figure things out before you involve him?"

"Can't. The gossip in this town is rampant. We don't want him hearing it from someone else, and after Jenna stormed out of Tosco's last night, we're on the gossips' radar. It's better if he hears it from us."

"It's your call, Bry. I just hope you know what you're doing."

Yeah, that would be nice, wouldn't it?

Chapter Fifteen

Jenna straightened the last magazine on the table and fluffed the last pillow on the sofa. This was silly. Bryan didn't care what her house looked like. Neither did Trevor. As long as he had room on the rug to build his football stadium—again—he was happy. She'd had to pry him away from the blocks to get him to take his nap, but take his nap he would. There'd never been a more important time for him to be well rested because once they told him Bryan was his father, Jenna had a feeling Trevor would never close his eyes again.

Bryan tapped the sidelight by the front door.

She had to smile. Already he was acting like a parent, keeping the noise to a minimum so he didn't wake Trevor.

"He's still napping," she said as she opened the front door.

"Good. That'll give us time to go over these." He held up a pile of papers, but Jenna wasn't looking at them. She was looking at him. At those eyes that were the spitting image of Trevor's, at the smile that crossed lips she wished she'd been the one to kiss four years ago, and down to his broad chest covered in that sexy as hell t-shirt that she wished she'd been the one to remove that night…

She shook her head. The only reason she was wishing she'd been the one that night was so that her parental rights wouldn't be called into issue. If she were truly Trevor's biological mother, she wouldn't be risking her son's family, stability, and happiness by bringing his father back into the picture.

It was a Catch-22: she wanted Trevor to have a father, she just didn't want that father to have any claim to supersede hers.

"Let's go into my office."

Bryan stopped in the doorway. "No wonder you wanted to toss my money back in my face." The room was ringed with eye-chart-like posters of letters and numbers and sentence structures and diagrams. A couple of timelines from the Revolutionary War were lined up on the wall on the far side. Her desk was covered with lined paper, rulers, and pencils, and stacks of notebooks where her students practiced their writing.

"I'd thought there was a lavish bed back here. Silk sheets, a waterfall, sensual music—"

The image was getting to her so Jenna took her seat behind her desk. Normally, she'd sit next to her clients at the conference table she'd shoved up against the wall to conserve space, but with Bryan weaving seduction—albeit unknowingly—into the room, she needed a buffer.

Bryan spread the papers out and handed her the ledger.

"You don't use the computer?"

He shrugged. "It wasn't a top priority cash outlay at the beginning since we had to hire staff, get a venue, and fix it up. Manually has been working for us."

She nudged the stack of unpaid bills. "Uh huh."

A black curl fell over his forehead when he ducked his head. "Well, it worked for a while."

"Okay, so show me your system. I might need to make some adjustments."

"As long as it's not diverting funds to the Caymans, be my guest."

She put her pencil down. "Look, Bryan, either you trust me or you don't, but I wasn't the only person there that night Trevor was conceived. You might think I'm cheap and trampy or something—most people do when they think of strippers—but I'm honest."

The words mocked her. Here she was, declaring her honesty when the biggest lie in the world just rolled off her tongue.

But she was doing it for the right reasons; that's what she had to remember. Didn't history treat Robin Hood much kinder than the Sheriff of Nottingham had? Sure, what he'd been doing was illegal by the letter of the law, but by the spirit, Robin Hood had been doing what was right.

Was she really comparing herself to a fairy tale?

"Jenna, it was a joke. I do trust you. You've proven yourself by getting yourself out of dancing and into teaching, and by how well you've raised Trevor. I didn't mean to imply anything."

"Oh." She picked her pencil back up, different factions warring inside of her. She hated lying. Really really hated it. Had never been good at it and hadn't wanted to be. And the fact that she was good enough at it that he didn't question her—and even trusted her—was scary.

It's all for Trevor.

Right. She had to remember that. "Okay, so show me what's current."

They worked on the books with Jenna pulling out her laptop to load a basic accounting program and typing in the data.

"This won't be hard, and it's not going to take me much time. I can probably get it done during his nap."

"I don't wanna take any more naps."

Trevor stood in the doorway to her office.

"Hi Bwyan. Can we pway football now?"

"Hey, Sport." Bryan hopped out of his chair and scooped Trevor into his arms before Jenna could make her way out from behind her desk.

And, yes, she was jealous that Trevor had his arms wrapped around Bryan's neck and was perfectly comfortable being in his arms.

She was jealous that Trevor was in his arms.

"Trevor, a growing boy needs his naps. That's when he grows."

"Nuh uh. Michael said that's a cwock. I don't wike cwocodiles. But his stories are cool."

"Everything was "cool" these days to Trevor. Except Bryan, that was. Bryan had been *awesome*.

"How about this?" Bryan sat down and settled Trevor on his knee. "How about if you take a nap for your mom, then I'll take you out for a cupcake afterwards? No nap means no cupcake."

She was going to have to educate Bryan on the merits—and lack thereof—of bargaining with a child. Especially Trev. He could be as stubborn as they came at times.

"Okay."

She did a double-take. Was this her son?

"I mean it, though," said Bryan. "Your mom will give me a report. If you give her a hard time, no cupcake."

"I won't. I wove Mommy and she only wants what's best for me."

Jenna could kiss Cathy right now; those words had *Cathy Mayfield* stamped all over them.

"That's right, your mom does. And you know what? So do I."

Trevor patted Bryan's arm. "Cool. So we can pway football now? And can we get a cupcake too?"

Seeing them in front of her, both in profile, Jenna's heart thudded. Same nose, same chin, same happy expression on their faces, same gorgeous eyes. Trevor was a mini version of Bryan and showed her exactly who her son would become.

"How about a little later? Right now your mom and I

have something we need to talk to you about."

Trevor's lips had that twisty pout Jenna had come to know so well over the years. He only used it when he wanted to be adorable, and she never told him that it didn't matter; he was always adorable to her. But there was no need to reveal his physical cues nor her understanding of them.

And maybe Bryan's were the same. Who knew? That knowledge could come in handy some day.

"Why can't you talk to me water? I'm stawving for cupcakes."

Bryan raised an eyebrow at her. "Is he always this much of a negotiator?"

She laughed. "Looks like that's an inherited trait."

Bryan laughed. "Touché." He set Trevor onto his feet. "Come on, Trev. Let's go into the living room to have our chat."

"Are you coming, too, Mommy?"

It warmed Jenna's heart to hear that little bit of worry in Trevor's voice. He needed her. "Of course, Trev. I'm not leaving you." She said that for Bryan's benefit as much as Trevor's.

Sure, things were good between them right now, but would they always be? Bryan had to know that she was in this for the long haul and if he wanted to be, as well, they had to work together.

She smiled as she followed her guys out the door—

Her guys.

She stopped. God, if only that were true. If only Trevor really was hers and if she'd made him with Bryan.

She swallowed. No use crying over things that couldn't be. The situation was what it was and if she wanted to keep it, she better get in there. Trevor might want a father, but she had no idea what was going to happen when he actually got one.

Bryan glanced back at Jenna. What was taking her so long to walk the twelve feet into the living room on the most important afternoon of his life?

"Didya see my stadium, Bwyan?" Trevor patted the top block. "It's for football."

"I did, Trev. You did a great job." Bryan smiled just enough to hide his laugh behind it. Trevor had the same Boston accent he'd had as a child—and neither one of them was from Boston. Bryan's mother had said it was the cutest thing, all his dropped *r*s and added *ah*s at the ends of words that'd disappeared when he'd started kindergarten. Now Trevor had it. Maybe that meant that *his* biological father had had the same trait.

Funny how the hollow feeling a thought about his father would normally have evoked was lessened by seeing the same thing in his son.

Bryan sat on the sofa and patted the cushion next to him. "Hop up here, Trev and we'll wait for your mom to join us."

Jenna looked up at that, startled it seemed, and finally walked into the room. "Sorry about that."

"No problem."

She sat on the other side of Trevor, nibbling her lip.

God, that got to him. *He* wanted to nibble her lip.

His jeans got tight enough to make him lean forward and rest his arm across his groin. "So, Trev." He glanced at Jenna. "Your mom and I have something to tell you. Jenna? You want to do this?"

He saw her swallow. This had to be tough for her. She'd had Trevor to herself for so long and, really, she didn't know him. Sharing her child with an almost complete stranger had to be one of the most difficult things for her. Luckily, he was a stand-up guy. He'd take care of Trevor and her if she'd let him. He wanted to do what was right for all of them.

"Trev, honey. I know how much you want a father,

and, well…" She looked at him. "What would you say if Bryan was your dad?"

Bryan wasn't sure he liked all the uncertainty and *if*s in the way she told Trevor, but the smile that lit his son's face took all the doubt away.

"Weally?"

For the first time in Bryan's life, he saw the beauty in violet eyes. His throat closed at the awe and happiness in that one mispronounced word.

He cleared his throat. "Yes, Trev. I'm your dad."

Trevor turned that same look toward his mother. "Why are you cwying, Mommy?"

She brushed a shaky hand over Trevor's curls. "Because I'm so happy for you, Trevor. Every child should have two parents, and now you do."

The last was said to him more than Trevor. Bryan closed his hand over hers and together they stroked their son's hair.

"This is cool!" Trevor jumped to his feet. "Can we pway ball now? I wanna pway with my dad." He tugged Bryan's hand. "Come on, daddy. Wet's go!"

Daddy.

It took his son less than ten seconds to accept him and call him dad.

This was the best day of Bryan's life.

Which was, of course, followed by the worst night of his life.

Chapter Sixteen

Bryan stared at the nightmare in front of him.

Gage had an offsite show; one of them always accompanied the dancers in case something happened , which, more times than not, did, so they would step in and dance if they had to or make monetary decisions or call a tow truck… whatever. Things like that were expected when they traveled to a show.

But *here*? At the club? Things were supposed to run like clockwork here.

Dancers dropping left and right was *not* clockwork.

"What was in that damn pizza?" he yelled to Tanner as Tanner was on his way to the bathroom to lose the dinner tonight's crew had ordered out.

He didn't get that; they had a fully functioning kitchen that served excellent food; why'd the crew order from somewhere else? Hell, he even gave them a discount.

"How the fuck should I know? I certainly didn't order it." Tanner slammed the door shut, but not soon enough for Bryan to miss what was happening inside.

Poor guy. It sucked to get yelled at while your insides were rebelling.

Tamra ran past him into another bathroom, her Vegas showgirl tail feathers whipping across his face.

They needed to plan for more bathrooms in the expansion area.

Melanie limped past him. "I don't think I can go on,

boss."

Considering her skin was paler than the angel wings she wore, Bryan had to agree.

Markus came out looking just as white. And he was black.

"Markus, go home. Or better yet, go lay down in the break room. You probably shouldn't be driving."

"I definitely shouldn't be away from a bathroom," he mumbled, heading toward the break room in the back.

Bryan and Gage had made sure there were plenty of sofas there in case any of the patrons needed to sleep off some drinks and didn't want to leave their car.

He had a feeling *that* wasn't going to happen tonight. No show meant very little booze.

He pulled out his cell and started making calls to the dancers who were off tonight. Hopefully, enough of them would come in that they could still have a show.

He looked at the time. A much later show than normal, but he'd comp everyone a couple of drinks. Better to lose a little income than an entire night's worth if he had to shut down.

Three of the off-call dancers were able to make it in. Typically, they had twice that number, so these three would be dancing their asses off. Literally. But he still needed some more.

"I'm leaving, Bry." Steve stuck his face around the office door. His green face. "I don't live too far."

"Take a bucket or something with you. You don't look good."

"Tell me about it." He grabbed the trashcan by Bryan's door. "Thanks. I'll bring it back tomorrow."

"Keep it. I don't want it back."

Steve's smile was wan—either from the bad pizza or the bad joke.

Bryan made the last call. Dominic had to make it in.

"You've reached Dom. I'm out. Leave a message."

Dom was usually glued to his cell. That he hadn't answered didn't bode well for Bryan.

Shit. He was going to have to dance.

He looked at the time again. The replacement crew would be here in the next half hour. Dom lived a good forty-five minutes away. If he didn't return the call in the next ten, Bryan was going to have to pull his own costume out of mothballs.

He picked up the box of noxious pizza and tossed it into the trash. Probably ought to have it analyzed then charge the pizzeria with attempted murder by poisoning.

He looked at the delivery number on the front and called the place, hoping to save other people from the same nightmare.

It didn't make him feel any better to learn that other people were calling in with the same complaint; his dancers were still out for the count.

"Tamra, go in the back and sleep it off. You'll feel better in the morning."

She looked like a showgirl who'd seen far too much of the Vegas nightlife. Even her tail feathers drooped.

"I can't get this damn tail off. Would you mind, Bry?" She turned her back to him.

It'd been a long time since he'd had to undo a showgirl's costume and the hook-and-eye's were hidden in a cloud of feathers. It probably didn't look all that great to have his hands all over Tamra's ass in the middle of the service corridor, but she was so ill *nothing* would happen between them and unless someone opened the door into the main dining area, no one would see any way.

Which was, of course, exactly what happened. And who was standing on the other side of that door?

Jenna.

So much for trusting Bryan.

Jenna stared at him. He had his hands all over that

girl's backside. Right there. In the hallway. Where anyone could see them.

Her included.

And she'd been worried about ruining *her* reputation? Bryan was going to ruin it for her.

"Jenna."

Yeah, he better look guilty. 'Cause he was. The snake.

"Jen, is that—?" Cathy peered over her shoulder.

"Yeah. It is." She hustled Cathy back the way they'd come. "Come on. Let's go."

"Hey, wait a minute. I want to see the show. I thought you did, too."

"I've seen enough of a show back there, thankyouverymuch."

"Hmmm, sounds like someone's jealous."

That got her to stop. "I am not jealous."

"Then why are we leaving? If you're not jealous, you shouldn't care that Bryan's feeling some girl up."

Leave it to Cathy to put it in its most crude terms. But yeah, feeling up a dancer in the middle of a hallway where anyone could see was a bit crude.

A lot crude.

"Come on, Jen, chill out. I'm sure there was a logical explanation for what he was doing."

Jenna arched an eyebrow at her friend. "I thought you said you knew exactly how you got in the position you're in?"

"They weren't having sex back there. Not unless he's one of those furry people."

Okay that got her to laugh. The thought of Bryan having sex with a mascot…

Not that there was anything wrong with that if that's what he was into. It's just that she wasn't and eeeew, the idea kind of turned her off.

Which could be a good thing actually. She'd found herself thinking about Bryan way too much after the afternoon they'd spent together.

That's why she was here tonight. Cathy had arranged for a babysitter for Bobby since her husband was out of town and she'd decided she and Jenna needed a girls' night out. And the perfect place to come was BeefCake, Inc.

Jenna was second-guessing that decision. Especially when Bryan came barreling out of the back.

"Jenna, wait." He grabbed her arm and, yeah, she'd wait. The man knew just how to touch her.

He'd also touched Mindy.

Jealous much?

Yes. She was. And there. She admitted it. She was jealous. She wanted him to touch her. To want her. To make love to her like he had with her sister.

Well, actually, no she didn't want him to make love to her like he had to Mindy. Hopefully, if she and Bryan ever got to that point, there'd be no drunken fumblings or forgotten names.

Her body heated at the thought. It'd been way too long since she'd slept with anybody, and with Bryan looking as gorgeous as he did… her pheromones were zeroed in on him like heat-seeking missiles.

Now *there* was an image.

"Jenna, that wasn't what you think."

"Oh?"

"Yeah, Tamra. She and I weren't, well, she needed me to help her out of her costume."

"Not helping your argument."

"Oh. Right. Look, she got sick. They all did. The dancers. They ordered pizza and the cheese is bad or something. They've been getting sick for the last hour. I told Tamra to go sleep it off, but she couldn't get her tail off."

There was something vaguely sexual in that statement, but Jenna was willing to let it pass because she believed him. Despite the evidence of her own eyes, his story was strange enough to be true.

"I swear. That's all it was. I've been running around trying to find replacement dancers, keep the bathrooms clear for them, and manage the general chaos that normally accompanies a show. I was just trying to help her. That's all."

She put a hand on his arm. Involuntarily—okay, maybe not so involuntarily—her fingers flexed on the strong muscles beneath his skin. "It's okay, Bryan. I understand. Have you had any luck? Is there anything I can do?"

"Oh my God, yes." It was his turn to grab her arms. "I hate to ask this, and I wouldn't if I weren't in such dire straits, but, yes, there is something you can do. Can you dance? I know it's been a while, but it's like riding a bike. The moves will come back. I'm going to be dancing, too. After all, the show must go on."

"Da… dance?" Jenna was going to faint. He wanted her to dance? On stage? In front of people?

And take her clothes off?

"You can keep all the tips."

For money?

Ohmygod…

"Uh, Bryan?" Cathy poked her head between them. "I don't think that's such a good idea. Jenna's out of practice. Probably out of shape, too."

Jenna looked at Cathy. Out of shape? She was *not* out of shape.

"Plus, there's her job. She's got a morals clause and I'm pretty sure stripping falls under the list of things she shouldn't do."

"We've got wigs. Theater makeup. No one will ever know it's her. Not even the other dancers. It'll be our secret." He looked at her. "Please, Jenna. I hired that company you used to work for because of recommendations, so I know you're good. You'd really be helping me out."

She couldn't. Of course she couldn't. She didn't know how to dance. Not like a stripper anyway. "I don't know the routines."

"We're going to be free-styling most of it anyway because only a few of these dancers have worked together. I just need to put bodies up on that stage who know how to move. Please?"

Bodies. That's all she was, just another body.

Spoke volumes about the night Trevor had been conceived.

Bryan's cell phone rang. He took the call. "Connie? No, please don't tell me that. You're sure? You can't get someone to drive you?" He exhaled and pinched the bridge of his nose. "No. You're right. I get it. Yeah, thanks for letting me know."

He cursed as he punched the button to end the call. "I'm down two females. Please, Jenna. I'm begging here. I have to give our guests what they want or it's going to cost all of us. Me, Gage, the dancers who are on their way in, the ones heaving their guts out, the wait staff… Please say you'll help."

But she *couldn't* help. She wanted to scream that at the top of her lungs. She didn't know *how* to do this.

Cathy nudged her shoulder. "Go ahead, Jen. You can do this."

Oh thanks. Support from the peanut galley who was probably going to be laughing her own ass off while Jenna made the biggest fool out of herself shaking hers.

"Remember, he's got wigs and stuff. No one will know it's you. You can be anyone you want to be. Channel your inner Marilyn."

It'd been a joke with them when they were teenagers. They'd stood in each other's rooms with their hairbrush-microphones, belting out the latest pop song, going all seductive in the way only sixteen-year-olds think is seductive, channeling Marilyn Monroe's famous stance over the air grate.

"Hey, we have a Marilyn costume," said Bryan, looking way too perky at the idea.

Cathy smiled. "See? It's fate."

"Your name isn't fate," Jenna muttered as she went to follow Bryan. "Paybacks are a bitch."

Cathy raised her eyebrows. "My name also isn't Payback."

"Very funny."

"Oh, I don't know. I think I'll be laughing a whole lot this evening."

Chapter Seventeen

Jenna was going to be as sick as the rest of the dancers—and she hadn't eaten any of the pizza.

She couldn't do this. She kept saying it, but no one would listen to her.

The fact that she only said it inside her head might have something to do with that, but still… she couldn't strip in front of people down to the tassels some girl named Desiree had glued to her nipples and the teensy tiny thong that barely covered the landing strip she'd thankfully let Cathy talk her into getting when Cathy's belly had first started to pudge out. Cathy had wanted to feel sexy and had wanted Jenna to do the same.

Jenna was not feeling sexy now. She didn't know if she'd ever feel sexy again. The heels were threatening to break her ankles, the wig was giving her a headache, the greasepaint weighed like five pounds on her skin and dragged it down her face, and the dress only needed one flick of her finger to blow off with the specially designed vent she was to stand over at the end of the number.

She so could not do this.

"Break a leg, Marlee." Desiree used the name Bryan had given her as the call came to go on stage.

Sadly, she just might do that as she wobbled up the stairs.

Bryan grabbed her arm. "Seriously, Jenna, I can't thank you enough. I really appreciate it."

He wasn't going to when she made a complete fool of herself.

And then he'd know she wasn't Mindy.

Oh, God. She hadn't thought about that. Mindy would know how to do this. Mindy would be great at it. Mindy would actually *relish* the moment in the spotlight.

Okay, so maybe Jenna didn't have to relish it, but she did have to put on a show. Had to convince not only the patrons, but *Bryan* that she was stripper material or he'd start wondering how on earth she'd worked that bachelor party.

The music started and the guys sauntered on stage one by one. "It's Raining Men." Seriously? Was there a more cheesy song for a strip club? She thought Bryan had said this was a classy place.

And then it was Bryan's turn.

Oh my.

Jenna forgot all about cheesy. She forgot all about the music because the real music was the rhythm in his body as he undulated and shook and swerved and flexed and did all sorts of good moves that could be cheesy but, on him, so weren't.

His hips rolled in perfect time to the downbeat and his vest came off so suggestively she knew every woman in the audience was running her tongue over her lips imagining what all that hard smooth sculpted chest tasted like.

She tucked her tongue back into her mouth.

He teased the audience taking the vest halfway down, then pulling it back up, looking over his shoulder while he did so, shaking his backside in perfect time to the beat, his black pants hugging him like her hands were itching to do.

She curled her fingers into a fist.

Then it was the next guy's turn. Jenna watched him for a bit, but she couldn't ignore Bryan at the back of the stage, his left foot taping to the beat, his hands on his hips, his broad chest, the vest giving her peek-a-boo glimpses of glistening skin.

The next guys followed, each one talented, but neither doing for her what Bryan had. They worked the stage, muscles flexing, butts straining against the tight pants—other parts straining too… God, they put on a good show. She was glad Cathy had suggested coming tonight—well, she would be when this was over.

And then it was the women's turn.

Oh, God.

Desiree was first. The woman could shake her booty.

Jenna's heart dropped into her toes. She couldn't do that. At most she'd get the cellulite jiggle.

Luckily, Marilyn's dress would hide that until the end, but they'd assured her that the lights would go down three seconds after her dress flew off. She could be exposed that long.

Maybe.

Keisha was next on stage, all done up in a Jessica Rabbit costume. She didn't shake her booty; she didn't need to. Hers undulated to the music like a snake, sleek and sexy and sensuous. She put her arms over her head, weaving them like a harem girl, tossing her head back so her long black hair—completely fake, but it was a good wig—brushed the floor, and the same movements she made with her body rippled through her hair.

Now *that* was talent.

And then it was Jenna's turn.

She refused to look at Bryan. She couldn't or she'd fall apart—which she couldn't do. She *had* to be convincing. Had to make him believe she knew what she was doing.

Jenna took a deep breath and curved her left hip forward while she ran her hands along her thighs. She'd seen enough Marilyn Monroe movies to get the walk down pat. Throw in a couple of shoulder shimmies, some dragging-her-fingers-along-one-arm, and enough *oomph* in her hips to knock a horse over, and she could do this.

And then she *was* doing it. The heat of the lights hit her, blackening out the audience, and the music ratcheted up until it was all she could hear, every downbeat, every low hum, thudding through her body like an electric current.

Oh, *this* was why they used that song. It was *made* for stripping. It was made for sex. Forget the words, it was all in the bass and beat below them.

Jenna worked it. She swished her hips. She tossed her head back, opening her mouth like she'd seen Marilyn do, with that little butt-push by bending her knees. She tossed her hair, thankful the wig was so tight so she *could* toss her head, then she slowly spun around and looked back at the audience, winking at just the right moment.

Then the lights went black and the rest of the dancers filed by her.

Bryan squeezed her arm. "Great job," he whispered as he passed.

Now all she had to do was get through that last blast of air.

Sucking up every ounce of sexuality that she'd felt out there under those lights doing those moves, Jenna channeled Marilyn once more and sashayed toward the vent, each move a measured step with just the right amount of sway and hip movement—and careful foot placement so she didn't fall on her face.

The dancers were taking their clothes off now, and, yes, she did see what Bryan meant about it being classy. Keisha's dress slithered off and if it weren't for the green fabric giving way to brown skin, no one would notice because it was so effortless and so sensual. Where the dress ended, her skin began, and it was one long continuous movement.

Keisha then slid her dress up her leg and caught it in the crook of her knee before she flung it offstage in a pure bedroom move that was sheer artistry.

Jenna could practically hear half the audience sighing.

The other half were growling.

The extended version of the song was coming to an end as Desiree did her number, and Jenna stepped onto the vent.

The lights were off her and there was a black curtain in front of her so no one would know where she'd gone. She listened to the words, knew the end was coming.

How should she pose? No one had given her any direction. How exactly would the dress come off? Was she supposed to have her arms up? Stretched out? Or should she pose with them clasped on one bent knee?

Well, no, the dress wouldn't be able to do what it was supposed to do if she did that.

"Ready in three," the stagehand said behind her.

Crap. She had to decide now.

And then the curtain dropped to the floor, and the blast of air hit her, and Jenna didn't have to decide. The air went straight up, her arms went straight up, and the dress went straight up.

And there stood "Ms. C." in all her tasseled, thonged glory.

Chapter Eighteen

The rest of the show had been much easier to get through. They'd done a quick costume change and she'd chosen another Marilyn outfit, knowing that this time, she only had to slither the dress down her back and walk off trailing it after her like a feather boa. She could do all the little wiggles and mouth pouts and short shoulder shimmies straight out of *Diamonds Are A Girl's Best Friend*.

"It's more the suggestion of sexuality than the actual nudity," Bryan had said when he'd handed her the first costume before the show, so she'd used that.

Sure, her ass had felt exposed out there in that piece of dental floss they called a thong, and she might have covered herself a little more than Desiree would have with the dress when she was walking off stage, but all in all, she didn't do too badly. Not enough to make Bryan suspicious, at least.

"Holy moly, woman!" Cathy grabbed her backstage when she came off from the final number. "Seriously, I think you missed your calling in life. That was *hot*."

Now embarrassment was creeping in. She hadn't felt any once she'd gotten over the initial shock of what she was doing, but now, back in real life, she was going to have to face people. Thank God only Cathy and Bryan knew who she really was.

Bryan.

Oh, God, how was she going to face him? Sure, she'd

pulled that off to protect Trevor, but Bryan had been watching her. Had he been thinking about their supposed night together? Was he wondering if he'd touched all the parts she'd revealed? And those she hadn't?

Or did he know he never had?

"You are never to mention this again, Cathy Mayfield. Do you hear me?"

Cathy smirked. "It'll be our little secret. Though, damn girl, I didn't know the set of ta-tas you've got on you. Nothing little about them."

Jenna rolled her eyes. "Go back to your seat and wait for me there. I can't deal with you now."

"But you'll deal with me later."

"You got that right."

Jenna headed back to the dressing room. She wanted to get her stuff and get out before anyone recognized her.

"Well, ladies, gentlemen, we pulled it off." Bryan high-fived them as they filed into the dressing room. "I can't tell you how much I appreciate each of you for coming in when you didn't have to and doing such a great job with no rehearsal. You are true professionals. And as a sign of my appreciation, there's a bonus in your check this week."

Cheers, more high-fives, the mood was festive as people started to change back into their street clothes.

Uh oh. It was a communal dressing room; she wasn't going to take off her makeup and wig in front of everyone. And she couldn't leave the club looking like this. That'd be a dead giveaway the minute she got in her car.

"Uh, Bryan?" she whispered in his ear. "Is there somewhere I could, you know…" She waved at the dress then nodded her head to the rest of the dancers.

"Oh, yeah, sure." He fished a set of keys out of his pocket. "Here. We have an apartment upstairs for when Gage or I have to stay late. There's a shower, too. Feel free to use it."

She ran up the stairs as fast as those platform menaces would allow her.

Actually, halfway up, she stopped and took them off, her arches protesting at the flatness of the floor beneath her.

She ignored the pain. If her nipples had been okay having pasties stuck to them, and her butt with the dental floss, her feet had no room to complain.

The apartment was minimalist at best. A sofa, a tv, two chairs, a toaster and microwave in the galley kitchen, and not a picture hanging on the walls. They *had* spent some money on the bedroom, however; the comforter looked fluffy and cozy and the high-def flat screen on the wall screamed *bachelor*.

Luckily, they'd carried their same sense of luxury into the bathroom with thick towels, a couple of shampoos and soaps to choose from, and nice hot water from a pulsing showerhead with the perfect amount of water pressure. Jenna couldn't scrub the show—and the tassels—off fast enough.

Still, she had to admit, it'd been fun. Playacting up there, knowing people were watching, seeing her as a fantasy, knowing none of it was real, that was actually a turn on.

She glided the soap down her body, every nerve ending standing up and paying attention. It'd been a long time since she'd felt sexy. A long time since anyone had looked at her that way.

She rinsed out her hair and turned off the shower, wrapping one of the thick towels around her, then rummaged through the cabinet below the sink for a hair dryer.

Half a dozen boxes of condoms, but no hair dryer in sight.

What, exactly, did Bryan and Gage stay late for?

Half a dozen boxes. Well, at least they were careful. Though that hadn't served Bryan well four years ago.

She thrust the thought of those condoms—and Bryan and Mindy using them—out of her head and scrubbed the towel through her hair. She was just going to go home; she didn't need to look all dolled up.

Still… She looked at the medicine cabinet. Maybe they had some product in there she could put in her hair—

Bryan? Product? He was about as alpha as you could get; she couldn't see him using product.

But still, desperate times called for desperate measures…

Or an excuse to snoop.

She shut her conscience up and opened the medicine cabinet.

No product. Just some dental floss, shaving cream, toothpaste and toothbrushes—a couple unopened ones.

Jenna closed the cabinet. She didn't want to think who would be using those unopened toothbrushes. It was none of her business.

Except it was. If he was going to be in Trevor's life, *he* was her business.

And what, really, did she know about him other than the man made beautiful babies and could kiss?

She rolled her eyes. *Seriously, Jenna, mind back on the present situation and all its possible ramifications, not wondering what he did with condoms. Set the hormones to* OFF.

She went through the mental checklist of what she knew about him. It wasn't much. He owned this place, worked as an electrician, and liked to jump to conclusions. And strippers. He liked to jump strippers.

And she was right back to those damn condoms.

She got dressed quickly and hung the towel over the towel rack to dry. It didn't matter who Bryan did what with. He had his life; she had hers.

But they both had Trevor's.

Her hand stalled on the doorknob. She did have to

consider what Bryan did with his life. What if he got married and then wanted full custody? What if Jenna didn't like who he married? What if the woman tried to steal Trevor's affections from her?

Jenna sank down on the toilet lid. Oh, God, what if Trevor wanted to go live with Bryan and his wife? What if Bryan had kids? Trevor would love to have brothers and sisters.

She started to shake. What was she going to do? What could she do?

"Jenna?" Bryan was right outside the bathroom door. "You okay?"

No she wasn't. And it was all his fault.

Literally.

All of it. Trevor's existence and this incredible worry that she was about to lose everything.

"Jenna?"

"Fi…" She cleared her throat. "Fine. I'll, uh, be right out."

With wobbly legs and a sick stomach. If the dancers who'd eaten the pizza earlier had felt like this, she could see why they hadn't been up to giving a performance. Yet she had to.

She opened the door. Damn. He was right there.

"You okay?"

His low voice rumbled through her, touching every pulse point she had. Just like the downbeat when she'd been on stage.

"Yeah, I'm okay." She tucked her hair behind her ear.

It didn't stay. It never stayed. She didn't know why she did it.

Bryan reached up and tucked it.

This time it stayed.

"I really want to thank you for tonight. You were great."

She slid her fingers up and untucked that hair. She

liked it falling in her face when he was staring at her so intently. "Well, like you said, it's just like riding a bike."

So were a few other things, one of which she hadn't done in over three years and him standing so close was reminding her of that fact with bells and whistles and big, crashing cymbals.

"So, um, thanks for letting me use your shower." She squeezed past him, willing all body parts and wayward arm hairs to steer clear. He hadn't showered and her nostrils were making her well aware of the fact and the rest of her senses were telling her that was a good thing.

"You still got it, Jenna."

Oh she had it all right. A bad case of the hots for Trevor's father. Whom she *hadn't* slept with. Or danced for.

"Have you thought about getting back into this line of work?"

Now she got a severely cold dousing of reality. Her? Strip?

She'd taken two steps into the room—his *bedroom*—then spun around, as much to avoid looking at his *bed*, as to remind him of one really important fact. "I'm a teacher, Bryan. If I danced for you, I could lose my job."

If she danced *with* him, she could lose a lot more. Her sanity, her inhibitions, all sense of propriety—

Her loneliness. Her non-self-imposed celibacy…

The latter had a lot to recommend it. But what if—oh God—what if he was suggesting this so she *would* lose her job? She'd *have* to work for him, then. She'd be beholden to him and be ripe for the picking should he ever want full custody of Trevor.

"Right. I forgot." He stood up from where he'd been slouching against the door jamb in that quintessential hot-guy-door-slouch pose that made her wonder if there was a photographer around here somewhere, before he headed into the bedroom.

Why couldn't the bathroom have led into the *hallway* instead of the one room in this place she did *not* want to be with him?

Because her luck had gone on vacation ever since that spur-of-the-moment trip to the grocery store she now wished she'd never taken.

The bed called out to her as she walked by. Especially since Bryan was standing right beside it to let her pass. All she'd have to do would be throw herself into his arms, dropping them onto that bed, and Nature would take care of the rest.

It was so tempting she practically flew out the door.

And tripped over her stupid platform shoes.

Luckily, Bryan caught her before she hit the floor.

He didn't, however, stop her from hitting his hard wall of a chest.

With her palms.

Flat against it.

Oh my, he felt good.

Especially when his hands tightened on her waist and she was snuggled up against him just a little more.

There was *nothing* little about Bryan Lassiter.

"Jenna…"

It wasn't a question. It wasn't a sigh. It wasn't anything she'd ever heard before, so of course, she had to look up. Had to look at his mouth. At his lips…

That were descending toward hers.

He had to kiss her. Just once.

One turned into two, doubled to four, and after that, Bryan lost count.

Holy hell, this was hotter than the other one. What had their very first one been like? The second? Third?

And what about when he'd come inside her…

Jesus, his cock got hard so quick it sucked the breath right out of him. Or maybe that was Jenna. But how in the hell could he not remember what she'd tasted like the night they'd met? Even in his drunken haze he must have noticed, must have realized how incredibly hot and sweet and sexy and good and delectable and luscious and… he was running out of words—which went with running out of breath which she stole with all the fire inside that lithe, sexy body she'd sauntered across the stage tonight with such confidence.

He hadn't expected it. With what she now did for a living, he'd thought she'd be shy. Demure. School-girl persona that some men fantasized over. But not Jenna. She'd out-vamped Marilyn for sexy and it'd been all he'd been able to do not to scoop her off that stage and carry her up here, the show and patrons be dammed.

If only he could remember how good it'd been between them. Because it *had* been good, of that Bryan had no doubt. But he wanted to find out *how* good.

He backed her up to the bed.

She went willingly, clinging to the edges of his shirt so tightly he had a feeling she was going to pop some buttons.

He knew some buttons he'd like to push on her.

Those damn tassels had mocked him that entire time she'd stood there almost naked, and he'd known every man was devouring those breasts with his eyes, while he'd had the chance to do so with his mouth and his tongue and his hands and why the *hell* couldn't he remember?

He lowered her onto the bed.

"Bryan?" She pulled her lips from his, her blue eyes wide with—dare he hope—desire?

"I want you, Jenna." He did. There was no hiding it and, hell, they'd done this once already. It wasn't as if it was new.

But it'd be like the first time again for him and Bryan liked that idea. He had a feeling *every* time with Jenna would be a new experience.

"Bryan, I..."

He held his breath. Held hers, too, inside him, tasting it, wanting more.

Her eyes searched his, looking for... something. He had a lot of something inside him and prayed to God he could give her what she wanted .What she needed.

Then she uncurled her fingers against his chest and pressed her palms to it.

Bryan blew out their mixed breaths, sucked in another one, and kissed her again.

God, she tasted good. Amazing. Fresh and sweet with a little bit of spice as if she'd eaten an apple pie before coming here tonight—or had one of their appletinis. He'd have to get her one of those the next time they were downstairs.

God willing that wouldn't be for hours yet.

He stroked her tongue again, thrusting against it, his cock doing the same thing against her mound. The one that'd been barely covered in that golden thong with the sequins... it'd sparkled in the stage lights, practically winking at him.

And then there'd been her ass, dear God that ass, shaking with just the right amount of jiggle for a woman, all firm and plump and right there, the perfect size and shape and contour and smoothness for his hands—

He slid a hand down to her hip, wanting to cup her. Did she still have the thong on?

Bryan groaned into her mouth and squeezed. He wanted to find out. Then he wanted to peel it off her. With his teeth.

"Bryan."

It took him a few seconds to realize that she'd wrenched her lips from his, she'd said his name so softly. Or maybe that was due to the blood pounding in his ears.

"Jenna?" His voice was raw. Hoarse. Raspy. Like every nerve ending in his body. He wanted her. Badly.

"I…" She licked her lips.

He would have been fine if she hadn't licked her lips. He would have stopped. Really. He would have. But those lips and that tongue and that look in her eyes…

She didn't really want him to stop, did she?

He kissed her, not crushing her to him like he wanted to, but giving her an out.

One she didn't take.

Instead, she sighed into his mouth and then, by God, all bets were off.

He rolled over, pulling her on top of him, and sunk a hand into that riotous bunch of curls that just demanded attention, screaming sexy-tousled-love-making-hair every single time he looked at her.

The other hand finally got to grab hold of her ass, kneading it, filling his palm with its softness, and his dick turned to stone. He had to have her. Here. Now. And then again.

Condom. He needed to get a condom. The thought mocked him given that they already had a child between them, plus the fact that he didn't want to move to get one.

He ran his lips along her jaw, down to her throat where the pulse pounded every bit as fast and strong as his own. She wanted him, too.

He peeled back the open vee of her shirt and licked her throat. She'd used the apple cinnamon scrub; that's what he'd been tasting. Best investment he and Gage had ever made was buying those edible flavored soaps.

Jenna was the first to go for apple cinnamon and he was now retiring that flavor from any other woman.

He didn't want any other woman using his soaps anymore.

That was enough to get him to stop.

"Bryan?" *Now* there was a question in her voice, and by God, there was a question in his head.

He didn't want any other woman? Was he out of his

freakin' mind? Just because he and Jenna had made a baby didn't mean they'd made a commitment. This wasn't a happily ever after. They weren't even a family. One of them—both of them—could go on to marry someone else.

Someone else…

Jenna could marry someone else and *that* man would raise his son?

Bryan looked at her.

"Jenna, marry me."

Chapter Nineteen

The words just popped out. He hadn't thought about them before he said them, but yeah, sure. Why not? It made sense. They couldn't keep their hands off each other and they had Trevor. This way they wouldn't have to share him with anyone and they could be a family.

"What?" She let go of his shirt and pushed herself up on his chest. "What did you say?"

He licked his lips, his cock jerking when her gaze shot to his mouth. "I said, 'marry me.'"

Now she scrambled off him. "You can't be serious."

He rolled to his side and leaned onto his elbow. He ran his hand down her arm. "I've never been more serious."

"But that doesn't make any sense. We barely know each other."

Oh they knew each other *barely*.

"But we have Trevor."

Now she scrambled off the bed. "But that doesn't mean we have to get *married*. What if we don't have anything in common *except* Trevor?"

He raised his eyebrows—and his cock went to full-on salute, too. "We have more than just Trevor in common, Jenna."

She knew what he was talking about and her gaze shifted right to his groin.

He saw the flare of interest in her eyes.

"That's just sex, Bryan, and if you'll recall, it's how

we got into this mess in the first place."

He sighed. She wasn't coming back to bed. Not with that tone in her voice.

He sat up. "First of all, I don't consider Trevor to be a mess. Yes, it's not optimal to create a baby with someone you don't know—and can't get in touch with—but we *do* have him so that's a moot point. We'll be in each other's lives for at least the next fourteen years, if not more. And then there are the grandchildren."

Oh, God, he hadn't thought about grandchildren. He'd be a grandfather some day.

"Grandchildren?" She felt for the dresser and leaned against it.

Looked like she hadn't thought about them, either.

"Well, yeah. We did, after all, just give our parents a grandchild." His *mom*. He had to tell his mom about Trevor. She'd be ecstatic.

"Are your parents still around?" Jenna asked.

"My mom is. My dad died when I was younger. What about you?"

"My dad died when I was in high school. My mom and I… we don't exactly see eye-to-eye."

"I've heard it's that way with girls and their moms. Good thing Trev's a boy, huh?"

She crossed her arms and made some non-committal response.

Bryan exhaled. "Look, I know it's unorthodox. This whole thing is, but I meant it. I think you should marry me. It's what's best for Trevor."

But was it best for her?

Jenna uncrossed her arms and stood up. She tucked hair behind both of her ears. Again.

It didn't stay. Again.

"Bryan, this is crazy." She started pacing. "We don't even know each other. I didn't even know your last name until yesterday. Now you want to marry me?" She shook her head. Here he was, saying all the right things, all the things she'd wanted Carl to say, yet she was waffling.

Because she'd have to lie to him every day for the rest of her life.

She didn't know if she could do that. Once Trevor turned eighteen it wouldn't matter if Bryan knew the truth—*if* they weren't married. But if they were, it'd kill him. It would destroy their marriage. He'd wonder what else she'd lied about.

Bryan grabbed her hand. "We have a lot more in common than a lot of people."

Heat sizzled all the way up her arm. "Chemistry doesn't make a good marriage, Bryan."

"It doesn't make for a bad one. But I was talking about wanting what's best for Trevor. I mean, you obviously do because you didn't deny that I was his father and make me jump through paternity-testing hoops. You want what's best for him; I do, too, and he'd love to see us together. We're both single, right?"

"You are?"

He shook his head. "Well, yeah. I wouldn't have come on to you if I weren't."

"Oh, right. Sorry."

He exhaled. "I guess I deserve that, given what I accused you of."

"I wasn't doing it in retaliation."

"I know."

"How?" She flung her arms to her sides. This was ridiculous. He couldn't just propose to her and expect her to jump up and down in gratitude. "*How* do you know? You really don't know anything about me."

He rubbed the back of his neck. It was a really sexy move on him. "I know you're a caring mom. A loving one. A hard worker. You've inspired the love and loyalty of your students. Trevor's a happy, healthy, fun, outgoing kid. The head of the police department likes you. You have a stable job, a nice home, and you were generous enough to give me a part in my son's life. And that's all without the window-dressing and insane chemistry between us. A lot of people have a lot less when they get married."

"But they at least know each other."

"Fine. Then let's get to know each other."

"Huh?" She shoved off the dresser and started pacing, both to give her something to do *and* work off some of the adrenaline that had come from her little dance number earlier.

And that kiss—

"Let's get to know each other, Jenna. Hang out. Play with our son."

"I thought we were already doing that."

"We were—with Trevor—but I mean *us*. As a couple. Date."

"You want to date me?"

"It's backwards, I know, but, yeah, I would like to date you."

Damn if that didn't cause a little flutter in her tummy. Of course, that tummy didn't know what it was like to get stretch marks from carrying his son so it didn't really have a say in the matter. "I don't want to get married just for the sake of my son, Bryan. Marriage should be between two people who love each other, because once Trevor's out of the house, it'll just be the two of us."

"Not necessarily."

"Huh?"

"What if we have more kids?"

"More?" She was halfway into her second turn on her pacing when that comment plunked her butt down onto his bed. Make *more* children with Bryan? Well, his *more*, her *first*.

And how the hell would she keep that from him? She's supposed to have gone through childbirth before. Going to Mindy's Lamaze class was nothing like giving birth. She'd breathed through the contractions for her sister as a spectator, not the main participant, and Mindy hadn't been anywhere coherent enough to go into detail about the experience. It'd hurt and that was all Jenna had needed to know at the time.

"You do want more kids, don't you? Trevor can't be an only child."

She rubbed her head. It hurt. For a whole bunch of reasons, not the least of which was an image of another black-curly-haired baby cuddled in her arms.

"I... I guess." She *did* want more kids. But she hadn't exactly planned on Bryan as their father and she wasn't ready to go there. To go near any of this. Because with the secret she was carrying, this had the very big, very real possibility of blowing up in her face.

But how was she going to convince him this was a bad idea without telling him the truth?

"Bryan, I'm sorry, but I can't marry you."

Chapter Twenty

First time he'd ever been shot down and it'd been when it'd mattered the most.

Bryan tossed back the covers on the bed in the apartment. He'd stayed here last night after watching her storm off down the steps to the back of the club. He'd wanted to go with her, but she'd insisted that she didn't need him because she'd been raising Trevor on her own for almost four years and had done a damn fine job of it without his help, *thankyouverymuch*, and he could take his marriage idea and go find some other woman who needed a man to make her life complete.

There'd been a lot unsaid in that diatribe that he'd wanted to explore, but figured, given the level of upset his suggestion had garnered, it'd be best to wait until she'd cooled down and had a night to sleep on it.

So he'd slept here. At least, that'd been the theory.

He'd flipped from channel to channel in an effort to distract himself, but it hadn't worked. So he'd finally given up, gone downstairs and closed up, then had come back to lay in the dark, trying not to think about what he'd just done.

What he'd been *proposing* to do.

He'd never even come near the idea of marriage. Had never thought he would.

'Course, he'd also never thought he'd be a dad, so that showed what he knew.

He scrubbed his face. He needed a shower. He hadn't wanted to get in it last night after she'd been in there because he was sure her scent still lingered. At the very least, that damn apple cinnamon soap would be there.

He was going to throw it out.

He got out of bed. Hmmm, he'd worn his boxers. A conscious decision he'd forgotten about since he usually slept in the nude, but since he hadn't wanted to give in to the temptation to *take care of business* with the image of Jenna in her tassels and thong and nothing else, he'd provided a barrier to deter himself. It just didn't seem right to jack off to the memory of his son's mother's hot body.

He ought to be making love *to his son's mother's hot body.*

His dick sprang to life.

Bryan shook his head and headed into the bathroom. It was a losing battle; he just couldn't get Jenna out of his head.

And when he caught a whiff of that damn soap, he realized he couldn't get her out of his skin either. She'd wrapped herself around him like a big ol' bear hug when she'd given him access to his son.

He hoped to hell he hadn't just scared her off.

He turned on the showerhead and stepped under it. Good. The cold water not only woke him up, but it got his dick to calm down, too.

He reached for the soap, fully intending to pitch it into the trashcan, but cinnamon wasn't something anyone could ignore.

It smelled like Jenna.

Or rather, she smelled like it.

Oh hell, he didn't know which smelled like which and did it really matter? He was transported right back to last night and that kiss and his royally botched proposal.

She was right, of course. They didn't know each other; getting married probably wasn't the smartest idea. At least, not yet. But why *couldn't* they date? Why *couldn't* they get to know each other? They had as good a chance as anyone in a new dating situation that they'd like each other.

Bryan rubbed the back of his neck where a headache was starting, and turned the water a little hotter. Standing here thinking about it wouldn't get them to know each other. Only one thing would: actually hanging out together. And he *had* promised Trevor some football.

Bryan ran the soap over his body. It was silky. Smooth. Just like her. He sniffed it, remembering the same cinnamon-y fragrance when he'd nuzzled her neck. How he'd nibbled on it.

He rolled his eyes and set it down, reaching now for his shampoo. Something strong and masculine. He'd hang on to the soap in the hopeful event that he could convince her to get to know him and maybe, someday, she'd shower here again.

Bryan snorted. Yeah, it was a long shot. But, still, he'd never given up during a game in his life, not even that last one with his torn mess of a leg. Coach had been the one to tell the paramedics to strap him to the board and get him to the hospital, so he sure as hell wasn't going to give up now even if she'd already shot him down.

His only saving grace was that no one but he and Jenna knew.

"He asked you to marry him?"

Cathy had kept repeating it the whole ride home last night and it was the first thing she said when she'd showed up at Jenna's house this morning.

"My answer hasn't changed since last night."

"Your answer to me or your answer to him? 'Cause, seriously, Jen, you really might want to rethink this. I mean, the man's a freakin' god in the looks department, *wants* to be part of his kid's life—do you know how rare that is among baby daddies?—*and* he's pretty well off. You could do a lot worse."

"Can we not talk about this now? Trevor will be down any minute."

"No, he won't. Bobby brought over his new book about T-rexes. We won't see them for hours."

Jenna sighed. Cathy was right. The only things more engrossing to Trevor than football were T-rexes.

"I wouldn't put it past you to have bought that book on your way over here." She handed Cathy a cup of apple juice with a dollop of whipped cream floating on top and sprinkled with cinnamon. Since Cathy had given up her normal lattes for the duration of her pregnancy, she and Jenna had gotten inventive with fruit juice.

Cathy raised her glass. "Do you really think I'm that conniving, Jen?"

Jenna raised her eyebrow. "Uh, wasn't your husband the one who only wanted one child yet here you are with number two on the way, due exactly four years after the first one in the same auspicious planning-for-college-tuition time frame we discussed *ad nauseum* when we were in high school?"

Cathy raised the glass to her lips. "Condoms have been known to break. You of all people ought to know that."

"Breaking is one thing. Purposely sabotaging them is another."

Cathy took a sip and lowered her glass. A whipped cream mustache curled above her lips like Snidely Whiplash's. "I did not purposely sabotage them. I just forgot to bring the box in from the car."

"For an entire year while they went through four seasons of extreme temperatures in the spare tire well?"

Cathy swirled her glass around. "You don't know that's where they were."

"I do now."

She stuck her tongue out. "You can't prove anything.

And besides, Mark's ecstatic about the baby."

Yeah, he was. He kept calling this new arrival their miracle baby because he'd never gotten anybody pregnant using that trusted brand of condoms since college.

Jenna was never able to look at Cathy whenever that discussion came up.

"You know…" Cathy sashayed over to the fridge, putting nine months of pregnancy waddling into a four-month-pregnant body. "If you did say yes, you two could start working on a sibling for Trevor, and you and I could have babies together." She pulled out the can of whipped cream and squirted another blob—or three—into her glass. "Just think how much fun that'd be."

Jenna was trying *not* to think how much fun *making* a baby with Bryan would be.

"You're nuts."

"Hey, don't make fun of the pregnant woman. We've been known to cry at the drop of a hat."

"You've also been known to cry at the drop of a credit card when not pregnant, so I'm not buying it, Cath."

Cathy opened her mouth to say something then shut it. She pulled out one of the chrome chairs and patted the placemat on the table next to her. "Here, Jen. Have a seat."

"I can't. I have to, um…"

"Right. You have to nothing. Come on. Just take a load off and let's discuss why you're so adamant about not marrying Bryan."

Jenna took the seat reluctantly. She knew exactly why she was reluctant and Cathy ought to be able to figure it out, too.

"I can't lie to him, Cath."

"Sweetie, you're already doing it. And normally, I'm not a big proponent of lies."

Jenna raised her eyebrows and looked at Cathy's belly.

"Bad lies, I mean. I knew Mark would be thrilled. But

we're not talking about me—"

"Convenient," Jenna muttered.

"We're talking about you. And Bryan. And Trevor. And Tabitha."

"Tabitha?"

"Yeah. Your little girl."

"I'm going to name her Tabitha?"

"Yes. You are. Because I'm naming this one Samantha."

Jenna rolled her eyes. Cathy like TVLand reruns a little too much.

"Anyhow, just think how great it'd be for Trevor to have not only his mama, but his daddy *and* a baby sister all under one roof."

"But Auntie Cathy is forgetting one teensy tiny detail. I'm not Trevor's mama. I'm the stand-in."

"Hello?"

The masculine voice at her back door had Jenna freezing as if the entire world had frozen over.

If that was Bryan, she really hoped it had.

How much had he overheard?

Cathy gulped.

It never boded well when Cathy gulped.

"Jenna?"

Oh, God, it *was* Bryan.

Now it was her turn to gulp.

"Ladies? Everything okay?"

He rattled the screen door and the only reason he couldn't come in was because Jenna typically locked it so Trevor wouldn't wander off into the backyard without her knowing. Why hadn't she shut the entire thing today? Locked it with deadbolts? And chains?

A hermetic seal?

And kept her big mouth shut?

"Jenna?" He rattled a little harder.

"Uh, yeah. Okay. Um, fine." She willed some bones

into her Jello-y legs and got to her feet.

Cathy squeezed her hand.

Wiping the sick look she was certain was on her face if Cathy's was anything to go by, Jenna tried to plaster an equally *un*-sickly smile on top of it. "I, uh, wasn't expecting you."

"Obviously." He swung a backpack off his shoulder and clasped it in his hands in front of him while he waited for her to open the door.

A backpack? She'd nixed marriage and he took that to mean that he could just waltz right over and move in?

Oh, God. What if he wanted to? What if he *demanded* to?

Jenna took her time getting to the door—mainly because she had to remind each group of leg muscles to move, but also to figure out what the hell she was going to do.

How much had he heard? Was that *obviously* in relation to her not expecting him because she wouldn't have been talking so freely about Trevor's parentage? Did he know?

She blew out a breath as she reached for the latch.

"It's good to see you," Bryan said all melted – chocolate-creamy-goodness in his voice—*not* what she'd expect to hear from him if he knew. Had she dodged a bullet?

Her heart felt as if it'd taken one.

Chapter Twenty-One

"I'm, uh, gonna get going." Cathy did an exaggerated pregnancy backward arch out of her chair, complete with the splayed feet and a hand on the chair and table.

Jenna rolled her eyes.

"Oh, hey, let me help you." Bryan dodged past her, dropped the duffel on the baker's rack by the door, and ran to Cathy's side, supporting that bogus pained back with one of his big hands.

He had really nice hands.

"Thank you, Bryan. You're such a gentleman." Cathy made some weird scrunching/head-knodding move over his shoulder at Jenna. "I can't believe some woman hasn't snatched you up yet."

Now it was Jenna's turn to make a weird scrunching face, but it was more to keep back the breakfast that was threatening to make a re-appearance.

"Thanks, Cathy, but I was never in the market."

"Not what I've heard…" Her sweet Southern charm—and Jenna knew for a fact that the only time Cathy had ever been south of the Mason Dixon line was the senior class trip to Orlando—disappeared in an instant.

Bryan looked between the two of them. Was that a blush creeping over his cheeks? "You told her."

He wasn't asking, so Jenna didn't really have to answer did she?

"Oh, was it supposed to be a secret?" Cathy even did

the fingertips-to-the-chest posturing. All she needed was a fan and she could be Scarlett with the Tarleton brothers, but if she said "fiddle dee dee" Jenna was going to squirt the whipped cream all over her.

"She's my best friend, Bryan. We share everything." She glared at Cathy to keep her big fat fake trap shut.

He grunted. "Yeah, I guess. I mean, Gage is my best friend, but I didn't tell him."

Jenna walked to the table and picked up Cathy's drink. "But was Gage at your house this morning at a ridiculously early hour to get all the dirt?"

"Hey, I resent that."

Jenna shoved the glass at her. "Thanks for stopping by, Cath. See you tomorrow."

Cathy took a healthy swig. "Fine." She set the glass down. "I'll go round the boys up so you two can talk."

"If you don't mind, could you leave Trev here?" Bryan asked. "I didn't get a chance to see him yesterday and, well, I did promise him I'd throw some passes with him."

Ah, that was what was with the backpack. He carried his balls—

Jenna tried not to giggle. She did. Really.

"Jen? You okay with that?"

Jenna bit her lip. Right. Trev. Here.

Hey, he didn't get to call Trev Trev. That was *her* nickname for him. "Uh, yeah, sure. That's fine. I mean, I know Trev*or*—"she emphasized that last syllable—"would like that."

"Okay. Fine. Suit yourselves." Cathy waddled out of the room.

"Was that what it was like for you?" Bryan startled her with a hand on her elbow.

"What?"

He nodded toward the doorway Cathy had just walked through. "That. Walking. She looks like it's painful."

Cathy was just as good an actress as Jenna was a stripper. What did that say about them?

Jenna didn't want to know. "Cathy's, um, shorter than me. Pregnancy is more of a trial for her." Technically, she hadn't lied to him, though why she felt compelled to make that distinction when she was telling him the biggest lie of all was beyond her.

"Bwwwwyyyyaaannn!"

Trevor thundered down the stairs and hung onto the doorframe for dear life as he skidded around the corner. "You're here!"

He launched himself into Bryan's legs, wrapping his arms around them as if *they* were his life.

As if *Bryan* was his life.

Jenna pulled out one of the chairs and sat down. This was going to get more complicated by the minute.

"Hey, Trev." Bryan pried the little arms off his legs, but he didn't let go, instead hunkering down to be eye level with him. "I brought my football. Want to throw a few passes?"

"You bet!"

Then Trevor did the one thing designed to rip Jenna's heart to shreds.

He hugged Bryan, a big, tight hug around the neck, and Jenna had to look away before she cried.

But not before she saw Bryan's eyes get misty.

"Hey." Bryan cleared his throat. "Hey, Trev, thanks."

Jenna peeked back. Bryan's big hands were plastered to Trevor's small back as if he'd never let go.

He wouldn't. She got that. Bryan was in Trevor's life for good.

Which meant he'd be in hers just as long, too.

***

Bryan and Trevor had thrown a few passes in the back

yard while Jenna had tried desperately to compose herself. This was a good thing. Trevor needed a father figure and Bryan wanted to be one. Cathy was right; there were plenty of "baby daddies" who didn't want to have anything to do with the children they'd created. She should be thrilled that Bryan wanted to be involved.

And she was. Really.

She was just worried as hell that she'd slip up somehow. Clue him in about Mindy.

And obviously she couldn't hide Mindy's existence. Her half sister had grown up in this town, and when Bryan eventually met her mom, Mindy and her "tramp" of a mother, as Ellen North referred to her, would definitely get mentioned—they were always a topic of conversation.

Her mother. Oh, God. Her mother was going to meet Bryan and if there was one thing the woman wasn't quiet about it was Jenna's "shameful" past. Especially since she thought Jenna had gone out and done the same thing all over again.

"Hey, Mommy!" Thirty-five pounds of little boy came barreling through the doorway. "Bwyan wants to take us to a fair! Can we go? Pwease? Pwease?"

Bryan shrugged as he followed Trevor back into the kitchen. "It's to benefit the children's wing at Community General and BeefCake, Inc. is sponsoring a booth. I said I'd stop by to help out. So if you're not doing anything and are interested, I thought it'd be fun."

He'd paid her to not be doing anything.

Actually, no he hadn't. And even if he had, it would have been too soon to cancel any of her students. So it was a good thing she didn't have any scheduled today.

Part of her wanted to tell Bryan no. Besides the fact that he shouldn't have mentioned it to Trevor without consulting her first—and making her look like the bad guy if she had to say no—he shouldn't be spending this much time with their son, insinuating himself into his life as if he'd always been there.

The other part of her, however, couldn't tell him no. It wasn't fair to Trevor. The circumstances of his birth weren't his fault—they weren't even Jenna's. They *were* Bryan's, but it wasn't as if he'd known anything about it. He certainly hadn't planned it, given the selection of condoms in that apartment.

"Sure, Trev. We can go to the fair." She'd been planning to take him anyway.

Bryan squeezed her arm and mouthed "thank you" over Trevor's head.

One of—or both—the actions caused sparks to *zing* through her.

Oh for Pete's sake, get over him. Get over this. He could be as good-looking as he wanted, but it didn't change the fact that she had to keep her distance. He'd already proposed, what more did she want?

The fairytale.

The thought haunted her for the rest of the day.

Especially when she saw the booth Bryan was supposed to work.

Chapter Twenty-Two

Of *course* BeefCake's booth would be a kissing booth. She had wondered how a strip club could sponsor a booth at a family event, but hot guys in suits selling chaste kisses on the cheek were the perfect cover.

It was also the perfect money-maker. Women were lined up two deep for their chance to get up close and personal with the hunk of the day.

Of which Bryan was now going to be one.

He pulled on a jacket one of the guys handed him, adjusted a bow tie around his neck, and Velcro-ed the tear-away pants on over his shorts, looking devastatingly attractive. As usual.

"Hey, Trev. Why don't you and your mom go see the pony rides while I work for a little bit? Then I can join you when I'm finished."

"You *work* here? Cool!"

No, actually, it was hot.

"*Can* I wide a pony, Mommy?"

Another thing she and Bryan were going to have to talk about. He needed to clear things with her before offering them to Trevor.

She kissed the top of Trevor's curls and looked at his father. "Of course you can, sweetheart."

"Everything all right?" Bryan asked, running his fingers down her arm.

Bryan was a toucher; she got that. She also got that

her skin liked when he touched her.

It was something else they'd have to discuss.

"How long will you be?" she asked, not willing to get into the parental rights discussion in front of half the town. The *female* half. "He's going to want to start riding rides and playing games and all that other fun stuff as soon as the pony ride is finished."

"An hour tops." He pulled out his cell phone. "What's your number? I'll call you when I'm finished and meet up with you."

Her number. Now he'd have access to her—to Trevor—twenty-four /seven.

Jenna took a deep breath and gave it to him. It wasn't as if she could deny him now. "I'll wait to hear from you."

She turned around to leave, but Bryan grabbed her arm again. "Aren't you forgetting something?" His violet eyes bored into hers.

She'd *like* to forget something… "I don't think so."

"Aren't you going to, you know, support the charity?" He nodded to his left. To the booth.

Then he tugged her close to him. "I'll even let you jump in line."

He smelled good. Really good. He felt even better, especially that hard sculpted chest her shoulder was snuggled up against—that *she'd* been snuggled up against.

"Come on, Jenna. It's for a good cause. I'll even make the donation for you."

She shouldn't have looked up at him. Not when they were that close together. Not when she'd been dreaming about making love to him all night long. Not when her body remembered every part of that dream and was demanding a real-life re-enactment.

But she did.

And he kissed her.

Again.

Oh it was different this time. G-rated. Well, maybe

PG. But it was still hot and she still responded and she still wanted him. Wanted this.

"Ewww, blech!"

Leave it to Trevor to put the situation into perspective.

They broke apart, laughing, though Bryan's gaze was searching hers. She ducked away. She couldn't look at him. Didn't want to look at him. Didn't want him looking at her because she'd seen the desire there. Kind of hard to miss since she'd been so up close and personal with it in that apartment—in that bed—and could recall every nuance to those few minutes in his arms.

"Come on, Mommy! I wanna wide the pony!"

She wanted to ride something else.

"Okay, Trev. Let's go."

She tugged away from Bryan as much for her own sake as Trev's.

It was one of the longest half hours of her life.

Hour.

Hour and fifteen minutes.

Jenna kept checking her phone. Both for the time and to make sure she hadn't missed his call.

How many women was he kissing anyway?

She tried not to think about it. Tried not to wonder what those other women felt when Bryan put his lips on their cheek. When they got close enough to smell his heat. Would they wonder what it was like to make love with him? Would they fantasize about him tonight in *their* dreams?

Had any of them wondered who she was?

Would they care?

Would *he*?

She waved to Trevor as he took his fifth ride on the pony. There were only five ponies at this ride so Bryan better hurry up because when this trek around the track was finished Trevor was going to be looking for something new to do.

"Miss me?" someone tall, dark, and gorgeous whispered in her ear, sending shivers down her spine.

"Trevor did." Jenna was very proud of herself for answering coherently and not babbling in a puddle of pheromones.

"What about you? Did you miss me?"

It was kind of hard not to look at him when he put his finger under her chin and turned her face to his.

His lips were right there. Close enough to kiss.

"How much did you make for the cause?" She had to ask. Had to get her mind off his lips.

Of course she watched them form his response. "About a thousand."

At two dollars a pop—a kiss—he'd—

"You kissed five hundred women?"

"Jealous?" He waggled his eyebrows.

Yes. "Or course not. It's… it's just… I'm concerned. About germs." Okay, that was lame, but it was the best she could come up with. "I mean, you could catch something. And hanging out with Trevor, you could give it to him. He doesn't need to get sick."

"And then there's you, too." Bryan circled around her like a predator eyeing its prey, and, yes, she did feel a bit hunted.

"Me?"

"Yes. You. If I'm sick, I can't really keep kissing you, can I?"

Okay, they were going to have to have this discussion now. "Bryan, I don't think it's a very good idea for you to keep kissing me."

"Okay, then you can kiss me. I'm not one to let chivalry stand in the way of a woman's kisses."

"That's not what I meant."

"Oh? Then what did you mean because you certainly can't tell me you don't want to kiss me."

"I don't—"

"Don't even try it. I was there, remember? In the apartment and back when we..." He nodded toward Trevor. "Then. Obviously we did some kissing. A lot more, though I don't think we're ready for that just yet."

Maybe *he* wasn't, but her hormones were doing the happy dance just from the mention.

"I don't think it's a good idea to be kissing in front of Trevor. He might get the wrong idea."

"I'm perfectly happy to kiss you away from Trevor. When and where? I'm there."

He looked so darn cute with that hopeful expression on his face she just had to laugh. "Does that really work for you?"

He shrugged. "I don't know. Why don't you tell me?"

Yeah, it worked. And, no, she wasn't going to tell him.

"Look, Bryan. Obviously there's chemistry between us." Full-blown, lethal contact, light-up-the-skyline sort of chemistry, but she had too much to lose for a few nights of unbridled passion.

Though unbridled passion did have a lot to recommend itself.

"But we have to look at this from the long haul perspective. Trevor isn't even four. We've got at least fourteen years, if not more, of dealing with each other. It's not a good idea to start something that could cause problems down the road. We need to just stay friends. Co-parents. Work together. Without any added complication."

"You've thought a lot about his haven't you?"

"Haven't you?"

He smiled and a dimple appeared in his cheek. Just like the one Trevor had.

God she was so screwed.

No, you want to be *screwed.*

Her subconscious was *not* helping matters.

"I *have* been thinking about it, Jenna. Ever since I blurted out that marriage proposal."

The woman behind him looked over.

Crap, he'd said that too loud. Jenna dragged him away from nosey ears. "Bryan, please. Keep your voice down. We don't need any more gossip going around."

"Why, has someone said something to you about the prostitution thing? Who was it? I'll go set them straight."

She'd never been into caveman tactics, but she did have to admit that she liked that he was indignant on her behalf and wanted to fix the problem for her. For so long she'd had to fix her own problems.

"No, nothing like that. But Trevor doesn't need talk going around about his parents. It's going to be bad enough when it's known that you're his father."

"Who do people *think* is his father?"

Yeah, this wasn't an area she'd wanted to get into with him. "I never really said. Just changed the subject whenever it came up."

"Like you tried to do with me."

"Um, yeah."

"We definitely need to come up with a story to explain me, Jenna. Something people will believe." He tugged her closer. "And to help get that ball rolling, I think I *should* kiss you. Let people see that we're together. It'll soften the blow when the truth comes out."

Nothing would soften *that* blow, but he wasn't talking about *her* truth. How ironic that they were going to lie about *his* involvement in Trevor's parentage when hers was the real lie.

"So, you with me?"

"With you?" She had no idea what he was talking about, her mind was spinning with all the implications of this situation.

And then her mind was spinning from something else entirely.

He kissed her. Again.

Luckily he kept it PG. His arms went around her, his lips found hers and he slid his tongue inside with just the perfect amount of slippage that no one would know where his tongue was but her.

And she knew. Whoa baby, did she know. Her nerve endings switched on as if he'd flipped a switch, her heart rate went into rumba mode, and her hormones were once more dancing with joy.

"Mommy? Why is Bwyan kissing you?"

Exactly the question she wanted to ask.

She pulled out of Bryan's embrace, tucked her hair behind her ears, and had to prevent herself from licking her lips because he'd tasted *that* good.

"I was thanking her, Trev." Bryan, damn him, sounded all cool and composed while she was a bundle of overactive nerves.

"For what?"

He lifted Trevor off the pony and stuck him on his shoulder. "For allowing me to be your new friend."

"Oh. Okay." Trevor patted the top of Bryan's head. "Can I wide up here all the time?"

"Well, I don't know about all the time, but you can for now."

"Cool!"

Bryan raised an eyebrow at her. "Cool? Where'd he come up with that?"

Jenna rolled her eyes and the levity was just what she needed to get her hormones under control. "The all-knowing Michael."

"Ah."

"Yeah, ah."

"Can I pway a game? I wanna win a teddy bear. Mr. Monkey wants a new fwiend, too."

"Where do you see a teddy bear?" Bryan asked.

"Over there." Trevor pointed to a row of carnival

games. "It's bwue. Mr. Monkey woves bwue."

"That's because he fell in a glass of punch," Jenna whispered to Bryan. She'd had to do some pretty quick thinking to keep Trevor from crying his eyes out over his "ruined" friend. But when he learned that Mr. Monkey "loved punch," it'd become his favorite drink, too. She was hoping Mr. Monkey would make the transition to orange juice soon. Didn't leave quite the mustache that punch did so she wouldn't have to fight as hard to scrub it off.

It took Bryan over sixty bucks in tickets—and assorted other prizes he'd won in the interim—to finally win the Trevor-sized teddy bear, but it was worth every cent to see the smile on their son's face and the hero-worship in his eyes. Bryan could seemingly do no wrong.

Then Bryan bent over to pick up a light saber he dropped and—yeah, pretty much everything about Bryan *was* darn near perfect.

Jenna exhaled and looked around. Anywhere but at the gorgeous set of glutes stretching a pair of nylon shorts tight.

Something else was a little tight...

"Can I go on the mewwy-go-wound, now? I wanna wide a tiger." Trevor swung his legs and bounced on Bryan's shoulder.

Bryan winced and grabbed Trev's feet. "Yeah, but you don't want to kick him like you just did to me. That hurt."

"Oh. I sowwy."

"I know you are. So which animal should I ride?"

"The felefant. It's big wike you."

Jenna blushed just thinking about how "big" Bryan was. Mother and son were on two different wavelengths.

Bryan however, was riding on hers and his smirk confirmed it. "An elephant, huh? Is it because of my long trunk?"

He was so not looking at Trevor when he said that.

And she was *so* not going to look at him.

"What do *you* want to ride, Jenna?" Bryan went with the touching thing again, his fingertips sliding along her arm in what could be considered an innocuous touch but wasn't.

She was *not* going to dignify that with an answer. Mainly because she doubted she'd be all that dignified answering him.

"Mommy can wide the poodle. She wikes poodles, don't you, Mommy?"

"Um, yes. I do. Poodles are nice." She reached up to ruffle Trevor's hair. It was curly like a poodle's.

Like his father's that she'd had her fingers threaded through.

Thank God the merry-go-round was just up ahead. A couple of spins on a stationary poodle would be just the thing to get her libido and imagination under control.

So was Trevor's chatter as they walked beneath the red, white, and blue mini triangles that stretched across strings tied between the rides and booths in a pergola-like mish-mash of festive, from the sea of families, to the game booths, to the face painting stations, fortune-tellers, tarot readers, stilt walkers, jugglers, and clowns, Trevor had to comment on each one. He also had to sample every food product between there and the carousel and Jenna could only envision a late night tummy ache.

But she hadn't been able to say no any more than Bryan had.

Trevor kept up a running dialogue about what animals were what on the carousel, what they ate, where they lived, surprising her at how much he'd retained from the animal videos she'd bought him at Christmas since he hadn't watched them in months now that fire engines and football and T-rexes were his favorites.

"I wike poodles, but boxers are better." He handed Bryan the half-eaten water ice so he could run up to the fence ringing the ride, Bryan being the repository of all things Trevor today and Jenna tried not to mind. Trevor had wanted a father and now he had one.

Who'd asked her to marry him.

"Penny for 'em." Bryan nudged her shoulder with the ginormous teddy bear.

She had no idea where she was going to put that thing in her house. Trevor's bedroom wasn't big enough for the collection he had, let alone another one.

"I'm wondering where we're going to put the bear."

"I could keep him at my place if you want."

"That apartment? With all those condoms?"

A smirk slid across his face. "Saw those, did you?"

She rolled her eyes. "Give me a break. You are not putting my son's toy in that… that… that den of iniquity."

Bryan stared at her for about one second before he started to laugh. And laughed some more. He laughed so hard he had to bend over to catch his breath and the teddy bear now had a big blue wet spot on his nose from hitting the ground right where some kid had spilled their snow cone.

Just like Mr. Monkey. Those two would get along famously.

"What's so funny?" Trevor asked oh-so-innocently as he ran back from the fence.

"Nothing." She turned his head back toward the carousel. Maybe if they ignored Bryan he'd go away. How could the man make her feel hot and bothered and just plain bothered all at the same time?

"Then why is Bwyan laughing?" He even looked like his father when his forehead was all scrunched up.

"Your mom said something funny," said Bryan, getting his laughter under control.

"Oh. Was it about a milkman and a showgirl?"

"What?" She and Bryan said it at the same time.

"Where did you hear about a showgirl?" She looked at

Bryan in a panic. Did someone know about last night? Had someone recognized her? Was she going to lose her job?

She couldn't lose her job. She couldn't. Okay, she had some money saved up, but not nearly enough to weather unemployment.

She should never have danced last night. She should have told him no. Told him she couldn't. Explained *why* she couldn't.

Oh yeah, like that was the answer. Then, instead of standing here at a fair with cotton candy stuck to her tank top and way too many ride tickets in her pockets, she could be facing a judge, explaining why she'd kept the truth from Bryan, and pleading for visitation rights.

She was so screwed. And not in a good way.

"Trevor." Bryan hunkered down to Trevor's level and Jenna didn't mind if the teddy bear's entire face was covered in blue sugar water. "Where did you hear that joke?"

"Michael told me."

Of course he had. Michael was the purveyor of pre-school filth now as well as a bully, a thug, and a disciplinary problem.

"What exactly did Michael tell you?"

"Are you mad?"

Jenna's heart twisted at that scared little look on Trevor's face. "No honey, we're not mad. We're just curious. We've never heard that joke so we wanted to know how you did."

"Well, it's not weawwy funny."

"It's not really funny?" She translated for Bryan who'd looked at her in confusion. Having been there every day since Trevor had said his first word at the age of two, she understood him.

Trev shook his head, his black curls bouncing. "No. It just made me firsty because the man wanted to drink the milk."

Jenna closed her eyes. She needed to have a serious talk with his teachers. And with Michael's parents.

"You handle the school and I'll take the dad?" Bryan helped her stand up.

"Deal." She held out her hand to shake his. It was nice that they were on the same wavelength on this. It was nice to have someone to share this with.

It was nice to have *Bryan* to share this with.

Chapter-Twenty-Three

The merry-go-ride unleashed a torrent of commentary from Trevor, especially about the wooden St. Bernard he was riding and the dog show in the next aisle over.

They headed there once the carousel had lost its appeal—after three rides—and saw dogs jumping through hoops, walking on their back paws, on their *front* paws, some hopping, and some skipping rope. One of them could even do back flips.

"The man said he twained the puppies when they were babies." Trevor looked at them from where he was hanging onto the plastic fencing the trainer had set up around the performing dogs. "He said you hafta do it weawwy weawwy young or they won't get it." He pointed to one of the dogs, an old sheepdog mix whose main job, it seemed, was to nip at the little ones who ran too close to the fence. A guard dog for dogs. "That one's firteen years old. The man said so. Am I gonna be firteen some day? Can I get a puppy for my birfday? I want to make it do what those do. I can feed it and wove it and it can sweep in my bed. Wight Mommy?"

Those violet eyes turned on her with enough fervor to make her heart melt. Just like his father—

Jenna shook her head. No, she wasn't thinking about anything melting when it came to Bryan.

"Aw, pwease Mommy? I'll take care of it, I promise!"

"Trev, this isn't really the pla—"

"Your mom and I will talk about it, okay, Trev? Why don't you go watch that puppy walk on the ball?"

"Oh, cool!"

Bryan, once again, to the rescue. It was getting pretty annoying.

She wanted to tell him she was perfectly capable of answering her own child, but the last thing they needed—the last thing *she* needed—was for them to be warring factions in front of Trevor. She knew a lot of people who'd pitted their spouses against each other during a divorce, her own mother included. It'd made Jenna all the more determined not to do that with Trevor.

"You're catching on to this parenting thing pretty quickly. That was the perfect way to get him to stop talking about it." She had to give Bryan props where props were due.

"Thanks. That's nice of you to say."

That was a warm fuzzy moment she didn't need to have happen between them either. She could *not* let her guard down around Bryan; it'd be too easy to do, and then who knew what she'd tell him?

"But he's still not getting a puppy."

"Why not? He wants one."

"But *I* don't."

"Aw, come on. What do you have against puppies? You don't like cute little furry animals?" He nuzzled her cheek with the teddy bear's big snow-cone-covered snout.

She wiped the residual goo off her cheek. "I do love cute little furry animals. Someone else's. School will be starting soon. Puppies are time-consuming and they require work. They need to be trained and walked, and they howl at night, and then there's the poop patrol in the yard and—

"You said poop."

She looked up at him. "What?"

He grinned that grin that turned her insides to snow cone mush. "You said poop."

"Well, duh. What else am I supposed to call it? That's what puppies do. They poop. All over the place. And I just put new carpet in the family room."

"I've never gone out with someone who said poop before."

"Really? Did they *eliminate* instead? Or didn't they do that at all?"

He laughed. "I don't know what they did. It never came up in conversation."

He could have sex with them, exchange bodily fluids with them, but no one ever brought up *that* particular bodily function? Had he dated Stepford ex-wives or something?

Okay, she didn't want to think about who he'd dated. She didn't want to think about any of it. Including poop. "No puppy."

"Spoilsport."

"Yeah, well if you want to come over and clean up the yard—and Trevor's shoes when he steps in it, not to mention the midnight potty breaks, and the oodles of fur to clean up. Puppies sound great in theory, but the only time anyone should get a kid a puppy is to teach him responsibility. That way the parent doesn't have to do everything, and Trevor isn't ready for that responsibility."

"Man, who died and named you Scrooge?"

Mindy, that's who.

The thought socked Jenna in the gut. This should be *Mindy's* conversation with Bryan, not hers, though Mindy would probably have said yes to a puppy because she'd never been allowed to have one.

"Jenna? You okay?" Bryan brushed some curls off her face, his expression all worried and serious.

Couldn't have that. Couldn't have him wondering what she was thinking about—*who* she was thinking about. "Yes, I'm fine. But can we nix the idea of a puppy around Trevor, please? I don't want to have to be the bad cop."

"Ah, sweetheart, we've got years to go before we hit the good cop/bad cop stage."

"Really? I seem to remember hitting it awfully early."

"You? I can't believe you were ever at that stage. I thought you were the good kid. The perfect daughter."

Until she'd been seventeen and had brought home a little *present* from that vacation to the shore her mom had finally let her go on with Dave's family.

Her mother hadn't spoken to Dave's mother ever since. And they lived right behind each other.

"Just… no puppy, okay? It's too much work right now. Maybe when he's older. Then you can be the hero."

He gave her a funny look and opened his mouth to say something when Trevor took off running.

Away from them. "Oh, wook! Fishies!"

Jenna went into full-on panic mode. She hated when he got so excited that he just upped and ran.

She and Bryan went after him. Amazing how fast little three-and-a-half-year-old legs could go.

"Yo, Trev." Bryan caught up to him first, scooping him under the arms with his free hand. "Buddy, you can*not* go running away like that. You scared your mom and me."

Trev looked up at her, his eyes wide and tearing up. "I sowwy, Mommy."

She cupped his face and kissed his nose, breathing in that sweet sweet scent of his that'd been ingrained in her memory from the first moment she'd held him in the hospital after Mindy had delivered him. She could *not* lose him.

"I know, baby. But remember what I said in the grocery store? You can't run like that. I don't want anyone to take you."

Bryan winced when she said that and put Trev down. "Maybe you don't want to say it to him like that? Make it a little less scary?" he whispered.

She whispered right back. "I *want* him to get scared. I

want him to be terrified that someone will take him so he won't keep doing that. What if he'd run into the street? I'd rather have him scared and alive than fearless and dead." She was shaking she was so… angry? Scared? Both?

"Can I go see the fishies now?" Trevor turned those big hopeful eyes up at the two of them.

Jenna was so toast. "Yes, Trev, you can. And Bryan and I will be right here." Two feet behind him. With no one in front of them. In a perfect, uninterrupted line of site.

"Guess I shouldn't have given him the cotton candy, huh?" Bryan said when their breathing had returned to normal.

Jenna wasn't sure her heart rate ever would. "Or the hot dog, or the hot fudge sundae, or the snow cone. But it's a fair. At least he'll sleep well tonight."

She on the other hand, would probably not. Just like last night, but for completely different reasons.

"Mommy! Daddy!" Trev turned around and waved at them. "Come here!"

Daddy. He'd called Bryan *Daddy.* This situation was just getting more complicated every minute Bryan was around.

Bryan didn't look at her, but she certainly looked at him. He swallowed. Slowly.

"Ah." He cleared his throat and walked over to Trev, then tapped the brim of the hat Bryan had won for him. "What's up?"

"If I can't have a puppy, I wanna goldfish." Trevor pointed to the hundreds of tiny goldfish bowls on the platform behind the counter. "Can you toss the ball into one of them since you're the bestest thrower ever?" Hero worship shone in his eyes.

Tears shone in Bryan's.

Which made them spring to life in hers. Jenna had to look away.

"Uh, yeah, Trev. Sure." Bryan's voice was a little

husky—no a *lot* husky. He cleared his throat again. "Where's the ball?"

"Here." Trevor held up a ping-pong ball he'd grabbed off the counter then smiled his big sunny grin at Jenna. "Watch, Mommy. Daddy's gonna get me a fish."

Bryan handed her the teddy bear and the light saber and the rubber duck and the half-eaten box of popcorn with the cotton candy paper cone center sticking out of it, his damp eyes saying everything he didn't.

She nodded at him, her throat too tight to speak as well.

But then he put his game face on, took the ball, and tossed.

The ball bounced off a succession of rims like a pinball game, then flew into the gutter.

"Oh no!" Trevor banged the counter. "I want a fish!"

Jenna jostled the prizes in her arms to get a hand free to ruffle his curls. "Trev, these games aren't really designed to win. They're more designed to take people's—"

"Jenna? If you don't mind?" Bryan cut her off as he waved the booth attendant over.

"Hey, Ms. C." It was Rocco, her repeat freshman in English 101 who she wouldn't be surprised to have as a client next summer. If not sooner. Rocco cuffed Trevor lightly on the chin. "Hiya, bud."

Normally, that would make Trev light up like a Christmas tree, but not now when his dreams of fish ownership were going down the toilet—where the fish would eventually end up anyway.

Bryan peeled a ten from his wallet. "I'll take however many balls this will buy."

Rocco took it, raised his eyebrows, and shrugged. "It's your money, dude." He then set a plastic slot machine bucket full of ping-pong balls on the counter. "Good luck."

"Come on, Daddy, I know you can do it. You'll win me a fish."

She saw Bryan's Adam's apple flutter again. All this pressure. Best thrower, *Daddy* … Trevor had a lot of expectations for Bryan, and Bryan was feeling every one.

The first five went the way of the previous gutter ball. The next one however, bobbled a bit closer to actually landing in a bowl and if there'd been another two rows of them, he probably would have gotten it in one.

The next one didn't do as well, getting stuck *between* the bowls.

"Aw, man! I wanna fish!"

Now Bryan shoved back a set of imaginary sleeves, went into a baseball pitcher wind-up, and lobbed the ball.

It took one bounce off a rim and went sailing off into the sunset.

Trevor banged the counter again. "Come on, Daddy, you can do it!"

Bryan was feeling the pressure. Three more balls disappeared into the gutter.

There couldn't be many left.

"How about if we let your mom try, Trev?" Bryan held out a ball. It was a pink one.

"Big tough guy can't throw a pink ball?" she teased, hiking the teddy bear under her arm, ready for the challenge.

"Big tough guy *can* throw a pink ball. But if it doesn't land where it's supposed to he'll never live it down."

She took the ball. "I'll never understand men."

"Aw, come on, we're easy. Football, cars, food, and se—uh, women. Not much more to us."

The problem was, he was wrong. There was a whole lot more to Bryan Lassiter and he'd just proved it by giving her the chance to be the hero in their son's eyes.

She tossed the ball.

"Oh, Mommy!"

Chapter Twenty-Four

Jenna's ball landed in the middle bowl with a splash and Trevor went nuts, screaming and jumping up and down, banging the counter with his fists. "I get a fishie! I get a fishie!"

Rocco was laughing as he scooped the pink ball out of the bowl, then poured their new pet into a plastic bag for the ride home. "You want the ball, Trevor? Your fish might like to have it for a souvenir."

"What's a souvenea?"

"It's something that helps you remember a special event."

"Oh, wike my new teddy bear? I'm gonna name him Bwyan."

Bryan started coughing and had to turn around. He was coughing so much his shoulders started to shake. Coughing so much he had tears dotting the corners of his eyes.

"So what are you going to name the fish, then, Trev?" Jenna took mercy on Bryan and got Trevor focused on the fish. She'd worry about the teddy bear later.

She'd worry about Bryan later, too.

"My fishie's name is Wocco."

Jenna laughed and hiked the offending teddy bear up under her arm. "I'm sure Rocco will be honored."

Bryan coughed once more then took the prizes back. "You ought to name the fish after your mom since she was the one who won it for you."

"That's siwwy. You can't name a fish Mommy." Trevor dropped his arm and dragged the bag behind him.

"Hey, Sport, let me carry that for you." Bryan held out his free hand before they ended up with a dehydrated fish in the bag. "I think we need to get him a bowl and some food and pretty quickly. We might want to think about heading home."

"Aw, but I wanna get a cupcake. You said we could get one and Wocco will wike a cupcake."

Bryan did some judicious juggling with the prizes and the bag with the poor fish that'd be lucky to live the next twenty minutes forget the hour or so it'd take them to buy his bowl, his food, and go satisfy cupcake cravings.

"You did promise him, Bryan," she said, chuckling. "I heard you."

"Well then, it's a good thing I know just the place, isn't it?"

"Do they have stwawbewwy ones?"

"I guess. They have lots of different kinds."

"What about snozzbewwies? Do they have them?"

Bryan looked up at her with a deer-in-the-headlights look. "You want to help me out here, Jenna?"

"Seriously? You don't know snozzberries?"

"Never heard of them."

"Really? Charlie and the Chocolate Factory? One of *the* classic movies?"

"No…"

"Trev? Wanna tell Bryan about the movie?" It was one of his favorites, especially when she'd recited the dialogue with the characters. Trevor had looked at her as if she was the smartest person in the world and Jenna had been more than willing to let him believe so. The teenage years would come soon enough.

They'd ended up watching the movie a few times back-to-back until he knew some of the dialogue, and still watched it at least once a month together, their little "thing."

"Watch me, Bwyan! I'm an *oompa loopma*!"

Trev had the song and the waddle down pat. The waddle wasn't hard since he'd walked the same way when he'd been in diapers; all he had to do was channel those days.

"You should watch it with us sometime. Daddies watch movies with their kids, wight, Mommy?"

Out of the mouths of babes…

"If he wants, Trev."

"Or course I do. What dad wouldn't want to?"

"Yay!" Trevor spun like an *oompa loompa* which was a lot like Charlie Chaplin with his pants bagging around his knees. "So, do they? Have snozzbewwy cupcakes?"

"Well, now, Trev, I don't really know. I guess we'll have to find out. You ready to go?"

"I'm always weady for cupcakes."

***

Bryan glanced in the back seat as Jenna tightened the seatbelt across Trevor's booster seat. The giant teddy bear—Bryan—was strapped in beside him. Trevor had insisted, and Jenna, awesome mother that she was, had agreed. Bryan was wishing he'd won another one so he could have latched it to *this* side of the cab, the perfect airbags in the event of an accident.

Amazing how his priorities had shifted in the twenty-four hours since he'd officially become a father. Three and a half years too late, but that hadn't been anyone's fault. What would be his fault was if he allowed any more time to be lost.

Unfortunately, he did have to get back to the job he was working on. The Vistons were due back from their vacation in two weeks and he'd promised to have the addition wired and ready for the drywallers by next weekend. Taking this time off to be with Trevor was going to make the schedule tight. Plus, he had a few shifts to cover for Gage this week at the club, which was going to make it even tougher to carve out some time for Trevor.

It was a good thing Jenna had turned down his impromptu proposal. He didn't have time to court her, get to know her, fall in love with her. Work had to be his focus so he could pay for his son.

He pulled into the parking lot at Gage's fiancée's bakery. In the year since Gage and Lara had been together, Lara and her cousin, Cara's business, Cavallo's Cups & Cakes, had grown so much that Gage had been spending all *his* free time building on an addition to the kitchen and expanding the front of the building to include a walk-in store where people could buy the products they made on-site. Business had taken off after the Fourth-of-July community picnic last year and Gage was complaining that he no longer had any spare time. Since he'd barely had any before that, that was saying something, and was the reason Bryan had helped cover his shifts whenever possible. With his nephew's surgery, Gage had a lot on his plate and Bryan had been able to help out.

But now, with wanting all *his* free time to be tied up with Trevor—and Trevor's mother—things were going to get tight across the board.

His heart ached for the time he'd already lost with his son. For what he'd missed. For knowing how Trevor had felt in his arms as a baby. How he'd smelled. How he'd cried and cooed and when he'd started sleeping through the night. If there were any foods he was allergic to, or anything he was scared of or what he liked to eat… Everything. He wanted to know everything about Trevor and he wanted to be part of every moment of his life from here on out.

Should he ask for custody?

Bryan jerked the car to a stop. *Custody*. The word had just popped into his head, but now that it was there, he couldn't not think about it. It was his right, after all.

But *was* it right for Trevor?

He climbed out of the cab and opened the back door to undo Trevor's seat belt. Things were going well with Jenna. Would a discussion about custody upset that balance? Was it wise to risk it? Suppose she said no and hired an attorney? She was Trevor's mother and a good one; no judge would take a child from her and it could limit *his* access to him.

Bryan helped Trev down. No, he'd hold off. For now anyway.

"What cupcake are you going to get, Bwyan?" Trev hopped up and down some more.

"I don't know yet. How about if you pick once we see what kinds they have?"

"Okay." He bent over and looked under the car. "Huwwy up, Mommy! Race ya!"

Bryan had to do a quick lunge to grab the kid before he went racing across the parking lot. Jenna was right. Better to scare the pants off the kid than have them knocked off of him. Gage and his family were already living that nightmare.

"Trevor, if you go running off, no cupcakes."

It stopped the little squirming monster in his tracks. "No cupcakes?"

"Your mom's right. Running away is dangerous. You're in a parking lot. People can't see you from their cars. They could hit you."

"And squash me like a bug?"

Bryan winced at the image. It'd probably come from that Michael kid, but in this instance, Bryan was glad for Michael's over-sharing.

"Yes, and then you'd never get a cupcake."

"Oh." Trev stuck his thumb in his mouth and twiddled

his hair with the other. "Okay. Can I hold your hand?"

Bryan could only nod.

Lara, Gage's fiancée was behind the counter when they went in.

"Hey, Lar."

"Hi, Bryan. And who do we have here?" Lara glanced at Jenna with a smile, but it was Trevor who got her full focus.

"I'm Twevor. Do you have snozzbewwy cupcakes?"

Lara tapped her lip. "You know, I think I just sold my last snozzberry. Do you like any other kind?

Trevor scrunched his face. "Oh. How about dinosaurs? I wike T-wexes."

"I do have some dinosaurs." She pointed to the glass case. "Why don't you look around and I'll take a look in the back to see if there's a spare snozzberry hanging around. Sound like a good idea?"

"Yes, pwease."

Lara raised her eyebrows at Jenna and Bryan. "Polite. Very nice."

It *was* nice. So was the little tug to Bryan's heart at the compliment paid to his child even though he knew he had no claim to it since Jenna's parenting skills had made Trevor the way he was today.

Okay, so he wouldn't bring up the custody issue. Not yet anyway. She was doing a good job and he didn't want to mess this up.

"Wook, Mommy! She has a T-wex! And a diplodocus."

"I see, Trev. You want one of those?"

"I dunno." He slid his sticky palms on the glass as he looked at the rest of the cupcakes.

"He can't say T-rex but he can say diplodocus?" Bryan whispered to Jenna before he walked behind the counter to grab some paper towels.

She shrugged. "No *r*s or *tr*s. You should hear him say *truck*. It's pretty embarrassing."

It took him a few seconds but he got it. He chuckled as he walked to the front of the glass case with Lara's vinegar spray bottle and wiped up Trevor's hand prints.

"Oh, wook, Mommy! They have a fire fu—"

"*Truck*. They have a fire *truck*. Yes, I see it, Trevor." She raised her eyebrows at Bryan.

Yep, definitely embarrassing.

"Hey, look what I found!" Lara walked out from the back with a smile on her face and a cupcake in her hand.

A red cupcake. With some weirdly shaped strawberry on top.

"What's that?" Bryan asked.

"A snozzberry," Jenna and Lara answered at the same time. They looked at each other and started laughing.

"You found a snozzbewwy? Weawwy?" Trevor's eyes lit up and his voice rose an octave.

Ah. The secret to successful parenting. Lie to the kid. Bryan liked it.

"Yes, Trevor. This is the last snozzberry cupcake in the whole place and since snozzberries are out of season, we probably won't get any more in for a while. But you're welcome to this one if you want."

Trevor held out his pudgy little arms. "Yes, pwease. I always wanted to twy a snozzbewwy."

Trevor peeled the cupcake holder back as if he were unwrapping a present, with all the awe and wonderment and happiness a kid could muster.

"So, what do you think?" Jenna ran a hand over his curls. She did that a lot. As if she *needed* to touch him.

Bryan completely got it. This parenting thing was—

"Awesome!"

Yeah, that summed it up.

"So, Bryan, how is everyone today? Gage told me what happened. Thank God those other dancers could fill in."

"Hey, Trev," said Jenna. "Why don't we go look at the dinosaurs again? Maybe we can take one home for later." Jenna steered Trevor to the far end of the counter while motioning toard the other end with a nod of her head.

Bryan got the hint and headed that way, Lara following. "I talked to everyone. Still feeling some residual stomach pain from the cramping, but they're doing okay. Best thing we ever did was get a bigger crew and rotate them. Of course, the team tonight will be on for their second consecutive night, but I doubt if many of the patrons are coming in two nights in a row."

"I heard there was a new dancer. Did the Marilyn Monroe bit."

Bryan rubbed the back of his neck. He hated sticky situations and this was about to get stickier than her buttercream icing.

"Uh, yeah. She was applying for the job, and since she was there, I figured it'd be the perfect audition."

"Pretty ballsy. What if she'd been awful?"

He resisted the urge to look at Jenna. "I had a feeling she wouldn't be."

"You had a feeling? Here, I've been looking at cost sheets and inventory and staffing needs and all I need is a *feeling* to make business decisions?" Lara put the back of her hand against her forehead. "Oh, my. I've been doing it all wrong."

"Okay, okay, your point's made. It didn't matter though; she decided she didn't want to work at the club. But she did help out and she did it well."

"Wow. That seems… counterproductive. Fickle, too." Lara rubbed his upper arm. "Good thing you didn't hire her. You've had enough fickle women in your life."

True. Most of it because of the night job. Gage had had the same problem. For a while, women liked the idea that he knew those sexy moves. Sex had never been a problem in his relationships. Jealousy, on the other hand… It took a secure, confident woman to be with a dancer.

"So what's the story there?" Lara nodded toward where Jenna and Trevor were huddled together, staring at the items in the display case. "Is she the one?"

"Gage told you."

She nodded, not that it was a surprise. News like this wouldn't stay quiet for long, though he hadn't expected Gage to keep it from her.

"Then you know he's my son."

"I do. How are you?" She rubbed his arm.

"Okay. It was a shock, obviously."

Her fingers tightened. "She should have told you."

He covered her hand with his and gently removed it. "She didn't know how to get in touch with me. My fault." It wasn't anyone's fault, but society was the way it was and it'd be better for Jenna if he took the fall. He didn't mind. "But she's fine with me being part of his life. It's going well."

"So far. Are you going to ask for her for a formal custody arrangement?"

It was his turn to put *his* hand on *her* arm. He squeezed. "Thanks for caring, Lara, but right now, it's working for us. I'll cross that bridge when I need to."

"I just don't want you to get hurt, Bry."

"I'm not going to. Not in this. Trevor's great, and so is Jenna. It'll work out. You'll see."

"Hey, Bwyan!" Trevor barreled into his legs again. "I'm gonna get a whole bunch of cupcakes. Want some?"

"Sure, Trev. What are you getting?"

Jenna walked up to them. "He's decided on two dinosaurs, one fire truck, and three footballs." She looked at Bryan. "One for each one of us for dessert. After dinner tonight. If you're interested, that is."

He glanced at Lara. Point proven as how well it was working out.

"Pwease, Bwayn! Pwease have dinner at our house. Mommy's gonna make pisghetti. I wove pisghetti."

Bryan laughed. He used to call it the same thing. "Sure I will, Trev. I love spaghetti, too."

Hell, he'd eat anything if it meant he could share it with his son.

And his son's mother.

Chapter Twenty-Five

"Wocco wikes his new home." Trevor stared into the glass bowl he'd *insisted* join them at the dinner table. He'd even set a place serving out for the fish so Rocco wouldn't feel left out.

"Now he has a weal famiwy too!" he said, melting Bryan's heart. He'd obviously missed out on having a "real" family, and Bryan was so glad he could give it to him. That he *and Jenna* could give that to him.

He cleared the dinner plates while Jenna scooped out ice cream for dessert. "Thanks for coming today," he said as he scraped the remainder of Trevor's "pisghetti" into the trash and set the plate into the sink to soak. "I had a great time and I think Trevor did, too."

"Thank *you* for suggesting it." She dug a scoop of vanilla fudge out of the carton. "I'd really wanted to take him this year. Last year the clowns scared him before we got past the ticket line. I was worried he'd be scarred for life." She plopped the scoop into Trevor's bowl.

Bryan unwrapped the football cupcake Trevor had claimed. "I never liked clowns either. I always thought the big red shoes were scary."

She chuckled and scooped some ice cream into another bowl. "He said the same thing. Genetics are amazing things."

"I know." He unwrapped another cupcake, the pink one Trevor said was Jenna's. "I'd like to see his baby pictures sometime. Compare them to mine."

The ice cream scooper clattered onto the countertop and Jenna got all flustered trying to grab the ice cream before it fell onto the floor.

Bryan set down the last unwrapped cupcake and turned on the faucet when she dropped the glob of ice cream into the sink, then handed her a dishtowel when she finished washing her hands.

"His baby pictures." She scrubbed her hands dry and got a funny look on her face. "I, uh… I have his baby album put away upstairs. Sticky kid fingers, you know. I didn't want him to smudge the pictures. Can I show you some other time?"

"Sure, no problem. But you must have some pictures around somewhere? Hanging up or something?"

"Uh, yeah. I do. I'll grab a few when we're finished with dessert if that's okay?" She wiggled her fingers. "Even grown-ups can have sticky fingers."

"Sounds good. " He picked up two of the bowls and headed back to the table. "Here you go, kiddo. The blue and white football, just like you wanted."

Trevor's eyes lit up. Bryan would never get over the feeling of making his son smile. It was so precious. So sweet.

"Thank you, Bwyan. I mean, Daddy. I wike having a daddy."

Bryan liked him having one.

"Michael's daddy wives wif him. Are you going to wive wif me?"

Jenna's spoon clattered to the table and she got a funny—though not in a *haha* sort of way—look on her face. "Trevor—"

"I have my own house, Trev." Bryan jumped in because this was as much for Jenna as it was for Trevor. He'd just shown up in their lives and, as great as Jenna was being about this, she had to be freaked out by having to share their son. Had to be wondering where this was all going. So was Bryan, but he had to set her mind at ease. For as much as he wanted to be part of Trevor's life, they had to take this slow. That everything couldn't suddenly be different. "Actually, Trev, I already have a house."

"You do?"

"I do. And you're welcome to come over anytime you want. We can even set up a room for you if you like."

Jenna's gaze flew to his and she wasn't looking any more relieved than she had when Trevor asked about him moving in here. Maybe he should have cleared that invitation with her before issuing it.

"I can have another bedwoom? Cool! Do you have a twee fort? Michael has one, but Mommy says none of our twees are stwong enough."

"Sorry, no, I don't have a tree fort. But maybe we can build one when you're older." The last was as much a question to Jenna as it was a stalling tactic for Trevor.

"I'm gonna be four soon, wight, Mommy?"

Jenna's smile didn't reach her eyes. "That's right, Trev. In a few months."

"What day?" Bryan suddenly realized he didn't know. The most important day of his life and he didn't know the date. Early in the year sometime, given that Brad's bachelor party had been in April.

"January third."The words were short, clipped, and she kept her eyes firmly on her cupcake.

He wanted to keep his eyes on *her* cupcakes…

He shook his head. He should be ashamed of himself, lusting after his son's mother—

Though that pretty much contradicted itself, didn't it? How else would she be his son's mother if he hadn't lusted after her at some point? And why was it bad to do so now?

The thing was, it *wasn't* bad. It also opened the doors to a lot of possibilities. Ones he really wanted to explore.

That proposal hadn't come from nowhere. While he

might not have been *consciously* thinking it, he'd obviously been *un*consciously thinking it.

"Can I take Wocco up to my woom, Mommy? Mr. Monkey wants to meet him."

"How about if I carry him up for you?" Bryan pushed back from the table. No need to sit here with temptation sitting across from him, looking utterly delectable with a smudge of icing on her upper lip. Lusting after his son's mother with that son sitting right here wasn't the part of fatherhood Bryan wanted his son to see. "That way the water won't slosh out."

"I can cawwy it, Bwyan. I help Mommy all the time in the garden and I cawwy lots of water buckets. Wight, Mommy?"

Jenna looked up. "Yes, that's right. You're a very big helper, Trevor." She helped him out of his booster seat, then picked up the fish bowl. "But why don't you let Bryan carry Rocco anyway and you can show him your room. I bet Mr. Monkey would like to meet him, too."

"Okay." Trevor walked around to Bryan and tugged his hand. "Wanna see my woom?"

"Sure." He took the fish bowl from her. "I'll be down to help with the dishes in a few minutes."

"No, don't worry about it. Enjoy Trevor."

"You sure? Really, I don't mind helping out."

"But *Trevor* might if you leave before he shows you his toy car collection. I can handle K.P. duty."

He touched her chin. "Now you said *doody*."

She swatted his hand away with a smile—the one he'd been trying to put back on her face. "Go on, will you? The kid isn't going to be three-and-a-half forever. Enjoy it while it lasts."

"Aye, aye, captain." He punched his heels together and saluted which got Trevor to break out in a fit of giggles.

"Her name's Mommy, not captain, Bwyan!"

"Don't be so sure about that, Trev," Bryan said as he followed his son up the stairs. The woman was definitely captain of the ship *he* was on these days.

Jenna exhaled the minute they were out of the kitchen. Trevor's baby album. She had to do something about it and quick.

Mindy's pictures were all over that album, which was why she didn't leave it lying around. Trevor didn't know about Mindy and Jenna wanted to keep it that way until he was old enough to understand. And, as she and Cathy had discussed, to keep him from blurting it out in the unlikely event that his father ever showed up.

And since the unlikely had happened, Jenna was glad she'd kept that secret. Now to *keep* keeping it…

She was going to have to make up a fake baby book.

She looked at the retro red-and-white clock hanging above the doorway. Too late to go to a store tonight. She should have bought a baby book when they were there earlier, but that would have raised some questions she hadn't been prepared to answer.

She finished cleaning up the kitchen and started working on the family room, all the while listening to the chatter going on upstairs. She couldn't hear all of it, just the low murmur of voices, and while she should be happy they were bonding, should be feeling good about it, she didn't.

She was feeling left out.

This was going to be hard, adjusting to having someone else in Trevor's life who was just as important to him as she was.

Jenna took a deep breath. She could do this. She *could*. She had to. And she had to make it work so Bryan didn't get curious and start delving into areas she'd rather he didn't.

Which made the baby book even that much more important.

Chapter Twenty-Six.

She was home by nine the next morning, having dropped Trevor off at Cathy's while she completed Operation Fake Baby Book.

The pictures were tough to look at. Mindy at every stage of her pregnancy, the sonograms, the copy of his original birth certificate, the inked footprints by his birth photo…

She missed her sister. Ached that she'd died so young and missed out on Trevor's life. He was a gift, truly a gift, and one Jenna would treasure forever.

She scanned copies of the photos and pasted them into the book. She added in some of the notes Mindy had written down, decorating them with exclamation marks and hearts like Mindy had to show how happy she'd been as he'd grown inside her.

The same information about his birth came next, the same comments about morning sickness and worries about stretch marks and the delivery, followed by his feeding schedule and when he'd rolled over and smiled and cooed and said his first word. Took his first step. Called her Mommy.

Those last few had been *her* memories, not Mindy's.

She loved this little boy with everything inside her. Couldn't love him more if he *had* been inside her—and she knew that because she'd carried a child. Granted, it'd only been for three short months and she'd been terrified the entire time, but she loved Trevor just as fiercely as she had that other child. And she would mourn losing him just as much if it came down to it.

But it couldn't. Trevor was hers and she would do whatever it took to keep it that way.

She called Bryan when she was finished.

"Hey, Jenna, what's up? Is Trevor okay?"

She had to smile at the question; it'd be the same one she'd ask him if he called her. "I was wondering if you're free for lunch. I have those pictures you were asking about."

"Great. Can you meet me at Mick's Deli in, say, a half hour? I ought be able to get away."

"Sure. See you then."

She checked her makeup in the hall mirror, then tucked her shirt into her shorts, and made sure she was wearing two matching socks. Not that Bryan would look, but when she went out in public she always tried to look professional in case she ran into students or their parents.

Hopefully none of them had been in the club the other night.

Oh, God, the other night. What had she been thinking? Why on earth had she agreed? She could have told him no. Being a teacher was a valid excuse, yet she'd opted to be naked on a stage.

Okay, she'd had tassels and a thong, but she might as well have been naked.

She hadn't been thinking. That was all there was to it. She'd been so worried about losing Trevor that she'd been ready to do anything.

It hadn't been that bad.

She stared at herself. It wasn't *bad*? Was she crazy? She could have lost her job. The respect of her students if this ever got out.

Bryan's?

No. Of course not. He'd *asked* her to do it. Hell, *he'd*

danced, too.

Yes he had.

And then he'd kissed her.

And proposed.

Why on earth had he proposed? Where had that come from? They barely knew each other and getting married for the sake of a child was *not* a reason to get married and she could just forget about last night's dream.

The dream.

Oh, crud. The dream. The one that had woken her with an ache between her thighs and the sheets twisted around her.

He'd been oiled down and muscle-bound in that dream, wearing nothing more than what he'd barely had on on stage, with moves designed to jumpstart any woman's libido, let alone someone who hadn't had sex in over three years.

Of *course* she'd dream about him. He'd be dream-worthy even if she hadn't seen him dance at the club.

He'd danced in her dream, too. This time just for her.

And she'd done the same for him.

She tucked her hair behind her ears. *Get a hold of yourself, Jenna. No flings with your child's biological father*. Bad enough she was worried about spilling the beans about Trevor's birth, but what would happen if something *did* start between them only to go south? That would open a can of worms she'd never be able to close.

She and Bryan were co-parents. That's it. They had to get along for Trevor's sake, but N.O.T.H.I.N.G. more. Ever.

***

Yeah, that was all good in theory, but then she got to Mick's, and Bryan was waiting there by the door in his butt-hugging jeans, work boots, and a t-shirt that could have been paint on, her dream rose up like a tidal wave and crashed over on her, drowning her in want and need and an aching desperate loneliness she'd never really acknowledged before. But she had to now because with him standing there, looking at her the way he was... she ached.

"It's good to see you," Bryan said as he held the door for her.

"You, too." Because it truly was.

She couldn't shake that dream. Or the memory of when he'd kissed her. With Trevor around, it'd been a little easier to put thoughts like that out of her head, but when it was just the two of them... Hard. Very hard.

She kept her eyes straight ahead as she headed inside. There would be no looking around to see anything *hard* on him.

His bicep flexed as she walked past him.

Okay, she could look at that.

And salivate over it.

She pasted a smile on her face when she saw Johnny, one of her students, behind the counter, hoping she looked normal. Friendly. Not frustrated and undersexed.

She really shouldn't have stopped dating. That's what this was. Just a build-up of frustration that Bryan had tapped into by kissing her. And because he did it so damned well. Then there was the fact that she'd seen him all but naked on the stage—

Actually his butt *had* been naked.

She walked up to the display case and practically ripped a ticket from the dispenser as she looked at the menu hanging on the wall that might as well have been in Greek for all she could see straight right now. It was going to be a long fourteen-and-a-half years until Trevor turned eighteen.

Bryan put his hands on her shoulders. "Find anything you like?"

Yes. She had. And his hands were on her shoulders.

"Uh… Roast beef on white. Mayo. Swiss. Lettuce." A fork to pry her tongue off the roof of her mouth.

"Number twenty-seven," Johnny called out, changing the electronic number ticker on the counter.

No one claimed it.

"Number twenty-seven!" he said a little louder.

"Jenna?" Bryan reached over her shoulder and plucked the ticket out of her hand. "That's us."

Us. Not *her*, but *us.* He was already lumping himself in with her in areas that didn't concern Trevor.

This was not good.

Bryan placed their order, then led her over to a booth. Jenna was more than happy to slide in because her legs were just the tiniest bit shaky.

"So you brought some pictures?" he asked.

Now her fingers got in on the shaky thing. Her stomach, too.

"I did." She ducked her head, thankful for once that her hair wouldn't stay behind her ears so she had a few seconds to gather her composure, and pulled the baby book out of her purse. This was it. Once she did this, there was no going back.

Bryan took the book as if it were made of glass, the look on his face only adding to her guilt.

Think of the bigger picture.

Right. Trevor. Custody.

Bryan opened the first page. It was the sonogram.

"I don't see him." Bryan turned the book toward her. "Can you show me?"

"Sure." She tried injecting warmth into her voice. Tried to keep her finger steady as she pointed out Trevor's features. He'd been sucking his thumb even in utero.

"I used to do that, you know." Bryan imitated the same movement Trevor made.

"I figured you must have because M—I never sucked my thumb. What got you to stop? I've been thinking about doing something, but all the books I've read have differing opinions. Some say to leave him alone, that he'll stop on his own, others say to end it before it becomes a life-long habit."

"How many adults do you know who suck their thumb?"

"Good point. Besides, it helps calm him down and sometimes I need him to do it."

"Yeah, he does seem to be pretty high-energy. All that jumping up and down he does."

"He's a little boy. Snakes and snails and puppy dogs' tails, you know."

"I seem to remember something like that." He turned the page. "How old was he in this?"

Jenna tilted her head and smiled. She remembered that moment as if it were yesterday. "About an hour."

"Who took it? Your mom?"

Oh, crud. Here came the lies. "No. My mother and I… Like I said, we don't see eye-to-eye on a lot of things."

"But this is her grandson."

"Trevor's one of those things." Jenna bit her lip. "I didn't tell her about him until after he was born. She has an issue with his… parentage."

"You mean how he was conceived."

She nodded, biting back the tears. She didn't want to have to tell him about the other baby, the reason behind her mother's so-called shame.

He dropped the book onto the table and sat back, blowing out a big breath. "Jesus, Jenna. You went through all of that by yourself? You must have been terrified."

"Well, not all by myself. My sister—my half-sister was with me." When lying, it was always best to stick as close to the truth as possible. In this instance, she just switched uteruses. Uteri? What was the plural of uterus?

"… is she now?"

Right. Focus on the conversation.

Jenna took a deep breath, this part of the conversation as tough as the other part.

"She's… gone. Cancer."

Cancer she'd known about while she'd been pregnant and hadn't done anything about because she hadn't wanted to jeopardize her child's health.

Yet Jenna's own mother would deny his existence and shun her own daughter for "shaming" her. Biology did not make someone a parent.

"And then you were on your own?"

"That's when I came back here. Moved home, hoping my mother would want to know her grandson and be able to overlook the circumstances of his birth, but she couldn't." Still hadn't.

"So Trevor doesn't know his grandmother?"

Jenna shook her head. It was her one regret about the lies she'd had to tell. But the truth of the matter was, if she'd told her mother who Trevor's mother *really* was, not only would Ellen never want to bother with Trevor again, she'd spread more venom and vitriol about how *the tramp's* daughter was as much a tramp as her mother had been. Trevor didn't need to grow up with that going around about his mother.

No, it'd been better for everyone that Trevor was hers.

"Well, *my* mother is going to be thrilled," said Bryan. "She loves her grandchildren."

Jenna looked up. She hadn't thought about that. By gaining a father, Trevor also gained grandparents. And cousins. An uncle.

"Does she live around here?"

"Yeah, over in Oaks. Not too far. I'd like to introduce them if you don't mind."

It wouldn't matter even if she did. Trevor deserved a grandmother to love him. "Have you told her?"

"Not yet. I wanted to discuss this with you. It's a big step and I know you're used to having him all to yourself.

Just letting me in must be tough. I want you to get used to me before I spring my mother on you. She's going to want to smother him."

"He deserves that. He's such a good little boy with so much love inside him."

"Love that you've given him, Jenna." Bryan reached for her hands and intertwined their fingers. "Obviously this isn't the most opportune way to bring a child into the world and not really the way I would have chosen, but I'm glad I had him with you. You're an awesome mother, Jenna. Thank you. For loving our son as much as you have and for putting his wants and needs first. It can't have been easy. That's why I want to help lighten the burden. Not because I want to take him from you, but because I want him—and you—to be able to enjoy being together."

"But we do."

"I know, but like with Jason the other day. Trevor didn't want to nap, but he had to because you had to work. Take the ten grand. Use it to relax a little. Focus on Trevor. Spend time with him. With me. With us as a family. I know it's not the traditional kind, but what is anymore? We both want what's best for him and who knows, maybe we'll find out my marriage proposal wasn't all that precipitous."

Why'd he have to be so nice. So perfect? Then maybe she wouldn't feel so guilty about lying to him and *could* explore what was between them.

Maybe even marry him.

For a moment—just one tiny moment—she let herself go there. Saw herself waking up in bed next to him every day. Saw him going into Trevor's room and helping him get dressed while she made waffles in the kitchen.

Saw Bryan putting Trev into his car seat in the truck and driving him off to school with the T-rex backpack and the fire engine lunch box.

Maybe even bringing a puppy home for Trevor's birthday.

He would love to get a puppy on his birthday.

"Jenna?"

Bryan's thumb rubbed over her hand, trailing sparks of want and need in their wake—and not just the sexual kind.

She wanted to be with someone. She *needed* to be. It'd been three years since Carl and even then, Carl hadn't been *with* her like Bryan was right at this moment. The love they had for their son bound them together.

Was it enough? Could it be enough?

Did she want it enough?

She did. And that was the problem. If she wanted it badly enough and allowed herself—and them—to have it, she would have to lie to Bryan for the rest of their lives.

Chapter Twenty-Seven.

Jenna managed to put Bryan off about the money—and his proposal—for the remainder of their lunch, but that didn't mean she didn't think about it.

She did. A lot.

"This picture's cute. What's it from?"

Bryan had needed a run-down on every photo she'd put in the book: when it'd been taken, how old Trevor had been, what were the circumstances, who'd been there, who'd taken the picture. That part had gotten easier after Mindy's death because she'd taken most of the pictures of Trevor. The occasional one with her in it had been because of Cathy.

"Oh, that was his first day of pre-school. He was so excited and he'd insisted that Mr. Monkey had to ride in his backpack. The teachers had said it was fine to bring in favorite toys. That it was common for the kids to have separation anxiety and the toys helped transition them. Mr. Monkey had started staying home the second week, so it worked."

"He does love that ugly thing, doesn't he?"

"Yep. He does." Mindy had bought it when she learned about her illness. She'd wanted him to have something from her that he could hug and cherish and take anywhere with him. She'd still had her Mr. Monkey from when she'd been a child—their father had given each of them one. Jenna's was packed away in her closet, a reminder of her father she'd taken out the night she and Mindy had brought Trevor home… and the night Mindy had died.

"Sweetheart?"

Jenna looked up. An older woman was approaching their table.

"Mom? Hey." Bryan got to his feet.

Bryan's mother?

Jenna froze. This was Trevor's grandmother.

"Mom, I'd like you to meet Jenna Corrigan. Jenna, my mom, Tabitha Lassiter."

"Tabitha?" Cathy must be psychic.

"A bit old-fashioned, I know, though I was quite popular when that show was on back in the sixties."

"It's nice to meet you."

"You, too. Well, don't let me interrupt you—oh is that a baby album?" Mrs. Lassiter cocked her head. "He's adorable. Looks familiar. Have we met—"

It was Trevor's school picture. The portrait.

With his eyes center stage.

"Who is this?" Mrs. Lassiter's voice went hoarse and she planted her hand on the table. "Whose child is this?" She looked at Bryan, her face losing its color.

Like Jenna was sure hers had.

Bryan held his mother's arm. "Mom, have a seat."

Jenna gulped. There was no hiding those eyes.

"Bryan?" His mother braced herself with her palms on the table then sank onto the seat. "What's going on?"

Bryan ran a hand over his mouth. "I have some… good news, Mom."

"Good?" She looked from Bryan to Jenna.

Jenna tried to put a smile on her face. Tried to because she had no idea what this was going to mean to all of them.

"Yes, Mom. Good. It'll be a shock, but a good one. You'll see."

"Bryan, what are you telling me?"

Bryan smiled, then he gnawed his lip, then he swiped his hand over his mouth again and drummed the fingers on his other hand on the table. "He's my son, Mom."

"Oh dear lord." Mrs. Lassiter slumped against the padded vinyl. "How? When? Why?"

He patted her shoulder and glanced at Jenna.

She tried to give him encouragement, but, really, she didn't know what to say. Part of her wanted this for Trevor and the other part was terrified for herself.

"Well, the *how* is pretty obvious. I mean we all know how babies are made."

"Don't get flippant with me, Bryan."

"Sorry." He cleared his throat. "Let's just say, it wasn't planned."

Interesting that he hadn't said Trevor was an accident. Because he wasn't. No matter that he hadn't been planned, Jenna would never call him an accident. A blessing, a gift, a surprise… but never an accident.

"As to the *when* and *why*… Let's just say that Jenna and I knew each other a few years ago and lost touch."

Mrs. Lassiter finally remembered there was someone else at the table and sat up, drilling Jenna with her narrowed eyes. "You didn't tell my son he was going to be a father?"

Jenna winced. This wasn't going to be good no matter what spin Bryan tried to put on it.

"I—"

"Mom, look, I'm not proud of myself. We weren't… together for very long and I didn't tell her how to get in touch with me. She tried, but couldn't find me."

Okay, maybe that spin did do the trick because Mrs. Lassiter turned her disbelief on her son. "You didn't give her your *phone number*? Your last *name*? Is this how we raised you? You mean to tell me you let this poor girl raise your son with no help from you?"

She turned back to Jenna. "Please forgive me, my

dear. I apologize for my son's... reckless behavior. Of course we'll help you now. If you'll let us. I can understand if you want nothing to do with any of the Lassiters, but I do hope you'll think about it for a while. A child should know his family." She dragged the baby book over and looked at the picture. "What's his name? How old is he? Is he here?"

Bryan covered her hand and squeezed. "His name is Trevor and he's three and a half, and, no, he's not here. Jenna and I have a lot to talk about and he doesn't need to be part of that. He's with a friend of his."

"Can I meet him?" This she asked to Jenna, woman-to-woman. Mother-to-mother.

"Of course." Jenna looked at Bryan. "But... would you mind waiting a day or two? He's just getting used to having Bryan in his life and I don't want to overwhelm him with a family he's never known before."

"Of course. I understand." Mrs. Lassiter fingered the photo. "He looks just like you, Bryan. He has your eyes." *Her* eyes were filling with tears and she flipped the page. "Do you mind if I look at this?"

Jenna shook her head, trying to keep her own tears at bay. Such a different response from her own mother's take on the news. That'd been full of recriminations and "all about me"s and the tears hadn't been happy ones.

Mrs. Lassiter's were coursing down her cheeks as her son explained each picture to her, as they read his schedule and his first words.

"Oh, look, Bryan. His first word was *cow*, too."

"I said that?"

"You did. We were out at the Mackerley's farm. We'd been there many times with you and you knew all the animal sounds, but for some reason the moment we drove up that day, you started shouting, "Cow! Cow!" She patted his arm. "Of course, we didn't have the heart to tell you it was a bull when you were so proud of yourself. After that, we couldn't shut you up."

"Huh. How about that? Who knew even that was genetic?" Bryan sat back and scratched his cheek. "So what does Trevor do that you did, Jenna?"

"Oh, uh, well…" Jenna swallowed around the big fat lie choking her. "I liked to, um, color. Trevor does that really well."

"Oh, and he builds things, Ma. With blocks."

"Like you used to."

"Yeah. And he likes to throw the football."

His mother smiled and it both warmed and broke Jenna's heart. Why couldn't her mother have been as thrilled to find out about her grandchild? She could already see the love Bryan's mom had for Trevor.

"Maybe you'd like to come to dinner tomorrow night, Mrs. Lassiter?"

The invitation just popped out, but the moment Jenna said it, she knew it was the right thing to do. Trevor shouldn't be deprived even one more day of all this love.

"Are you sure, dear? I don't want to overwhelm him. Or you either. This can't be easy for you, giving up your personal time with him to share him with what must seem like a bunch of strangers." She socked Bryan in the bicep. "I'll never forgive you for not keeping in touch with her. How many other grandchildren might I have floating around from previous girlfriends?"

Bryan winced. As well he should. God, Jenna hadn't even thought about that. What if he did have other kids? Condoms weren't a hundred percent effective, regardless of whether someone pricked a hole in them with a pin or not.

"Contrary to your rather low opinion of me, Mom, I don't make a habit of leaving my DNA behind with random women. Jenna was… Well, let's just say that night wasn't the norm for me."

"Night?" Mrs. Lassiter's perfectly arched eyebrows almost reached her hairline. "I don't want to know. You two have to deal with that. I just want to make sure you've both learned your lesson and are at least practicing safe sex. Just because you've had one baby together doesn't mean you should have more. At least not until you're married. You *are* getting married, aren't you?"

"Ma, slow down. One step at a time. I just learned about him four days ago."

"Bryan did propose, Mrs. Lassiter. I turned him down." She owed Bryan that much at least since he'd taken the fall for their supposed night of debauchery.

"You did? Why, dear? It can't be easy raising a child on your own."

"Ma, really, I don't think—"

"It's okay, Bryan." Jenna tapped the table in front of him. With all the lies she would be telling for the next fourteen or so years, she could give him the truth now. "I said no because Bryan and I don't know each other very well, and we should if we're going to commit to spending our lives together. Right now, we need to be friends and focus on what's best for Trevor. It's a big enough adjustment. Marriage and all that entails will only muddy the waters."

Mrs. Lassiter pursed her lips and looked between them. "You're right, of course. No need to rush things. The important thing is that you're there for this little boy." She took one last look at Trevor's school picture and shook her head. "He has your eyes. I'll be…"

She sniffed then shooed Bryan out of the booth. "I'll let you two get back to your arrangements. And thank you, Jenna, I'd love to come for dinner tomorrow. I'll get all the particulars from Bryan." She cupped his cheek and kissed the other one. "Goodbye, sweetheart. I love you."

"Bye, Mom."

He watched her walk away then waved when she was out front of the deli.

"You have a great relationship."

"Yeah. We do. I knew she'd be thrilled. Ever since

Dad died, she's practically smothered Kyle's girls."

"Now she'll have someone else to smother."

"You sure you're okay with having her tomorrow night? You didn't have to do that."

Jenna took a bite of her sandwich more for something to do than any hunger issue. Because she wasn't hungry. All the ramifications of the situation were starting to hit her. Bryan's mother was coming for dinner. Trevor had a grandmother—a real one who wanted to know him and would probably want to take him to the Mackerley's farm and show him the cows.

"Does she bake?" Jenna's mom used to make the best chocolate chip cookies—up until her daughter had disappointed her.

"Bakes, cooks, sews, can plan a party with nothing more than a frying pan and a grill—don't ask. My mom has loved being a mom and all she's ever wanted is to have half a dozen grandkids."

"Looks like she got her wish."

"Well, half of it. So far there are only three, which leaves three slots open. I'd like to fill them someday." His fingers stole across the table and wound around hers.

Great. Something else for her to dream about.

Chapter Twenty-Eight

"So you're spreading your shame around again, I hear."

As usual, Jenna's mother didn't bother to knock, storming into her home as if she were the one paying the mortgage, and not giving a thought to keeping her voice down so Trevor wouldn't hear any of this.

Luckily, he'd spent the night at Cathy's and wasn't yet home. Jenna had wanted to make sure her house was up to snuff for the dinner with Mrs. Lassiter and Bryan—in two hours!—and had cleaned the place top to bottom.

If only she could dust her mother under the rug as easily. "Ellen, I don't know what you're talking about."

Mom had insisted on *Ellen* once Dad's affair had come to light. She hadn't wanted the *mom* moniker—said it worked against her in the dating arena and since Jenna had been about to become a mother herself at that point, she most definitely didn't want to be known as *Grandmom.*

It was just as well. Ellen had proven she really didn't have the Mom gene anymore—as proven by her next sentence.

"There's some dumpy old broad going around telling people that Trevor is her grandson."

Leave it to her mother to boil everything down to its most basic. Ellen had always been a glass half-empty sort, but Dad's affair had pushed her over the edge of negativity.

Of course, that could have been the reason for Dad's

affair, but Jenna had chosen to stay out of her parents' marital battles.

"Her name is Tabitha Lassiter and she *is* Trevor's grandmother."

"So am I."

If only she'd act it. Jenna fanned the magazines on the coffee table. "I didn't say you weren't."

"So what does she want?"

"What are you talking about?"

Ellen fanned the magazines a little bit more. "Well, she was going on and on at the post office about being able to see him and she wants to take him shopping for clothes for school and toys for Christmas. And she wants to have him over at Thanksgiving. How come I don't get to do any of that with him?"

It took all Jenna had not to go fix those magazines. Instead she straightened the picture frames on the mantel. "Because you've never wanted to. I seem to remember you telling me to keep 'the little bastard' away from you so people wouldn't look down on you." The words had hurt when she'd first heard them and every time ever since. They were especially hurtful now that Bryan's mother had so readily embraced Trevor's existence simply because she was thrilled to have another grandchild.

"I never said that, Jenna Marie."

"Okay, fine. You didn't." Jenna gave in. She'd never win anyway and, hey, if this was what it took for her mother to have the slightest iota of interest in Trevor, she'd take what she could get. For his sake.

"Are you being flippant?"

"Look, Ellen, I said, okay. You can take him shopping if you want. But right now I'm trying to clean the house before they get here, so if you don't mind, I don't have time to have this discussion. Christmas is six months away." And by then, Ellen would probably have forgotten her indignation.

And her grandson.

"Before *who* gets here?"

Leave it to her mother to zero in on the one thing Jenna didn't want her to. "I'm having some people over for dinner."

"Who?"

"People."

Ellen was across the room with her finger in Jenna's face faster than Jenna had ever seen her move—except when she'd thrown Dad's things out the window.

"You're having that woman over, aren't you? If you were having Cathy and her husband, you would have said so, but you didn't. The only reason you won't tell me is because it has to be *her*. Is Trevor's father coming, too?"

Jenna shoved her hand with the dust rag onto her hip and refused to back down. This was her house, dammit. She could have whoever she wanted over for dinner. "Fine. If you must know, yes, Bryan and his mother are coming to dinner. She wants to meet Trevor. So, if you don't mind, I have a lot to do to get ready."

"I don't mind." Ellen moved two of the frames around. "But I'm staying."

"What? No, you're not. This is a dinner for Bryan and his mother to spend some time getting to know Trevor."

"I could use the time to get to know him, too."

"It's been your choice *not* to know him before now

"One that has been grossly misguided." Ellen twirled around, sashayed over to the sofa, planted her butt on it, kicked off her heels, and crossed her ankles on the coffee table. "I'd like to rectify that situation."

"Only because you don't want Mrs. Lassiter to one-up you on the grandmother scale."

Ellen flicked her fingernails. "Now what kind of grandmother would I be if that were the truth, sweetheart? At least *I* have a grandchild, unlike that mealy-mouthed tramp your father had to hook up with."

Jenna clamped the truth behind her lips. No one would win if she came out with it now.

"How about if you come tomorrow night? Then you can have Trevor all to yourself."

"You're ashamed of me?" Ellen patted her brand new haircut that she'd been sure to let drop had cost over two hundred dollars. She'd relished spending her husband's life insurance money, hence the cut and color, the gym membership, and numerous sessions with the personal trainer to keep herself looking good.

If only she'd work on the inside as much.

"I'm not ashamed of you." In the looks department, no. But in the way she'd supported her and been there as a mother? Yes, that was embarrassing. But hurting her mom wouldn't change the past and Jenna wasn't that person.

"Good. Then there's no reason why can't I come to dinner tonight and meet them."

"I don't think that's a good idea."

"You *are* ashamed of me. I knew it."

Were those tears in her mother's eyes? Couldn't be. Ellen North sucked up her disappointment and swallowed it so no one would ever know.

Jenna sat on the opposite end of the sofa and dumped the dust rag onto the table. "Mom, what's going on?"

Ellen blinked. "I'm trying, Jenna. I am. Everyone knows what you've done. First you got pregnant as a teenager and then you turn around and do the same thing as an adult. And now, suddenly, the father shows up and his mother is pleased as punch—"her voice rose an octave—"to spread the word that my daughter has given her a grandchild. How do you think I feel? Everyone's looking at me as if I'm the bad grandmother. Do you know that Marla said she didn't know I even *had* a grandson."

Marla was one of the women in the bridge club that Ellen had been playing with weekly for years. Shame on her mother for not letting her supposedly closest friends know about him.

"Maybe if you took him out on occasion and showed your friends, they might." Of *course* this was all about Ellen. Jenna was a fool to think it had any deeper meaning, like missing out on Trevor's younger years. She stood up. She couldn't do this now. She had to get ready for the people who actually wanted to know Trevor for him, not for what other people would say.

Ellen flicked her nails again. "I already raised my child, Jenna. *Also* without a husband. Did you see me pawning you off on other people?"

"I was *sixteen*. And Dad was still around."

That got to her mother. Ellen slammed her feet to the floor and leaned forward. "Just because we were still legally married doesn't mean he was around for us. In our lives. He was too busy with *her*."

Okay, so maybe she *did* have to do this. At least some of it. For so long she'd listened to her mother rail against Dad and had just kept quiet. She'd sat back and taken her mother's barrage of insults when she'd gotten pregnant. But tonight was about Trevor. She couldn't allow her mother to ruin it.

"Ellen, you can't come tonight. Every conversation I have with you ends in a diatribe against Dad. I don't want Trevor or the Lassiters exposed to it. I know he hurt you, but he's gone. We're not. Enjoy us."

It felt good to finally say it. For so long she'd kept it bottled up inside her.

"That's what I'm trying to do, Jenna. Starting tonight. One big, happy family. It's what you want for your son, right?"

"Hello?" Cathy's voice sing-songed in through the kitchen. "Trevor and Bobby and I are here. Okay to come in?"

Cathy would have seen Ellen's car and figured out the necessity of making her presence known before bringing the boys in.

"Ellen—"

"Oh, good. My grandson's here." Ellen shoved her feet into her heels, stood up, and headed toward the kitchen. "Wait until he sees what I brought him."

Jenna closed her eyes, gritted her teeth, and counted to ten. Twice.

She wasn't going to be able to get rid of her mother.

Chapter Twenty-Nine

"Hello, I'm Ellen North. Trevor's grandmother." Ellen held out her hand to Mrs. Lassiter with all the faux grace of her country club membership's set. "Or, I guess I should say his *other* grandmother, shouldn't I?"

She could be very charming when she chose. She was choosing to now.

"So nice to meet you." Mrs. Lassiter was just as charming and genuine as she'd been at lunch.

Bryan was just as gorgeous.

Jenna hadn't seen him since yesterday. He'd gone back to work after lunch, and then to the club—and Jenna was *not* setting foot in that place for a long time because A) she didn't want to get roped into dancing again, and B) she didn't want to have to watch him do it.

Granted, he said it'd been a fluke, but still, the possibility was there, and now that she'd been up close to the physical perfection that was Bryan, now that she knew what he felt like and what he tasted like, and that he wanted her… She didn't need that kind of temptation. She was juggling enough as it was.

"Wook, Bwyan! Mr. Monkey wikes Wocco."

Trevor walked into the room, juggling the fishbowl—via Mr. Monkey's slippery, sockpuppet hands.

She and Bryan both ran over and grabbed the bowl before it crashed to the floor.

"You know, Trev." Bryan steered their son toward his

grandmothers. "Rocco doesn't like to get moved around. It sloshes his water all over his bowl."

"Does he get seasick?"

"He can, yes. Fish don't hang out in the waves, they like to stay in the calmer waters."

"Oh. Did I scare him?" Trevor's thumb zoomed right into his mouth.

Bryan patted him on the shoulder while Jenna dealt with the fish crisis. "You didn't mean to scare him and Rocco knows that."

Jenna looked at the fish. Typically they didn't live longer than a day or two. Rocco was on his last gills even without the wild ride. She'd better visit a pet store and find one that looked like him just in case. Trevor didn't need to carry the death of his fish around on his shoulders for the rest of his life.

"And, hey, I'd like to introduce you to my mom." Bryan hiked Trevor onto his hip. "Mom, this is Trevor."

There were tears in Mrs. Lassiter's eyes as she held out her hand. "Hello, Trevor. I'm very happy to meet you."

Jenna moved next to him when he started twirling his hair with his other hand. For all that he liked Bryan, the fact that he'd gone back to using his name instead of "Dad" meant he wasn't quite as secure with Bryan's place in his life as everyone would like.

He slurped his thumb harder.

Jenna tugged it free and wiped it off. "It's okay, Trev. She's… She's your grandmother."

His violet eyes got big and round. "I have a gwandmofah?" His for-whatever-reason-Bostonian accent always got thicker when he was emotional.

Jenna felt tears sting the backs of her eyes and she had to swallow around a lump of emotion before she could answer him.

But Ellen got there first, her laugh a little too loud. "Of course you have a grandmother." She rubbed his arm a little too roughly. "Don't forget about me, Trevy."

No one called him Trevy.

Bryan looked at Jenna.

She gave a little shake of her head. "That's right, Trev. Ellen's your grandmother, too." She looked at Mrs. Lassiter. "My mother prefers to be called by her first name rather than *grandmother*. She said it gets confusing at the playground with all the kids calling out for their grandmothers." No one ever called out for Ellen—but that was her own choice.

"Oh, well he can certainly call me Grandma," said Mrs. Lassiter, sagely removing her hand. "Or Nana, like my other grandchildren do."

"You have other grandchildren?" Ellen's once-over of Bryan's mother was far from subtle. "Aren't *you* the little homemaker?"

"Thank you." Mrs. Lassiter smiled with genuine pride. The woman was no slouch; she knew Ellen had meant it as a slur, but she honestly didn't care. And there *might* even be some pity in that smile.

Ellen wouldn't like that.

Jenna liked Mrs. Lassiter even more for recognizing what was important in life.

"Okay, then. Now that the introductions are out of the way…" Bryan set Trev down. "Want to see what my mom brought you?"

Trevor reached for Jenna's hand. "Is it my birfday?"

"No, sweetheart, but since this is the first time she's met you, she wanted to bring you a present."

"Oh. Cool."

"I brought you something, too, Trevy."

Ellen's voice grated across Jenna's nerves. "Mom, let's have him open one gift at a time so it's not so overwhelming."

Her mother's smile went brittle.

Just like Jenna's nerves. This was going to be a long

dinner.

***

The dinner wasn't quite as bad as it could have been—even though she was seriously tempted to use a steak knife to cut the tension—Mrs. Lassiter had mentioned rib-eye was Bryan's favorite cut when she'd called to ask if she could bring dessert—but Bryan did an excellent job of keeping everything friendly and moving forward while they ate.

Trevor was happily playing with the T-rex figurines Mrs. Lassiter had brought—a tidbit about her son Jenna had shared during that same conversation about Mrs. Lassiter's son. She was a lovely woman, just so thrilled to have someone else to love.

Ellen settled down once the focus was off Trevor. Well, the direct focus, since he *was* the reason they were all having dinner together. But Mrs. Lassiter—Tabitha as she insisted Jenna call her—knew how to handle children and was content to watch him as his dinosaurs stomped on a pea that had rolled off his plate.

"He has one more year of preschool, but then he'll go to kindergarten. It's a full day program and I think he'll do well." Jenna scooped some more buttered noodles onto Trevor's plate. They were his favorite. This week.

"Jenna didn't go to preschool. I taught her everything she needed to know. We were inseparable back then."

Jenna looked at her mother. She hadn't known that. Wouldn't have figured it either. "Really?"

Ellen munched on a pea. Just one. She was fanatical about watching her figure. "Oh, yes. I was so thrilled to have you. We'd tried for so long, you know, and then when you came along, I just had to spend every minute with you. I gave up my career, my friends, all the traveling we'd done so I could."

Was this a guilt trip or one down Memory Lane?

"You're lucky you could spend that time with her," said Tabitha. "My boys were like monkeys, and school was the only thing that saved my house from complete disaster. I guess that's the difference between boys and girls."

"You had a monkey, Daddy?" Trevor's little voice stopped conversation. Or maybe it was the use of *daddy* that did it.

Ellen's mouth drew into a tight line; Tabitha's curved into a smile.

Bryan looked like he wanted to cry. Which made Jenna want to. She was so thrilled for Trevor that his father loved him.

All the while being terrified that he did.

"No, Trev. My brother and I just acted like them."

"I wish I had a bwother."

The table went very quiet.

Everyone's eyes flicked all around the room.

Except Bryan's.

He looked at her. "We'll have to see what we can do about that, Trev. Every kid should have a brother or a sister."

"I don't want a sister. They're yucky. Michael has two and he says they weave their dollies all over the place and they don't pway football."

Jenna tried to look away, but she couldn't—and it had nothing to do with those gorgeous eyes of Bryan's.

No, it had to do with the image she had in her mind. Having Bryan's child. For real this time.

She wanted to. Really really wanted to. All of a sudden, it hit her, a consuming need to have a child—*his* child. To create a new life, one that she could call hers, that no one could take from her, and she wanted to do it with Bryan.

She was in so far over her head she ought to feel as if she were drowning, but she didn't.

It felt right. That image felt right. Sitting here, having dinner with him and Trevor and both grandmothers… it felt right. As if this were the way things were supposed to be.

But this whole scenario was based on a lie.

"I don't know if Jenna's up for a third pregnancy." Ellen scooped another teaspoon-ful of peas onto her plate. "I mean, the body can only take so much, even though she was so young the first time. But, really, Jenna, you should be happy with one healthy child. You just never know what can happen."

Reality came crashing down with a vengeance. Her mother's vengeance.

Ellen had never gotten over the "humiliation" of Jenna's teenage pregnancy, but Jenna would never have imagined she'd bring it up now like this, with the sole purpose of returning that humiliation.

"*Third* pregnancy?" Bryan looked at her.

"She didn't tell you?" Ellen looked shocked—but she wasn't. She knew exactly what she was doing. She'd never forgiven Jenna for not siding with her against her father.

What parent wanted their child to choose sides? She'd tried to remain neutral, loving each one on their own merits.

Her mother just lost a lot of those merits.

Jenna stood up. "I won't have this discussion in front of Trevor. Bryan, if you'll join me outside? Ellen, I'd like you to leave. Mrs. Lassiter—Tabitha—if you wouldn't mind watching Trevor for a little bit, I would appreciate it."

"Of course, Jenna." God bless Mrs. Lassiter's graciousness. The woman moved right over into Jenna's chair, picked up one of the T-rexes, and started making growling noises.

Trevor returned them, laughing.

Ellen, however, was scowling. "You are not letting that woman, that stranger, watch my grandson."

Jenna gripped the back of her chair, trying to keep a

tight rein on her anger. She would not do this in front of her son. "He's her grandson and I am. Now leave, Ellen, before it gets any uglier than it already is."

Bryan stood behind Jenna and put his hand on her shoulder. "Yes, Ellen. I think it'd be best if you left. My mother has more than enough experience to keep Trevor occupied for a few minutes. I'd trust *her* with my life. Matter of fact, I did for years."

Ellen hadn't missed the inflection on the *her* any more than Jenna had. Her lips pursed and she stalked out of the house, slamming the door behind her.

"Please excuse us, Tabitha."

Mrs. Lassiter waved her hand and engaged Trevor's dinosaur in a battle for another pea.

Jenna led Bryan out to the back porch. The crickets were just warming up for their nighttime symphony and the lightning bugs were just starting to twinkle through her backyard. Usually this was one of her favorite times of night with the pale purple dusk and the quiet, but now…

She leaned against the railing and looked at the weeping willow branches swaying in the soft breeze.

This wasn't a conversation she'd ever wanted to have. Especially not with him.

Chapter Thirty

Bryan was staring at her. He walked over and leaned on his elbows on the railing, but he wasn't watching the lightning bugs; he was watching her.

She took a breath, willing the pain not to overpower the memories. "I was sixteen. He was my boyfriend. We were stupid like teenagers are. We never thought it'd happen to us."

"What happened? Where's the baby?"

The twinkling fireflies got blurry. Jenna blinked. "She didn't make it. I was in a car accident, the one where my father was killed and…" She cleared her throat. "My mother thought it was a blessing."

Bryan exhaled. "I'm sorry, Jenna."

She looked at him then. "You have nothing to be sorry for."

"I'm sorry that you had to go through it with that woman as your support system. It can't have been easy. You needed to be held and comforted. A blessing? Didn't she realize she lost a grandchild?"

Jenna tried to shrug, but the weight she'd carried around on her shoulders ever since—guilt, grief, relief, horror at that relief, more guilt—wouldn't let her. "It happened. There was nothing I could do about it. I had to deal. And, you know, I was sixteen."

"Sixteen, twenty-six… Does it really make a difference?" He turned toward her, leaning on his left elbow and running his hand up her arm. "Where's the guy now?"

She bit her lip and looked away. "He was gone the minute he heard about the baby. Even asked if it was his."

"Wow." Bryan stood up now and pulled her into his arms. "I am so sorry no one was there for you, Jenna. I'm sorry I wasn't there for you with Trevor. But I am now and I'm not going anywhere."

She let herself melt into his embrace. Just a little. She couldn't help it. He was right; no one had been there. She'd been dealing with her father's death, her baby's, the end of her relationship, and the realization of just what Dave had thought of her. And then her mother's betrayal on top of it. Was it any wonder she'd clung to Mindy so tightly? She'd been the only family Jenna had had.

And now Mindy was gone. She couldn't lose Trevor, too.

She straightened. She couldn't lean on Bryan. He had the power to take away the last person she could call hers.

"Thanks, Bryan, but I'm okay. Really. It was a long time ago." Twelve years, eleven months, nine days, and about six hours ago. She'd put it behind her and moved on. It was what she'd had to do.

But then she made the mistake of looking up at him.

He was right there. His lips were right there, his eyes worried, his expression thoughtful. Concerned. Caring. And the night was quiet, Nature's music serenading them, his aftershave and that scent that was all his own wrapping around her every bit as comfortingly as his arms, every bit as *excitingly* as his arms. Every bit a enticing and alluring and teasing and solid and welcoming as his arms.

"Jenna…"

"Bryan…"

She didn't know who spoke first. It didn't matter. She was in his arms and he was there for her and she had to kiss him. Had to. As if every part of her life spiraled down to this one moment in time, this one all-important moment that she couldn't run from.

Her fingers curled into the seams of his golf shirt and held on, keeping her upright, anchoring her to something tangible, as the world spun around her in a whirlwind of sensation. Of want, of need, of feelings and emotions and the all-consuming desire for a connection with another human being.

Bryan was so strong. So tall. So solid. So *there*. He *wanted* to be there. Hadn't flinched at all when it came to hanging around for his son. He'd even proposed to her to make sure he *could* be there.

Why had she refused him? Why hadn't she jumped at the offer? It'd be best for Trevor, and with the way Bryan's kiss was affecting her, it wouldn't be so bad for her either.

His tongue swept inside her mouth and, all of a sudden, the kiss was no longer comforting. It was no longer safe and protective and embracing. It was hot and it was carnal and it had nothing to do with the child they shared; it was all about the *chemistry* they shared. This driving want and need and the desire to burrow beneath his skin and never leave. To know him inside and out, be a part of him, to share with him, and to ride the waves of this pleasure with him to the heights and tumble over the edge.

He tore his lips from hers and buried them in the hollow of her throat, her head tilted back as she gasped for breath, her breasts thrust against his chest as his hands trailed hot sexy magic down her back to cup her butt, heat spiraling out from that spot in her belly, infusing every part of her with heat and an aching, driving need.

"I want you, Bryan." The words just tumbled out. She couldn't stop them. She didn't want to stop them. She didn't want to stop *him*. She wanted him. She did. It'd been so long since she'd been with someone, and no one, not even Carl before she'd talked about adopting Trevor, no one had ever made her feel as wanted and desirable and special as Bryan had since the moment she'd met him.

But then he pulled back.

He *pulled back.*

"Jenna—"

"Oh God." She stumbled from his arms, wrapped her own around her waist, and stood in the corner of the railing looking anywhere but at him. He'd *pulled back.* "I'm sorry, Bryan. God, I'm sorry. I shouldn't have said anything. It's… just… Forget I said it. Don't think it's… I mean… Just forget it."

He walked up behind her again and gripped her biceps. "Jenna."

She shook her head. She couldn't face him. She just couldn't. This rising tide of want and need and, yes, desperation, was threatening to overwhelm her and if she looked at him, she'd fall apart.

"Jenna." He put pressure on her arms, urging her to turn around. "Jenna, look at me."

But when he said it so kindly and softly, it touched something inside her. Some lonely, wanting part inside her.

She turned around—but stared at the bottom button on the neckline of his golf shirt.

"Jenna." He tilted her chin up with one finger. His eyes were so intent up on hers, they'd darkened to a deep purple. "I want you, too."

The desire in his voice threatened to buckle her knees. She gripped the seams of his shirt again.

"But you have to want *me*. Not the comfort I can offer. Not gratitude for acknowledging your pain and how everyone failed you. Not even because of Trevor. I want to move forward with you, Jenna, not relive the past. I want you in the here and now with me. We can't change the past, but we can change the future. When you're ready for that, when you want me for that, that's when it'll be right for us."

He kissed her forehead. Then her nose. Then a soft

soft brush of his lips across hers. "I'll be here, Jenna. When you're ready, I'll be here. I'm not going anywhere."

She swayed into him. This was what she wanted. What she'd always wanted. What Carl hadn't been man enough to be or do or say. What Dave hadn't been able to give. What her father had taken when he'd destroyed their family by choosing someone else.

But Bryan… Bryan was here for her. And for Trevor.

He kissed her again and rubbed her arms. "Come on. Let's go in and relieve my mom. It's been a long time since she's entertained a three-year-old."

Jenna nodded and sniffed back… something. Not a tear. Not an apology. But something…

He held the door open and it was all she could do not to close it and wrap her arms around him and stay just where they were right now with nothing—not the past, not her lie, not any of the ramifications of that—intruding on this most perfect of moments.

And then she heard Trevor's giggle.

"Weawwy?"

"Really," answered Mrs. Lassiter. "And then your daddy ended up covered in mud. All gooey, icky, sticky mud. He had to take four baths."

"Blech! I hate bafses."

Jenna could just picture the look on Trevor's face as he said that and she smiled. She knew all his looks. Knew every smile and every twitch when he slept and every droopy expression when he was tired. That was her reality. That was what she had to focus on, not this dream-out-of-time-moment with Bryan.

She nodded at him and walked into the house.

"But baths make you all clean and shiny and you smell good afterwards." Mrs. Lassiter looked up when Jenna stopped at the entrance to the living room. "And I bet your mommy gives you lots of hugs after your bath."

Trevor nodded quickly, his curls bouncing around his

head. “Yeah, she does. I wike hugs.”

“Would you like one now?”

Trevor stopped nodding. His curls stopped bouncing.

Jenna held her breath. Would he let her?

And if he did, how would Jenna feel about it? She’d been the only one to give her son hugs.

“Yes, pwease.” Trevor held out his arms and let his new grandmother sweep him up in hers.

Jenna slumped against the doorframe. It’s what she wanted for Trevor.

It was. Really.

“He still loves you most,” Bryan whispered in her ear. “No one will ever replace you, Jenna. The heart’s like any muscle; it has the capacity to grow and expand. Trevor can love many people in his life, but he’ll never stop loving you.”

It was the perfect thing for Bryan to say. The perfect sentiment and Jenna was grateful to him for giving that to her.

Too bad he didn’t know that Trevor *might* actually stop loving her when he found out about his birth mother some day.

And what about Bryan? What would he say?

He’d hate her for lying to him.

“You give good hugs, Nana.”

Mrs. Lassiter cleared her throat. “Thanks, Trevor. I gave your daddy lots of them when he was little.”

“My mommy gives me wots of hugs. I wove Mommy’s hugs.”

Jenna swallowed the lump in her throat. That was why she had to lie to Bryan. Why she could never tell him the truth. She couldn’t risk losing her rights to her son.

She cleared her throat and walked into the room. “Hey, Trev. Did you have fun with your grandmother?”

“Uh huh. She wikes to pway dinosaurs.”

The adults smiled at each other and Jenna just wanted

to scoop Trevor up in her arms and hug him until next week, her sweet sweet baby.

Mrs. Lassiter got to her feet. “I’ll just clear off the table then get out of your hair. I’m sure this young man needs to get started on his bedtime routine and I wouldn’t want to interrupt that.”

“Awww, do I have to?” Trevor pouted.

“Yes, Sport, you do if your mom says so.” Bryan looked at Jenna. “Jenna? Does he get a bath tonight?”

Jenna pointed to their son’s hands. “Looks like someone’s been playing with buttered noodles. I think that calls for a bath.”

Trevor pouted some more. “Can Wocco swim wif me?”

Bryan laughed. “Soap is bad for fish, but how about we bring his bowl in while I give you a bath. Is that okay with you?”

Trevor’s eyes sparkled. “Can he, Mommy? Can Bwyan, I mean, Daddy, give me my baf?”

She wanted to say no. Trevor was hers. *She* gave him his baths.

But he was so darn excited she’d be the mean mom for saying no.

“Sure, kiddo. I’ll clean up while you guys do the bath thing.” She looked at Bryan. “There’s a seat in the linen closet. It’s got suction cups on the bottom to stick to the tub. There’s also a bunch of colored soaps. He likes to draw pictures on the tiles.”

“Gotcha. Anything else I need to know?”

“Washcloth over his lap. It’ll save *you* from needing a shower.”

“Thanks, I’ll remember that.”

Rocco accompanied the two of them to the bathroom while Mrs. Lassiter helped Jenna with the dishes.

“You’ve done a wonderful job with him, Jenna,” Bryan’s mom said as she rinsed the plates off.

"Thank you. It's been a challenge, but I wouldn't change a minute of it."

"I'm just so sorry you had to go through it alone. I wish my son had been a bit more responsible."

Jenna pretended to find something on the floor so she wouldn't have to look at Bryan's mother. Talk about an uncomfortable conversation to have with her son's grandmother… "It takes two, Mrs. Lassiter. He can't shoulder all the blame. Plus, it wasn't planned. Sometimes things happen."

"Well what's important now, is that you both do the right thing. Thank you for allowing us to have a part in his life. It's what's best for Trevor. And you, too, you know. You now have a new family."

Jenna hadn't thought about it that way. Sure, Trevor had a new family, but, yes, she did, too.

And she was lying to all of them.

They finished in the kitchen just as Bryan brought a damp and powdered Trevor out to say goodbye, his footie pajamas topped off with the baseball cap Bryan had won for him at the fair.

Jenna didn't have the heart to tell him that Trevor would be too hot in that outfit during the night, so she'd change him after Bryan left.

"Goodbye, Nana! Fanks for my T-wexes. Wocco is gonna keep them company tonight so they don't miss you."

She kissed his cheek. "Goodnight, sweetheart. I'll see you later."

She tugged Bryan's ear and he bent down for his own kiss. "Take care of him, son. There's no more precious gift than a child."

Bryan swallowed. Loudly. Jenna saw it and heard it.

Heard the emotion, too, in his voice when he kissed his mom and thanked her.

They stood there, the three of them in the doorway, waving and watching Mrs. Lassiter get in her car and drive away, and it was Jenna's turn to swallow loudly. It was as if they were a real family getting ready to settle down for the night.

"So now what, Sport? Do we read a book? Watch some television? Eat some cook—"

"A book." Jenna jumped in, not wanting to give Trevor any ideas about cookies as a bedtime snack. "And he has to brush his teeth."

"I did that awweady, Mommy. Daddy sang me a funny song."

Jenna raised her eyebrows and was amazed when Bryan blushed.

"Something my dad used to sing to get us to brush our teeth long enough."

"And I got to spit at the end! Mommy never lets me spit." Trevor looked at her as if this was a bad thing.

"Well, your mom doesn't want you spitting at anyone, just in the bathroom sink and only the toothpaste. And just at bedtime."

"So I can't spit when I brush my teeth in the morning?"

"Oh, well then, too." Bryan scratched the back of his neck. "Lot of stuff involved in this parenting thing, huh?"

Jenna laughed. "You'll get the hang of it. It just takes practice."

She picked a book off the shelf. "Here. Read him this one. It's one of his favorites."

"Oooh! I wove the choochoo. He can go over the mountain."

The bed groaned when Bryan sat on it. Jenna leaned against the wall just outside the door, shamelessly listening in. Was this what it'd be like if she'd accepted his proposal? Would he move in with them and put Trevor to bed and bathe him and read him books and cut up his pancakes and toss the ball, bandage his knees, take him to ballgames…

"I fink I can!" Trevor shouted his favorite line from the book and Bryan laughed just like she did every time Trevor said it like that.

Someday his lisp would disappear and she'd miss all the cute little sayings he had.

She didn't want to miss anymore of his life so she walked into the room. "Is there enough space on that bed for me?"

"Yay! Mommy's here!" Trevor wiggled closer to the guardrail on the outside of his bed. "You can sit next to Bwyan, Mommy, 'cause Mister Monkey wants to sit next to me."

She picked the stuffed animal off the floor and set him next to Trevor and pulled the covers over his lap, then climbed onto the bed and leaned against the wall beside Bryan.

How wrong was it that she was super-aware of his long muscular legs next to hers on their son's bed? She probably wouldn't be thinking this way if she'd actually created Trevor with Bryan, but since she'd only gotten a teaser about what it'd be like to go to bed with him, it was the only thing she could think of as she was *actually* on a bed with him.

"Can you wead it again, Bwyan?" Trevor lifted his head when Bryan finished the story.

"I could, but I don't think you're going to make it, kiddo." Bryan adjusted Trevor's pillow and settled him down in a way Jenna envied. She could never get him to snuggle in so easily.

"Will you wead it tomorrow?"

Bryan slid off the bed, pulled the covers up, and kissed Trevor's forehead. "Sure will, Trev. Sleep tight. Keep Mr. Monkey company."

"And Wocco, too. He misses his fwiends."

"But he has the dinosaurs now, so he'll be fine." Bryan stepped back so Jenna could say her own goodnight.

"Night night, Mommy. I wove you."

"Love you, too, Trev." Her throat got tight as it did every time he said those magical words. There was nothing like being loved so unconditionally by this little boy.

She picked up the book, then flipped on the night light and closed the door as she followed Bryan out into the hallway—with one last look at the sweet little guy already almost asleep. She could never get tired of watching him sleep.

"It's a miracle, isn't it?" Bryan whispered above her head.

She looked up. He was staring at Trevor, too. "He is. He definitely is."

She put her finger to her lips and led him to the living room. "Thanks for reading to him. He usually doesn't go down so easily."

"Too much excitement, that's all. He would have done the same for you after the day he had."

Dinner had been enough excitement for *her*. And that kiss afterwards…

"So do you need anything else, Jenna?"

Jenna looked up. *Need* anything? Where should she begin? She needed. She needed help. Someone to share the burden and the worry of raising a child. Someone to take over so she could have a few hours off. Someone who cared about her as more than Trevor's mother or Jason's teacher or the neighbor across the street, or someone her mother gave birth to.

She needed to matter to someone.

"Jenna? You okay?"

No, she wasn't. And she really didn't want to be alone tonight.

Or ever.

She set the book on the bookshelf and turned around.

And then she kissed him.

Chapter Thirty-One

One moment Bryan was reveling in the warm fuzzy feeling of having put his son—his *son*—to bed and the next… the next he wasn't warm and fuzzy at *all.*

No, he was *hot* and *sizzling* and Jenna was in his arms with her lips on his and her sweet, tight, perfect body rubbing against him and there was no mistaking what she needed.

What *he* needed.

Bryan crushed her against him. This probably wasn't the best idea, but, hell, it'd be worse to stop.

He wanted her. In the four years since he'd had her—though he couldn't remember it—nothing seemed to have changed. There was a reason they'd gotten together that night, and though alcohol had been involved, it'd only helped things along, because they would have gotten there anyway.

But he'd be forever grateful for that night and that alcohol and that party, because all of it had gotten him to this moment and all he wanted was to take her to bed and rediscover everything he'd learned four years ago.

She mewled in the back of her throat when he thrust his tongue into the hot recess of her mouth, the sound curling along his spine like a lick of fire, igniting every inch of his skin.

She thrust her fingers into his hair, tugging on it, and he felt every tug right in his groin. The want, the need, the desire to make her his in the way man had been doing since time began. She was his. He'd created a life with her, a living breathing being who was the best parts of the both of them, and he wanted to discover all those parts in her.

He swept her up in his arms, never once breaking the kiss. He didn't think he ever would, and if the world ended right now with her in his arms, kissing him, wanting him, groaning for him, he'd die a very happy man.

He carried her up the stairs and strode down the hall past Trevor's room. Hers had to be around here somewhere and, hell, even if it wasn't, he'd take her up against the wall. He wasn't letting her go. Not now. Not tonight.

Not ever if he had any say in the matter.

"Door on the right," she muttered as she dragged his bottom lip between her teeth, the sting of that little nip zinging through him as he wedged her door open with his shoulder.

The room was floral and pretty, typical woman, but it could be a stone cold cave for all Bryan cared; he just wanted her naked and writhing beneath him on the—thank you, God—king-sized bed.

He closed the door then fell onto that bed without his usual finesse, but he didn't care about that either. He didn't want to take one hand off her any longer than he had to, so he barely broke their fall.

Jenna didn't seem to mind, curling herself into him, her knees tossed over his thighs, one arm trapped beneath him, the other hiking up his shirt.

Bryan managed to raise himself just enough—and pulled one hand away just long enough—to yank that shirt over his head and fling it somewhere. Something might have crashed to the floor—or that could be the beat of his heart as she traced her fingertips down his abdomen.

And then her lips.

Her tongue.

Bryan groaned and fell back on the comforter. Jenna's

hair brushed his skin like a feather—an electrified feather because every nerve ending jumped to attention and if she didn't stop soon, he was going to be the one writhing beneath *her*.

Which had all sorts of interesting possibilities attached to it.

But he wanted to enjoy her first. Wanted to get to know her all over again. Discover what made her groan. What made her tummy flutter. What made her cry out his name.

He cupped her head and tilted that beautiful face up to his. "Jenna, come here."

She licked her lips, "But Bryan—"

He sat up—sort of—and kissed her, pouring everything he felt, everything he wanted into that kiss. This was Jenna. The mother of his child, the woman who'd given him the greatest gift one human being could give another, and he wanted this moment to be about them. Not just about him, or just about her, or any combination of the two, but *them*. They deserved this, deserved to be together, to rediscover each other.

He laid her back on her pillows and brushed her hair off her face. Her eyes were so blue. So beautiful, like a clear summer day with the sun shining, every bit of that warmth as she looked up at him, clear and honest and true.

And if that wasn't a thud in the vicinity of his heart, Bryan didn't know what was.

He loved her.

Bryan let the thought settle in, warming his entire body that had nothing to do with the way Jenna made him feel, but everything to do with it, too. He loved her.

"Jenna…" He stopped. He shouldn't tell her. He *couldn't*. Not yet. It was too soon. Wasn't it? Could he be making more of it than it was?

"Make love to me, Bryan." She slid her hand into his hair and tugged him down to her, and, yeah, he could do it this way, *love* her this way. Let his body say what he couldn't.

Yet.

He kissed her again, pouring everything he felt for her into the kiss. He nipped her lips for that playful smile she'd had when she'd missed the football he'd tossed her the other day. Licked her lips for the cotton candy that'd been stuck on them at the fair. Swept across the seam for the hot, delicious feel of her moving against him, and he plunged inside like the rest of him wanted to do, feeling her around him, taking him into her heat, surrounding him with the very essence of all that was Jenna.

Her nails scraped his back and she shoved her hands beneath his pants and suddenly they were both wearing too many clothes.

He lifted himself off her—just enough that she could work the button and zipper at his waist and he could drag her shirt up over her smooth, toned abdomen, revealing the sexiest peach lace bra he'd ever seen, her nipples teasing him just beneath it.

He tugged the lace down and tasted her. Dear God, how could he have forgotten this? How could he have had enough beer to drown out the sweet heaven that was her body?

He rolled that tight nipple on his tongue, sucked it between his lips, taking her breast inside, and he feasted on her soft delicious flesh, the utter femininity making him shake with need.

Her palms found his ass and she squeezed and, God Almighty, he felt that action in his cock that was already so tight and hard and jerking against her thigh, wanting to claim her. Wanting to be buried inside her and moving… moving to ease this ache that was threatening to spiral out of control.

He kissed his way to her other breast, needing to see if it tasted even half as good as the first, and, hell, yes, it did.

Jenna was a sensation for his palate and he didn't think he could ever tire of her.

And then her hand found him.

Bryan sucked in a breath, her touch destroying any sense of composure he wanted to lay claim to.

Her skin was like silk, her fingers wrapped around him and squeezing just enough to have his blood boiling. He rocked into her grasp and dear sweet Jesus, it felt utterly amazing.

His orgasm curled in his balls and he couldn't stop thrusting. Couldn't stop rocking into the tight sweet hold she had on him, and if he couldn't move faster he'd die.

"Jenna." He bit out her name wanting her to do… something. He wasn't sure what, but he couldn't go on like this much longer. But if she stopped, he'd die.

She stopped.

He, interestingly enough, kept breathing. Harsh, ragged, tight, not-enough-air sort of breaths, but there was still air going in, keeping him alive, torturing him with the desire to thrust inside her so long and so hard and so deep and forever that he trembled trying to hang on to his sanity.

"There's a box. Top drawer." She nodded to the bedside table to his right.

Figured, the left one was closer.

He dragged himself over to it, yanked open the drawer, and pulled out a black case with a lock on it. "What's this?"

Jenna took it from him and he was so damn glad to see her fingers trembling as she tried to unlock it with one of the smallest keys he'd ever seen.

"I didn't want Trevor to see them," she said, all her concentration going to that tiny key.

He laughed for a brief second, but it was long enough to diffuse some of the tension—enough to let him be semi-coherent. "Smart thinking."

"Occasionally I do have a brilliant idea or two."

"Dinner was one of those. Thank you."

She dropped the key. Luckily, it was attached with a ribbon. "Unlocking this earlier would have been a better one," she grumbled as she finally, thank God, slid the key into the lock.

The image almost put him over the edge.

Yeah, he was a horny bastard, but he was only horny for her and it wasn't "horny" for horny's sake but desire for *her* sake. For his. For theirs.

A bunch of condoms spilled out of the box, falling across her chest, onto the bed, behind her neck, and Bryan grabbed the closest one, ripped it open with his teeth, and handed it to her. "Will you?"

She nibbled her lip again, damn her. Bryan almost came from that image alone.

Then she licked her lips.

The strength in his right arm gave out and he fell onto the bed, twisting so that his back was against it—and his cock was right in front of her, perfect for putting on the condom.

Which she did so well.

Too well. He sucked in a huge shaking breath as her fingers circled the base of him.

Then he lost that breath when she leaned over and sank her mouth down on his length.

"Jenna…" The words were strangled from him as his fingers found her hair. He had every intention of pulling her away, but then she licked him and oh dear God, he couldn't do it. Couldn't do anything but try to breathe as her mouth and her tongue and her lips and her fingers—holy hell, her fingers!—hit him like a ton of bricks, and Bryan knew—he *knew*—that nothing would ever be the same again.

Jenna couldn't believe what they were doing. What *she* was doing. Oh, she could because this was what she'd wanted to be doing but how had it happened? How had she gone from dinner with their mothers, to putting their son to bed, to ending up in her bedroom, naked and getting sweaty, with her mouth wrapped around his cock?

She'd wanted to be wrapped around him, that's how.

Bryan groaned her name and Jenna stopped thinking. She'd worry about all the ramifications later but right now, she had Bryan in her bed, in her mouth, and …

In her heart.

Her heart? Bryan was in her *heart*?

She closed her eyes and let the feeling wash over her.

Yes, he was.

"Jenna… Please. No more. Can't. Take. It."

His urgent plea pulled her back to what they were doing. She'd have time enough later to examine her feelings, but right now, she was feeling this. *Wanted* to feel this. *Needed* to.

And so did he, even if the grip he had on her head said he wasn't sure he wanted her to continue. But he was straining against her lips, part pull-part push, in-out, the perfect movement for where this was headed, so she licked him.

It wasn't the same with a condom, but they needed that condom. And maybe a few more because she didn't think once was going to be enough tonight.

"Sweetheart, please," he groaned. "Stop. I don't want to come this way. Not our first time. I want to be inside you."

She didn't remind him that, technically, for him, this wasn't the first time, but she wasn't going to ruin the moment and pull the past up when it wasn't *their* past.

Tonight *was* their first time. And hopefully not their last.

She pulled her mouth from him with a *pop*, smiling when he fell back on the bed with a groan. "Sure you want me to stop?"

He turned his head and smiled to the one side—the

one with that adorable dimple. "Oh I'm definitely sure I don't want you to stop, but I'm equally certain that you need to because if you don't, you're not going to enjoy yourself."

"Now that's where you're wrong. I'm thoroughly enjoying myself right now." She licked him again just to prove it, every taste, every nuance that much more incredible because of what she'd just discovered.

He groaned again. "Come here, you. I want to see you. I want to watch you. I want to watch us. Tonight's all about rediscovery." He sat up and cupped her face in both hands, drawing her toward him for a kiss that would have knocked her socks off if she'd been wearing any.

It invaded her senses, wrapping around her heart and tying it up a neat little bow that was so not what their relationship was, but what she wanted it to be.

He pressed her back onto the pillow, sliding her pants down over her hips, skimming her panties with them and then he was there, touching her, stroking her, cupping her, pressing against her as the ache built—the one between her legs. The one in her chest had been growing since the moment she'd seen his eyes and known just who he was.

But she wouldn't think about that now. This wasn't about Trevor or Mindy or anyone or anything but what was between her and Bryan because *that* was what was real. She couldn't fake it or lie about it and neither could he. He felt something for her here and it *had* to be independent of the fact that he thought they'd made a child together because how she felt certainly was.

His fingers picked up the pace and Jenna moved against them, the ache growing, demanding attention.

She speared her hands into his hair, loving the silky texture and that it gave her something to hold onto as he trailed fire along her skin and her hormones started dancing like they'd done in the club the other night.

Oh, God, there was an image she didn't need. Of him

dancing on that stage…

She slid her hands down over his shoulders, then down the middle of his back where the muscles dipped toward his spine, then followed that curve down to his butt, the one he'd shaken so delectably in front of the audience—and in front of her—while he'd danced. She cupped him, smiling when he moaned as her fingers stroked his sac.

So she did it again.

"Yeah, baby, that's it. Touch me again."

She did, her reward being when he thrust his tongue deep into her mouth and she sucked on it just as she'd sucked on him.

He groaned again and deepened the kiss, angling her head to the side, his fingers slipping inside her folds, and suddenly Jenna couldn't figure out what was where or who was where; all she knew was that this was where she was supposed to be and this was where Bryan was supposed to be and this was where *they* were supposed to be, wrapped around each other, inside of each other, and it was so perfect she'd cry if she could take even the smallest breath but she couldn't because every time she tried to Bryan would do something wonderful/exciting/novel/amazing/spectacular and steal her breath all over again.

He stoked her body, he stroked her feelings. He stroked her heart as he gave her pleasure. As he murmured sweet words and promises against her neck, as he promised her things that she'd longed to hear from the man in her life

"I want you." I need you." "I'll never leave you."

His words, his touch, the look in those gorgeous violet eyes… Every sensation whirled through her, spiraling her up towards that peak. Toward that one shining moment where everything hovered, the entire world below them just waiting for them to claim it, the pleasure filling her, surrounding her, teasing her with the promise of what was to come.

And when he took her over the edge, pounding into her in a rhythm she'd never forget, her name a litany on his lips, the strength of his arms and the hold he had on her, Jenna knew… She was in love with Bryan Lassiter.

Chapter Thirty-Two.

"You are so fucked."

Bryan picked up his coffee. That wasn't the first thing he'd been hoping to hear on this, the most perfect morning after the most perfect night that had followed the most perfect dinner he'd ever had in his life.

But then, given that it was Gage saying it, Bryan shouldn't be surprised. His oldest friend loved to give him shit, though, seriously? Since Gage had gone through this wild ride a year ago, the guy should have some sympathy.

"You're in love with her."

Nope. No sympathy. Matter of fact, if Bryan were to guess, he'd say Gage was enjoying the moment.

Whatever. Bryan wasn't going to bother answering him, then.

Of course, given the stupid-ass grin that was on his face, he didn't have to. And besides, if he was going to admit he loved her, shouldn't the first person to hear it be the woman he was in love with?

He'd come close in the wee hours of the morning with her in his arms as she stroked the back of his hand and he'd played with her hair in the sweet aftermath of the… sixth? round of lovemaking.

The moment had been ripe for it, but he didn't want to be that cliché. Bad enough they'd brought Trevor into the world in one; he wanted to do this right. He wanted them to have a story they'd be proud to tell their families and grandchildren someday, not some drunken night neither could remember, or a grand moment of passion that had dragged the words from his soul.

"Any chance you can get your head out of the clouds long enough to have a meaningful business discussion, or are you pretty much toast for the rest of the day?" Gage tapped his desk with the eraser on his pencil.

Bryan looked up from the cup of coffee he wasn't sure if he'd put cream in or not.

Wait. Did he take cream in his coffee?

He didn't know. Didn't care.

Which didn't bode well for the discussion Gage wanted to have.

"Yeah, sure, I'm good." He was a hell of a damn sight better than *good*, but he wasn't sharing that with Gage either. He took a sip of his coffee. Yeah, he took cream and, no, he hadn't put any in this cup.

"Well, you *look* good. Like someone got to you good and thoroughly and, hey, man, I'm happy for you." Gage tapped the pencil some more, an annoying habit guaranteed to grate on Bryan's nerves—and it did. Gage loved to egg him on. "So when's the wedding?"

Bryan almost choked on the coffee. Oh, his buddy was in *rare* form today. "What makes you think there's going to be a wedding?"

"Experience." Gage sat back and put his feet onto the desk. He had a goofy smile on his face and was wearing the cowboy boots from the costume he wore only on the rare occasions when they were called on to dance.

Hmmm… If Gage had worn the boots to work today, that meant he'd had to have taken them home last night, and the only reason for Gage to do that would be to…

It was Bryan's turn to smirk. Gage had danced for Lara in that costume on at least two occasions that Bryan knew about—though he didn't want to know about any other times he *didn't* know about.

But, yeah, Gage knew what he was talking about when it came to weddings and women and goofy smiles.

"I don't think this constitutes a business discussion, Gage." Bryan sat on the corner of the credenza instead of in the chair across from his partner. At least, here, he had the height advantage. Gage's mocking smile was tough enough to stomach from over here, let alone being condescended to in that low chair in front of him.

"All right. Whatever." Gage let out a big, put-upon, suffering sigh and tapped the pencil on the blotter again. "I need you to cover for me tonight."

"I can't. I promised Jenna I'd watch Trevor."

"Shit." Gage flung his pencil at the wall.

"Whoa. What's up?"

"It's Connor. I promised him I'd take him to a game and the tickets just became available. Right behind home plate with a locker room pass from one of the press guys whose wife went into labor. I already told Connor I'd take him." He put his feet on the floor and pinched the bridge of his nose. "Oh well. I guess I'll get Tanner to close."

"Except Tanner's not here." Bryan set the coffee down, the afterglow from his night receding in light of the headache that was about to come. Sometimes being in business for himself wasn't all it was cracked up to be because, ultimately, the buck stopped with him—literally at times.

"Is he still sick?"

"No. He took off for parts unknown, no notice. Again."

"What's with him? He's been doing that a lot lately and he won't say a friggin' word about where he's going."

Bryan shrugged, more a frustrated one than a nonchalant one. Tanner's absences were becoming both a habit and a problem. "His prerogative, but, yeah, it's weird."

"Darryl then."

"He's off tonight. Out of town."

"Shit. We need a manager. You sure Jenna doesn't need the night work?"

"I don't want her working here."

"Yet you had her *dance* here."

He didn't need the reminder. One, it did his composure no good to remember what she'd looked like in those lights ,and two, it did his *jealousy* no good to remember that other men had seen her on that stage in those lights—and not much more. "Yeah, well, that was before."

"*Before*? Or shouldn't I ask?"

"You shouldn't need to."

"Ah, right." Gage coughed, swallowing the laugh Bryan would have to punch him for if he let out. "So, I guess there's no way you could ask her for a rain check on babysitting?"

Bryan shook his head. "Her friend called this morning with a last-minute plan to go to some spa thing. Jenna hasn't had a day off without Trevor since he was born, so I said I'd be more than happy to watch him. She's gone and they're not going to be back until late tonight. He's at a morning camp with her friend's son until eleven. After that, I'm on kid duty." And damn glad to be doing it, too. He'd have a whole day and dinner with his son. He was probably more excited than Trevor was about it.

Gage sighed. "I'd ask Lara but she's elbow deep in preparations for a client's wedding this weekend. What about your mom? Would she babysit?"

It was an option, but… "I don't know about closing time. My mom's not as young as she used to be."

"So put him to bed upstairs. Use the back entrance so he doesn't see anything about the club. I'll run up and make sure it's kid-friendly and tell everyone it's off limits tonight. I even have a baby monitor up there for the few times Connor's been here so he could keep in touch with me." He rubbed his forehead. "I wouldn't ask if it weren't important, Bry. Connor's been looking forward to a game all summer since that last surgery turned out not to be the last."

Connor had been the victim of a hit-and-run over a year ago and was still recuperating from the extensive surgeries needed to get the seven-year-old back to his former active self. And Gage had sacrificed so much to help with the bills—almost even Lara. Bryan couldn't deny either one of them this game.

"I'll work it out, Gage. You go."

"Seriously?" Gage got to his feet and held out his hand. "Thanks, man. I owe you."

Bryan shook it. "Nah, you don't. You'd do the same for me if the situation were reversed."

Oh well. He'd have a few hours with Trev at least, and his mom would absolutely love it.

Chapter Thirty-Three

"You have to tell him, Jenna."

Cathy's words came out garbled through the hardening seaweed mask she had on her face as they stared at the beautiful sky above them. Jenna wasn't all that convinced that half-naked massages and facials in the open air were the best relaxation technique—given that she'd been naked less than five hours ago with Bryan—but it was all part of the spa experience Cathy had said she needed.

She didn't, however, need to bring up the one thing that was scaring her more than the acupuncture needles that were next on the agenda.

"I can't, Cath. You know that. And weren't you the one telling me to lie? To take his money and sleep with him?"

"And look how well you listened. You still got to sleep with him but no money." Cathy reached across the small space dividing their massage tables and squeezed her hand. "Look, I was wrong, okay? You need to come clean. If last night was anywhere near as wonderful as you said, and judging from the glow you haven't stopped giving off yet, I'm guessing it was even better, you're not going to want to start your life together with a lie. He'll understand. Everyone will. Of course you don't want to lose Trevor, but if you accept Bryan's proposal, you won't have to."

It made sense, and it was the fair thing to do, but, hell, Jenna knew first-hand the pain of a parent walking out. Not that she'd leave, but if Bryan ever wanted to push the matter, Trevor could end up without her. She couldn't risk his life, his stability, for her own selfish reasons.

"I'll think about it." It wasn't a lie; she'd done nothing *but* think about it all night. Well, that and make love to Bryan.

The goofy smile that kept reappearing all morning cracked the mask on her face. The technician hurried over, clucking like a hen as she scooped some more seaweed by the corners of her mouth.

"Don't talk," the woman whispered.

If only she'd tell Cathy that.

"I just think that the longer you let this go on, the harder it will be to come clean later on. You were planning to tell Trevor anyway when he was older, so Bryan will eventually find out. Why don't you rip that bandage off now and tell him? Get it over with. Then you can start a life together for real. With no secrets, no lies, no hidden agendas between you. He deserves that, and so do you, Jenna. Not every man is your dad. Not everyone will walk out on you. Give Bryan a chance. Hell, he had the perfect opportunity to run away—baby daddies aren't known for staying around, yet yours has. And he wants to do *more* than just stick around."

"We don't know that for sure. He hasn't said anything."

"Did he revoke his proposal?"

"Well, no, but—"

"Exactly. And then he spent last night with you *and* he's babysitting your son. Seriously, Jen, grab the man up. Another one like him might never come along."

She knew that. She also knew that if she didn't have the lie hanging over her head, she would have snatched him up. She loved Bryan. It was as plain and as simple and as earth-shattering and profound as that. She loved Bryan. Three words, a wealth of emotion and planning and probable disaster in each one.

The pedicurist rubbed some oil into her feet, working the muscles. Reflexology had a lot to recommend it as Jenna tried to hold back a moan of pleasure.

Bryan had caused the same reaction last night, and it hadn't just been physical. He'd touched her heart. Her soul. That special place inside her where she kept close watch on her wants and dreams and hopes. He'd breached that lock as easily—no easier—as she had the one on the container of condoms.

She smiled, remembering how many of those condoms they'd used. She should probably pick up another box on her way home.

Home. For the first time, that word meant something because Bryan was going to be there, waiting for her with their son, when she returned.

"I'm just worried that if you don't tell him now and he finds out on his own, he's going to be even more hurt. You had a reason for not saying anything before he showed up. But now that he has and he's proposed, you don't have a defense when this comes out."

"I'm not doing this for me, Cath. I'm doing it for Trevor. Whatever happens, I'm willing to deal with it so that Bryan doesn't find out the truth and tries to take my son from me."

"Give the guy some credit. How much more does he need to prove to you, Jen? He's here, he wants to be here, he doesn't plan to go anywhere, he babysits, he can toss a ball—and looks damn good doing it—and he wants you. Take a chance, Jen. For all of your sakes."

***

Cathy's words stayed with her all day. Meditating during her massages and facials and pedicure had ensured she'd nothing else *to* think about all day. It'd gotten a bit embarrassing when they'd been wrapping her body in seaweed. Peaked nipples weren't easy to disguise.

It didn't help that Cathy kept talking about it the whole way home. She'd even solicited some of the other guests' advice during dinner. For a day that was supposed to be so relaxing and taking her away from her daily life, it had only added to her stress.

"Thanks for the day, Cath. I really appreciate it." Cathy had meant well and Jenna appreciated her good intentions and genuine caring, but to tell Bryan…

She just didn't know.

She waved as Cathy drove away. She better figure it out soon though because with as close as they'd been last night, she was afraid he was going to be able to read her like a book and know something was on her mind.

Jenna took a deep breath and mentally prepared herself to see him again. To hide her inner turmoil and put on a good face until she could figure out what she was going to do.

Except, when she turned around, Bryan's car was gone.

Chapter Thirty-Four

He'd taken Trevor.

Jenna knew it was a ridiculous thought. Bryan hadn't kidnapped Trevor. Probably just taken him to visit his mom or the movies or out for ice cream…

Except it was after midnight and there was no note or no phone call.

The hospital?

Oh, God, no. The last time she'd talked to him, they'd been at a T-ball game watching one of his friends play. There'd been a lot of cheering, a bunch of "I wove you, Mommy"s and Bryan had told her to enjoy her day. Had something happened at the game? Had Trevor gotten hit on the head with a ball? A bat? Fallen from the stands?

She pulled out her phone. Maybe she'd missed his call—except the thing was dead. Great. Of all the times for her battery to die.

She ran back to her bedroom for her charger, passing Trev's room on the way.

Mr. Monkey was gone. Trevor wouldn't have taken him to the ball game, though, so that only upped the odds for a hospital trip. The blue teddy bear was gone, too. As were the dinosaurs and building blocks. Poor Rocco sat all alone on the shelf.

Jenna did *not* want to relate to a fish.

Where could Bryan have taken him?

She plugged in her phone, counting the interminable

seconds until the thing lit up, then punched in his number.

She got his voicemail.

"Bryan, it's me. Where are you? Where's Trevor? Is everything okay?" She wasn't successful in keeping the panic out of her voice.

She dialed his mother next.

A groggy Mrs. Lassiter answered. "Hello?"

"Mrs. Lassiter, I mean, Tabitha, it's Jenna. I'm sorry for calling so late, but is Bryan there by any chance?"

"Bryan? Oh no. He's at the club."

The *club*? What was he doing at the club when he was supposed to be watching their son?

"Is, um, is Trevor with you?"

"Oh no, dear. I left him with Bryan."

She left a three-year-old at a strip club?

Jenna couldn't get off the phone fast enough. She couldn't get in her car fast enough. She couldn't drive to the club fast enough.

Well, yes, apparently, she could. At least fast enough for Sarge to see her and pull her over.

"Sorry, Jenna, but I have to ticket you. We clocked you at fifty-five in a thirty-five mile an hour zone." He scratched his forehead. "Just 'cause I like you doesn't mean I can bend the rules. You know that."

She did. She'd done enough rule-bending in her life to know that it would someday catch up to her.

"And you might want to stay off that phone." He nodded to it in her lap. She'd been getting Bryan's voicemail the entire drive. "If I'd caught you on it, that'd be another ticket since it's against the law to be talking on a phone while driving unless it's hands-free."

It wasn't and he knew it. She had a feeling he also knew that she'd been on it the whole way, too. He wouldn't know why and she didn't really think telling him that she'd let Bryan, her child's father, the one who'd accused her of prostitution and now had their son at a strip club, babysit

Trevor and practically kidnap him without telling her where he was going. Sarge loved Trevor too much for her to worry or anger him like she was.

She thanked him—which made no sense given that this traffic stop was going to cost her a hundred and fifty bucks—and stuck to the speed limit the rest of the way to BeefCake, Inc.

Dear God, Bryan had their son at a *strip* club. Trevor was going to be scarred for life.

She parked the car next to Bryan's. They were here, thank God.

She ran to the front door.

It was locked.

Locked?

She dialed Bryan's number again.

He didn't answer *again.*

What the hell was wrong with him?

She ran around back, trying to peer in through the frosted windows that prevented people from getting a free show, but she couldn't even see a light on inside.

Where *was* he?

She ran around to the back entrance. If that didn't work, she'd take the fire escape stairwell up to the apartment and try to get in that way.

Luckily, the back door was unlocked.

A light from one of the rooms off the back corridor lit it enough for her to see and she headed that way.

Bryan's Domain was on a plaque by the door. She peeked inside. A desk covered in paperwork, a sofa covered in costumes, more costumes hanging from pegs on the wall—including her Marilyn Monroe dress—a computer monitor with a rotating screen saver, but no Bryan.

She walked toward the dressing room she'd shared with the other dancers. Dark.

The kitchen was dark, too, so Jenna headed to the stage door entrance into the club.

Low lights lit her way as she climbed the stairs backstage like when she'd danced the other night, and a soft glow beyond the curtain gave her hope that someone was here. Part of her wanted it to be Bryan and Trevor and the other part wanted to believe he'd never bring their son there.

And then the music started, soft, low, seductive… Was Bryan actually letting their son listen to this? It sounded like liquid sex.

She took a deep breath, not wanting to rant at Bryan in front of Trevor, and walked across the stage to feel for the opening in the center of the curtain.

"Who's there?" Bryan's voice cut through the sensual melody.

Jenna found the opening. "It's me," she said just as the stage lights came on, blinding her.

"Jenna?" Bryan leapt onto the stage. "What are you doing here?"

She put a hand up to keep the lights out of her eyes. She'd forgotten how bright they were. "Where's Trevor? I got home and no one was there. Your mom said you were here." She looked around, but couldn't see anything beyond the lights. "Where is he?"

"Upstairs. You didn't get my voice mail?"

"My phone died and I've been checking the entire drive here. There's no voice mail."

"It must not have transferred with your battery dying. I called you over five hours ago to let you know he'd be here."

"*Why* is he here? What could possibly make you bring him to a strip club?"

"Something came up and I had to close tonight for Gage, so I figured I'd put Trev to bed here rather than have to wake him up from my mom's in the middle of the night to take him home. I was planning to stay with him upstairs and bring him home in the morning. That's okay, isn't it?"

The whole time they were talking, Bryan's hands were roaming over her. First her shoulders, then brushing some hair off her face; he even shielded her eyes from the lights, moving closer with each motion, his eyes studying her, his fingers tracing her features, and drawing her closer, his body—and now hers—swaying to the beat of the soft music.

She was having trouble concentrating. "He's here? Asleep?"

Bryan moved a step closer. "Uh huh. Upstairs. Sound asleep. With Mr. Monkey and the blue bear as bedmates."

"Bryan."

"What?" He trailed his fingertips up her arm.

"I meant, the bear's name is Bryan."

"Lucky bear." His fingertips curved over her shoulder then headed south, trailing all sorts of fire in their wake.

"Arrogant." With good reason. The man could turn her on like no one else.

"I meant that *that* Bryan has a bedmate." He took another step closer until there were no more steps to take. "I'm hoping *this* Bryan will be as lucky."

And then he was kissing her.

Right there, in the lights, on the stage, dancing as a couple, their bodies in perfect rhythm, knowing each other's movements instinctively.

Just like they had last night.

"Mmm, you smell nice," he whispered as he nuzzled her neck. "I missed you."

"I missed you, too." She couldn't not say it when he was doing such delicious things to her nerve endings since it was true.

"Have fun?"

Not as much fun as this… "It was nice."

His lips were sending shivers all over her body just by nuzzling her earlobe.

"*You're* nice." He caught her earlobe between his

teeth.

Jenna shivered, sparks zinging through her body. This was so much more than *nice*. It was sexy and sensual and driving her nuts. Last night hadn't been enough. She'd never have enough of Bryan.

She wrapped her arms around him and held on tight, sliding against him in time to the music, remembering what it'd been like here on this stage, in the hot lights, the music infusing her body with a sensuality she hadn't known she'd possessed and she felt it again.

He grabbed her hips and tucked her up against him, the music affecting him—physically—as much as it did her.

He kissed her lips, sucking them like he had her breast last night, and Jenna moaned. She wanted him.

"I want you," he growled against her lips, yanking her hips even closer as if there were any doubt of how much he wanted her.

He slid his hands beneath her shirt, his fingers trailing heat wherever they touched. He cupped her, his thumbs caressing her nipples and Jenna reveled in the sensation. "Yes, Bryan, touch me."

Thank God they were alone here, on the stage, in these lights, in this club because Jenna didn't know if she could stop. It was the sweetest feeling imaginable, so hot and heady, being wanted by Bryan. Desired by him. He ran his hands back down her sides, following the curve of her waist, and curving over her hips to cup her backside, and she gasped into his mouth as he kissed her, hot, and open-mouthed, his pelvis thrusting against her.

"Here, Jenna." He growled. "I want you here."

"Here?" She gasped when his lips left hers to slide down her neck and over her collarbone, all the while undoing the buttons on her shirt.

And then he separated her lapels and kissed down between her breasts, undoing the clasp of her bra with his teeth.

His *teeth*.

That was when her knees gave out. Thankfully, he held her, but only long enough to lower her to the stage floor.

"Here." He laid on top of her, bracing his weight on his elbows, his thighs around hers, and Jenna didn't care where they were so long as he didn't leave her.

"Yes, Bryan."

It was all he'd been waiting to hear.

Bryan wouldn't have believed he could want her this much. He would have thought nothing could surpass last night, but now tonight, this, did. He wanted her with a fierceness that almost scared him. She was his. That little boy upstairs was his. They were his. This family was *his*.

He bared her breasts. She was so pretty. So perky and pouty and waiting just for him.

So he took. He took one sweet perfect breast in his mouth and tasted the essence of Jenna. Some other scent, floral or fruity, mingled there, but nothing would ever mask who she was from him.

She arched against him, her pelvis hitting him right where he wanted it to, but it was too soon. They had all night; no one would be at the club and he didn't want to waste the time going anywhere else.

Thank God, he'd had the foresight to put some condoms in his pocket.

"I want you, Bryan," Jenna whispered when he moved to her other breast.

He looked up, resting his chin on that sweet flesh. "You can't want me anywhere nearly as much as I want you, Jenna. I feel like I've been waiting for you my entire life." Yes, he laid himself bare with that comment, but his feelings were already there and if he didn't tell her, didn't take the chance, he'd never know.

"But I do, Bryan." She ran a hand over his hair then

traced his lips with them.

He kissed them.

"I want you so very much. Make love to me," she whispered, her voice as shaky as he felt.

"It will be my pleasure." And it would.

So he did.

He worshipped every inch of her body there, on that stage, the lights hiding nothing from each other, bodies bared to each other, eyes open, souls…

Souls shared as each movement, each touch was fraught with meaning. Each stroke so very personal and so very necessary.

He ran his palm over her belly where she'd carried their son. Not a stretch mark on her, though it wouldn't have mattered if she'd had thousands. He'd kiss each and every one and be thankful for all they represented.

The concave hollow of her hips, too, showed no sign of her pregnancy, but then, her mother was trim. Good genes. And good *jeans*, too. He smiled as he kissed her navel. Jenna looked good in anything and nothing.

He kissed lower, loving the feel and scent and taste of her in his mouth. Loved watching her climb the heights, her legs clamping around him, loved watching her rock against him as the sensations overwhelmed her, and he loved that soft smile when he kissed her at the end, that soft sweet smile that said he'd given her pleasure.

He grabbed a condom from his discarded pants, sheathed himself, then laid beside her on the stage, feeling her body recover from the ride he'd just taken her on, and he wanted more. He'd never get enough of Jenna. "We should go upstairs. I can't do to you what I want without hurting your back on this floor."

"And what do you want to do to me?" She rolled over and nipped his jaw.

"Ah, Jen… So much, sweetheart. I want to be inside you so deep and so long that you'll never remember what it was like without me there. That you'll never want to *know* what it's like. I want you, baby. Forever."

A tear slipped from the coroner of her eye.

Shit. Too much too soon.

He wiped it away. "Hey, no pressure. Please don't cry. I'll wait. I told you, I'm not going anywhere."

"It's not that…" She shook her head and bit her lip.

Then she grabbed his face and kissed him. Hard. Demanding. Forceful.

And then she rolled herself on top of him and lifted her hips and took him inside her body.

It was heaven. He'd died and gone right to heaven with no idea what he'd done to deserve such a reward but when she moved on him, he didn't care. He gripped those supple hips and held her above him and plunged into her.

"That's it, Bryan, take me." She had her hands on the floor by his head, her fingers catching some of his hair and he couldn't move his head.

Not that he needed to. He worked her up and down on top of him, the slick wet heat of her body driving him on, in and out, over and over, as if he were searching desperately for something that only she could provide.

She arched against him, her breasts right in front of him and Bryan tore his hair from her fingers as he surged forward, taking one sweet breast into his mouth, sucking it awhile he worked her down onto him.

Then somehow they were sitting and she was on her knees, taking him into her to the hilt, her thighs stroking his sides as she moved on him, driving him crazy with need and want and desire, the feelings coiling in his balls and threatening to shoot up through her like a rocket.

"Come for me, Bryan," she panted in his ear as she swirled her tongue around it.

Bryan slid a hand between then, finding that tight bundle of nerves that would take her over the edge. If he were going to go, he wanted her with him.

Jenna leaned back when he touched her, her breasts still within kissing distance, but her eyes… she was watching him with those gorgeous blue eyes and Bryan ever so slowly, bent forward to take her nipple in his mouth.

He flicked the tip gently—in time with the motion he was doing between her legs.

"Oh my God," she breathed, her moist lips parting, and it was the most beautiful sight he'd ever seen.

"Like that?"

She couldn't answer. She bit her lip and nodded, and her inner muscles clenched him.

Bryan drew in a ragged breath. God, yes, that felt so damn good.

He did it again.

So did she.

And again. And again.

Until soon, there was no conscious thought, there was no waiting for her reaction, but rather, it was both of them reacting. Both of them wanting.

Jenna cradled his head as he sucked on her breast and she tightened her muscles around him as she slid down, then tightened them again as she slid up, releasing all but the tip before sliding back down, and the rhythm kept increasing, their cries of pleasure getting louder , the sound of their flesh meeting quicker, and Bryan felt the end begin. Felt it coil inside him until he couldn't hold it off, and he spread his hand low on her back, working her onto him grinding her against him, his other hand working between them to bring her to the same point, and then suddenly, they were *there*.

Jenna cried out his name and gripped him as the waves of passion spasmed through her, milking that very same passion from him, and in a blinding rush, Bryan felt all that desire, all that want and need and all that was in him for her, spill out into her—metaphorically thanks to the condom—and he shouted out her name. Claimed her.

She was his. Finally and completely, as sure as he knew they were there on that stage together, he knew that she was his.

And then the condom broke.

Chapter Thirty-Five

Jenna never scrambled so fast in her life. The high of orgasm one minute and the crashing reality of her thighs dripping with Bryan's semen.

"Oh my God, oh my God, oh my God." She grabbed her pants—underwear—whatever—and tried to wipe it away.

On your legs isn't the problem, Jenna.

Yes, she realized that, thankyouverymuch, but short of a turkey baster, there wasn't anything she could do…

Jenna sank to the stage, her legs giving out with that realization. One. It only took one. One tiny little strong swimmer and her life would be changed forever.

"Jenna."

Though it already had been.

She looked at Bryan. He was sitting there, rolled onto his hip, his one hand supporting him, the other resting across the knee he had propped up in all his naked glory. And it was glorious. Except for the remnants of the condom on his…

"What are we going to do?"

"It'll be okay, Jenna." He reached for her hand.

"Okay? Bryan, in case it's escaped your notice…" She pointed to his groin. "You are batting oh-for-two in the condom department. How can that be okay?"

He looked down and released her hand to remove the three percent statistic she'd never wanted to see evidence of.

But then, she already had the evidence, didn't she? She was *raising* that evidence. Tucking him into bed at night.

Bryan sat up then, cross-legged, and grabbed his t-shirt to toss over his groin. "I know it's not optimal, but if it happens, I'm okay with it, Jenna. I'm sticking around and I'll love a new baby just as much as I already love Trevor." He took her hand in his. "You won't have to go through it alone this time."

Oh God, a baby with Bryan. It was everything Jenna could ever want and her biggest nightmare all tied up in one. She couldn't keep the pretense going through an actual pregnancy. She couldn't pretend she'd gone through it already when he'd want to come to every doctor's appointment, every sonogram, every Lamaze class, and the delivery.

He'd know.

Too late now, sweetheart, her conscience mocked.

No it wasn't. She could run out to the closest all-night pharmacy and get the morning after pill…

But she wouldn't.

Her hand went to her abdomen. If they *had* created a child, she wouldn't get rid of it. And not because it would be Bryan's, but because it would be *hers*. This one would be the one *she'd* decide to keep. No one else. Not her mother, not Bryan, and not some dumb drunk driver who should never have been behind the wheel, ruining and ending other people's lives. This child would be *hers*.

"Jenna? You okay?"

Bryan got to his feet and his voice pulled her out from that dark, intense moment, and she uncurled her fingers that had curled into her stomach protectively. "Um, yes. Sure. I'm fine."

And she was. Jenna let her hand drop to her side, standing there, naked, exposed, and she *was* fine. If they'd made a child, she would deal with it. Just like Mindy had.

And by the same man.

The irony was… well, ironic. What were the chances of her making a child with Trevor's father? It couldn't *really* happen, could it? God, the Universe, Karma, they couldn't all have that same twisted sense of humor. One surprise child in Bryan's world was enough.

Bryan walked over to her and slid his hands up her arms. "You're scaring me."

"I didn't mean to." She ran a finger along his jaw. Such a nice jaw. Strong. Dependable. Like him. "I'm okay."

"It will be okay, Jenna. If there's a baby…" He rested his forehead against hers. "We'll deal with it. The right way this time."

Question was, what *was* the right way? But she didn't ask it. She'd wait until she had to make the big decisions. Right now… right now she just had to deal with what they'd done. "I can't believe we just did that here. Anyone could have walked in."

"Only someone with a key, and that limits it to me, Gage, and his wife, Lara—and if they have an ounce of sense, they're home doing what we were here doing."

He tilted her face up. "What I want to do again." Those violet eyes searched hers and Jenna felt herself falling under his spell. "Join me upstairs?"

"I thought Trevor was sleeping up there?"

"The sofa pulls out. You didn't think two unattached guys would have a place with only *one* bedroom, did you?" Bryan waggled his eyebrows. "Best part is, I know the owner so we don't even have to put our clothes on to walk through the hallways."

"Wow, that does come in handy." Jenna patted his jaw. "But if it's all the same to you, I'd at least like to bring them with me so Trevor doesn't wake up to a naked mother and I can leave with some semblance of dignity."

"I'm with you on the no nudity thing for Trevor's sake, but trust me, Ms. Corrigan, I plan to work anything dignified out of you for the next six hours."

"You're welcome to try, Mr. Lassiter."

"I'll take that as a challenge."

"It was meant as one."

And it was one Bryan was more than *up* for meeting.

Chapter Thirty-Six

"Huwwy, Mommy! Me and Bobby wanna cwimb the tweefort."

"Yeah, *Mommy*, let's get that cute behind moving." Bryan swatted her on it as he passed her, then had the nerve to turn around and run backwards toward the playground in the park, looking way too good for someone who'd gotten as little sleep as they both had.

"This cute behind is dragging," she muttered. The price one had to pay for a night of lovemaking with Bryan Lassiter.

"Then, by all means, allow me." He ran behind her this time and literally held up her behind.

"Bryan! You can't do that! Someone might see." She took off running. That's all she'd need; one of her students spreading it around school that she was letting some man feel her up in the park. Of course, if she were pregnant, that'd pretty much null the feeling-up story.

Jenna refused to think about that and whatever repercussions a pregnancy would entail. She was having too good of a time with her son and the man she loved.

"Damn, woman, you're a spoilsport." Bryan caught up to her and once more ran past her.

This time, though, he didn't turn around so she got a nice show of *his* behind.

"Like what you see?" he tossed back over his shoulder.

"Matter of fact, I do. And if you'd let me catch up, maybe I'll even show you how much."

"Now there's a promise I can't resist." He stopped running and waited for her. But then he swung her up in his arms, twirled her around, and planted a big ol' kiss on her right there for anyone and everyone to see.

"Ewww!" Including two almost four-year-olds.

"Mommy's kissing Daddy!" Trevor looked charmingly disgusted.

His father just looked charming. "Hey, kiddo. Don't knock it 'til you've tried it. One day you're going to be kissing girls and it won't see m so icky to you."

"Nuh uh. I'm never gonna kiss a girl. Come on, Bobby, wet's go in the fort."

Bryan led her over to the bench in full view of the tree fort while the boys ran off to play. "So about last night."

"Yes, about that." She drew her knees up to her chest and wrapped her arms around her legs.

He checked out her legs. "It was… nice."

"I was thinking of a different word than nice, but okay."

"Oh? What word was that?"

Oh no. She wasn't showing her hand first. She shrugged and dropped her feet to the ground. "Nice fits, I guess."

"Aw, come on, Jenna." He put his hand on her knee and squeezed gently, violet eyes sparkling with amusement. "What were you thinking?"

She tweaked his nose. "You don't need any more reasons to get a big head. I'm not going to be one more in the list of women who fall at your feet and feed you lines about how magnificent you are."

The teasing light disappeared from his eyes and Bryan got solemn. "First of all, there aren't any long lines. Second, even if there were, do I really seem like the guy who'd take advantage of that? Bachelor party notwithstanding. That was too much alcohol and mutual desire. I was in no shape to resist a sexy woman coming on to me."

"How do you know she—I mean, *I* came on to you? Maybe *you* came on to me."

"Did I?"

Damn. Snagged. She didn't know the answer to that—because Mindy hadn't known it either. "There was a lot of alcohol all the way around that night."

"Exactly. So let's take that night out of the equation for what I was trying to say."

"What *were* you trying to say, Bryan?"

He took a deep breath and looked at her, the look in those gorgeous eyes one she'd never seen before. Then he looked away.

"I was going to say… " He looked back—and then he dropped to one knee in front of her.

Right there. In the dirt, beside the wooden bench that lovers had carved their initials in.

Oh my.

Bryan picked up her hand. "Jenna Corrigan, what I was going to say was that, while I might dance for a lot of women and maybe even inspire fantasies in some of them, you're the only one I've fantasized about. I wish I could say I've been doing that since I first met you, but there was that alcohol thing and, well, let's just say that since I've *re*-met you, since coming to your house and seeing you being so fiercely protective and supportive of your students and our son, of seeing how you welcomed me, *and* my family, into Trevor's life, of how beautiful you are when you smile, how adorable you are when you're determined to do something, and how utterly you rock my world with just a simple glance… I want to ask you something again. And this time, it's not because of Trevor and it's not because of what might or might not have been created last night, but because I can't get you out of my head and because spending this time with you and coming to know the person you are—and the way you turn me on—I want to ask you again if you'll marry me."

This time, he pulled out a ring.

"Where… where did you get that?"

"It was my mother's. I asked her last night if I could give it to you and she said she would be honored if you would wear something that symbolized the love she and my father shared for over forty years."

Jenna couldn't speak. She couldn't respond. She couldn't even shake her head.

He wanted to marry her. He hadn't said he loved her, but surely it was there. Surely, it was implied. Surely if he didn't now, he was on his way?

And what's going to happen when you tell him the truth?

"Jenna?" He squeezed her fingers. "Will you?"

God, she'd made the man ask her twice.

Maybe because you're having second thoughts?

"Yes. I will." She was *not* having second thoughts. She'd tell him. She would. And he'd understand. Now that they were going to get married and be together forever, he'd understand her need to protect Trevor. He said it himself: he loved the way she loved and protected their son.

His son.

"As soon as possible, Bryan." *Then* she'd tell him the truth.

Coward.

She preferred to think of it as self-preservation. Of *Trevor* preservation.

He slid the ring on her finger, then caught her head in his hands and kissed her. Long, lingering, full of promise and commitment and happiness and, yes, even love—it was there—Bryan sealed their souls and healed her heart.

"Ewww!"

They broke apart laughing. The two boys stood less

than a foot away. Trevor was looking at them so very innocently. "We want ice cweam."

Bobby on the other hand… "Are you gonna kiss the whole time because it's gross."

"I just might keep kissing Trevor's mom, yes," said Bryan, wrapping an arm around her. "You have a problem with that, Trevor?"

Trev shrugged. "I don't care. I just want ice cweam."

"Well I think it's gross." Bobby crossed his arms. "My mommy said that's how she got a baby in her belly again. Are you gonna get one, too, Jenna?"

"Cool! I want a baby bwother!"

Jenna looked at Bryan and something… magical? emotional? forever? passed between them.

Yes, he loved her. It was there.

"Kissing doesn't always put a baby in a woman's belly, guys, but it can sometimes." Bryan sat beside her on the bench again. "But what do you think if I said I wanted to marry your mom, Trev?"

Trevor's smile disappeared and his violet eyes turned her way. "Do you wanna mawwy Bwyan, Mommy?"

"I do, Trev. What do you think?"

Those eyes, so like Bryan's, started to sparkle and his mouth dropped open. And so did his arms, and then he threw himself at them, catching them both in a hug bigger than an almost-four-year's-old's arms could hold, but not more than his heart could. "We're gonna be a family!"

She just hoped Bryan remembered this moment and all it represented for all of them when she told him the truth.

Chapter Thirty-Seven

"Since you volunteered to cook, I'll run to the market," Jenna said to Bryan, scrubbing her hair with a towel after her shower. The jog to the park, followed by a dusty Trevor's enthusiastic hug, along with a few more covered in melted ice cream, had ensured they'd all needed to wash up when they returned from their morning outing. Even Bobby had been bathed and now the boys were building with blocks on the living room coffee table. "Think you can hold down the fort?"

"It's a castle, Mommy," Trevor said, concentrating so hard on setting the block just right that he didn't even look over.

"Sorry, Trev. Castle." She looked back at Bryan. "He's anal like that. Likes to make sure everything's lined up perfectly, and if something is a castle, it can't be a fort. Or a dungeon."

"Yeah, I get that. I was like that as a kid." Bryan stacked the napkins on the table.

Jenna looked at it and raised her eyebrows. "Just as a kid?"

He blushed and it did amazing things to her insides to see that side of him. Especially when he was in one of her aprons, getting ready to bake his mother's homemade apple pie recipe. Apparently the ring wasn't the only thing he'd asked his mother for last night, so not only was Jenna getting an amazing father for her son, an amazing lover in the bedroom, but also a chef in the kitchen.

"You sure you can handle this?"

"Of course I can. They're just kids, not a gang."

"Just remember you said that."

He swatted her butt with a dishtowel. "Go. Before I change my mind and make *you* stay here with them."

"I'm going, I'm going!"

***

She grinned the entire ride to the supermarket. And through half the aisles.

Matter of fact, the only reason she stopped smiling was because her mother was in aisle nine and saw her before Jenna could turn away.

"Ellen."

"Has *that woman* moved in yet?"

No greeting, no warm peck on the cheek. Ellen in a mood was someone Jenna didn't want to be around. She grabbed a bottle of ketchup and dropped it into her cart. "Her name is Tabitha."

"Named after a witch. How perfect."

Jenna turned to the shelves. She was low on mustard, wasn't she? She picked it up. Even if she wasn't mustard wouldn't go bad. Unlike this conversation. "Stop it, Ellen. Tabitha has nothing to do with this."

"She has everything to do with it. She tried to horn in on my daughter and her family—"

"A family you had ample opportunity to get to know and elected not to, if you recall." Jenna pointed the mustard bottle at her. "So you can't blame Trevor for being thrilled to have a grandmother in his life, or for her to love him and want to be around him. Or me, either, for that matter. You can't blame *me* for welcoming the woman into my home when she is probably the only grandmother Trevor will ever know."

"He could know me."

"He could—*if* you ever bothered to get to know him. But you haven't, Ellen. You've chosen to distance yourself from us. Just like you've been doing to me ever since you found out about Daddy's affair."

"*Daddy*." Her mother's lips curled back. "You call him that as if you loved him, but how could you when he chose *her*, that woman, *and* her bastard child over you. How could you, Jenna? How could you want to even think about being with him, visiting him, spending time with him when he did you wrong?" Ellen had a death grip on the back of Jenna's cart, her knuckles white as she practically rattled the thing off its wheels.

Jenna tugged the cart away. "Because I didn't want to lose the only father I'd ever known, Mom. Because he still loved me even if he fell out of love with you. And I'm sorry for that. I'm sorry you thought it had to be an either or situation. That *I* had to choose, even though you hadn't gotten to. I know what he did sucked. I get that. He shouldn't have done it. But I was a *kid*. His child and I needed my father." *Especially when you turned on me.*

But Jenna didn't say it. No good could come of hurting her mother with the past. Jenna just wanted to move forward. Focus on the future.

"*I* loved you. *I* carried you. You of all people ought to know the bond between a mother and child, Jenna, and you broke that."

Apparently, Ellen, didn't have the same moratorium on inflicting the pain of the past on the here and now. "How *dare* you. How *dare* you dump that on me. I was a child. A *child*. Yours *and* his. I couldn't choose. No child should have to. And he wasn't the one making me. *You* were. And you still are."

She spun the shopping cart around. "My door is always open for you, Ellen, but be sure that you're willing to accept me as I am, and Trevor as he is, and Bryan and

Tabitha and any other Lassiter who shows up to be part of my son's life because I will *not* make my son choose who he can love. It wasn't fair to me and it won't be fair to him."

She stormed off, fighting back the tears as she steered the cart to the check-out lane. How *dare* her mother do that to her. How *dare* she try to lay that guilt at her feet. Whatever Ellen had felt about their marriage, she should have kept it to herself. Dad had. He'd never bad-mouthed her mother once in all the divorce proceedings. He'd said that they weren't the people they'd fallen in love with and were no longer happy together. That much had been obvious to her even back then. Dad had been much happier with Mindy's mom—and Jenna had certainly been happy to have a sister. Yes, she'd felt bad for Ellen, but Ellen had let the bitterness and hatred fester and it'd affected everyone around her, until Jenna had gone looking for love and acceptance in the arms of her boyfriend.

It'd been a stupid thing to do. She knew that. She'd known it then. And Dave had proved just how stupid when she'd found out about the pregnancy and he'd called her a liar.

The irony was that, *then*, she hadn't been lying, yet Dave had left her. Now… with Bryan, she *was* lying and he wanted her.

Granted, he didn't know she was lying. And though she had a very good reason, she couldn't keep doing it. It wasn't fair. Not to him, not to Trevor, and most definitely not to her. She deserved to be loved for who she was and as long as she had this lie hanging over her, she could never truly be that person.

She had to come clean. Now.

Chapter Thirty-Eight

"Eighteen… Nineteen… Twenty. Ready or not, here I come!" Bryan uncovered his eyes and looked around the living room. They'd figured out there weren't any other places to hide in the five previous times he'd been "it" and had had to find them. Thankfully, they'd wizened up because it was hard pretending not to see two giggling, squirming little boys.

"I wonder where they could be." He made a big production of stomping around the living room as he made his way toward the stairs. They hadn't been at all quiet as they'd run up them the minute he'd closed his eyes.

"I wonder if they're in here." He opened the coat closet door and rattled the hangars loudly on the bar. "Nope. Not here."

He repeated the action with the dining room and the kitchen, opening doors and cabinets and moving the noisy stuff inside them around, then closing them with a big crash.

Giggles floated down the stairs.

"Hmmm, it doesn't look like they're down here. They must be upstairs."

Tiny footsteps went clattering down the hallway as he walked over to the stairs. He *thunked* his foot down loudly on each tread with an extra huff-and-a-puff thrown in every so often for good measure. God, he loved playing with his son.

"I don't know… If I can't find them, I'm not going to have anyone to throw a football with." He peered through the railing on the landing, but didn't see any little legs. Good, the boys were getting better at hiding.

Or maybe that wasn't so good…

He'd made it to the top step when he heard the crash. Then a wail. Then some thumping.

Definitely *not* good.

Bryan ran down the hallway toward Jenna's room. "Trev? Bobby? Where are you, guys?"

"In here!"

More thumps came from Jenna's closet.

Bryan pulled on the doorknobs to the double doors and out tumbled two little boys, a big blue teddy bear, a slew of clothing and boxes, and a bunch of DVDs.

"You guys okay?" Bryan helped them up, checking for broken bones and bumps and bruises while trying to get his heart rate out of heart-attack range. "What happened?"

Bobby's bottom lip quivered. "We were hiding and I got scared."

"I told him you'd find us, but he didn't think so. He thought we were gonna be stuck in the dark forever." Trevor hugged the teddy bear tighter. "See, Bobby? I told ya my dad would find us. He can do anything."

Now Bryan's heart was swelling—with pride. And love. And the feeling of being a superhero in Trevor's eyes. Being a parent was the best feeling in the world.

"My dad can do anything, too."

"Nuh uh. He can't frow a football. His bounce."

Bryan tried not to laugh. Poor Bobby. The kid was going to need some help in that area. "Hey, guys, how would you like to help me test the apple pie? It's going to be finished soon and I need someone to tell me if it's good or not."

Trevor's chest puffed up. "We can do that, Daddy. We're good tasterers."

"Yeah. Good tasterers," said Bobby, following Trevor out of the room.

Bryan scooped up the mess and put it on Jenna's bed. He'd help her put her closet together later…

The DVD cases had white labels on the front. *Trevor's First Smile. Trevor Rolls Over. Trevor's First Steps.*

He flipped through them. A little more than a dozen, all noting significant events in his son's life.

Trevor's Birth.

He wanted to see that one.

"Daddy! We want pie!"

Right. The boys. He needed to get down there before they took it upon themselves to open the oven—

Shit.

Bryan grabbed that last DVD and ran down the stairs. He'd watch it after Jenna came home. They could watch it together and she could tell him everything she was feeling and thinking as their son came into the world.

***

Bryan couldn't wait until after dinner. He couldn't even wait until Jenna came home; that DVD was burning a hole in his palm. He'd barely put it down to get the pie out of the oven and serve two slivers to the boys—he *had* promised them after all. Merely as a means to change their focus from being scared in the closet and everything fallen on them, but Bryan added some ice cream to the pie to keep them occupied a little longer. What was a little pie in the face of such grave danger?

And if it had the added bonus of keeping them occupied so he could take a peek at the video, more's the better.

He watched it for a lot longer than a peek. A lot longer than he should have, but Bryan hadn't been able to look away.

Jenna was not the one giving birth to his son.

Oh she was there—she was *filming* the birth. For a woman named Mindy.

A woman he actually *did* remember. Vaguely.

"That's it, Mindy, come on, you can do it. Just like in class."

Mindy's hair was stuck to her face, pain evident as she gripped the rails of her hospital bed, her knees pulled up, and she bore down.

And there… there was Trevor's head.

"That's it! I can see him! I can see Trevor!" Jenna jiggled the camera in her excitement. "Come on, Mindy, just one more!"

Mindy took a deep breath and bore down and pushed Trevor—*his son*—into the world.

"Bryan, what are you—Oh."

Jenna had opened the front door. She was standing in the living room.

She was looking at the television.

He was looking at her.

And didn't know who he was looking at.

"I… I can explain." She looked at him now, her eyes worried, her hands wringing, a tear coursing its way down her cheek and he…

He couldn't. He couldn't stay. He couldn't listen. He couldn't hear what she wanted to explain. Because it'd be a lie. Just like the one she'd been telling him for the last week.

She wasn't Trevor's mother.

Was he even Trevor's father?

That thought sucked the breath out of him more than the other one. Had she been trying to trap him into paying for this kid that she…

She *what*?

If Trevor wasn't hers, what did she hope to get out of

him?

But there were those eyes. Even at birth, he could see the resemblance—no they weren't violet yet, but there, on the screen, that was the face in his baby pictures. Trevor *was* his son.

But not hers.

He stood up, kind of amazed that he could. That his legs hadn't been cut out from under him because it sure as hell felt like they had. "Don't leave town. If you do, I'll find you. I won't *stop* until I find you."

"Bryan, I can explain—"

"Save it for my attorney." He walked past her and headed toward the kitchen. He was taking Trevor and getting the hell out of here.

"But you don't understand—"

"Damn right I don't. And I can't right now. But you *will* explain this to me. Or I'll have you thrown in jail for kidnapping, extortion, fraud, and whatever other charges I can find on you. So I suggest you pack his bag and meet me at my car or I'll call Sergeant Benton right now and no sweet smile on your part will save you from being hauled off in handcuffs in front of my son. Is that what you want, Jenna? Do you want Trevor's last image of you to be in the back of a police car?"

More tears were streaming down her face, but Bryan steeled himself against them. He wasn't going to fall for that act. No way. She might have gotten to him on her sweet and innocent loving mother charade, but his eyes had been opened. He wasn't that foolish.

"You can't take him from me."

"Can't I?" He walked to the DVR and removed the evidence. He put it in its protective case and waved it at her. "This says I can. This proves he's not yours."

"It doesn't prove he's yours."

"I'll get a DNA test, but we both know what it's going to say, don't we, Jenna?"

That hair that never stayed behind her ears didn't do so again as her head fell forward and she buried her face in her hands. "Please, Bryan." Her words were muffled. "Please don't take him from me."

"You took him from me." He stormed over to the kitchen, stopping and pulling himself together before he went in. Didn't need to scare the kid. "Hey, guys. We're going to go take Bobby home and then, Trev, you and I are going to do something fun."

"Cool! What?"

"It's a surprise." To both of them because he didn't have a clue yet what his next step was going to be. All he knew was he had to get out of this house. "So, come on. Let's get going."

"But I have to wash my hands." Trevor slid off his chair then held his hands in the air. "They're all sticky and Mommy doesn't like me to touch stuff wif sticky hands."

"Well, I'm not Mommy, and it's okay if you have sticky hands in my truck. How's that?"

The two little boys grinned at each other as if they'd struck gold. He knew the feeling. "Cool!"

No, it wasn't cool. Nothing was cool. Not now.

But it would be.

Bryan let the door slam nice and loud on their way out.

Chapter Thirty-Nine

Jenna didn't know how long she sat there on the living room floor. Had no idea how long it'd been since Bryan had taken her son and walked out of her life.

Her son.

His son.

Their son.

Her fingers curled over her belly. What if there was another one on the way? Bryan hated her. Would he try to take this child from her, too?

She drew in a deep, ragged breath and pushed herself onto her knees. She had to get off the floor. She couldn't just sit here and do nothing. Her child was out there. He was gone from her. Taken.

Granted, by his father. Whom he loved. And who'd never hurt him, but still… Trevor was *her* son. Aside from the legal piece of paper she had proclaiming it, her heart proclaimed it. She loved him as much as if he'd come from her body and nothing Bryan could say would change that.

And it wouldn't stop Trevor from loving her, either.

He would miss her. Oh, sure, this time with Bryan would be fun, but he'd want to come back to her. To his home. To Rocco and Mr. Monkey, and the blue bear and his blocks and his dinosaurs and his backyard and Bobby and…

Jenna made it as far as the sofa before she crumpled onto it in tears. Her baby. Her child. Bryan was going to go for custody.

She couldn't fight him on it. Well, she would if he went for full custory, but if he would see reason to sharing Trevor—for Trevor's sake—then she'd have to go along with it. Just like she'd told her mother, a child shouldn't have to choose between parents and she had to make Bryan see that.

She dragged herself off the sofa and went into the kitchen. She'd talk to him. Make him see reason. He loved Trevor; he'd do what was best.

And what about you? Does he love you?

God, what was with her conscience? It'd been mocking her since Bryan had shown up on her front porch, taunting her with the failings of her life.

Jenna swiped at the tears on her cheeks. She wouldn't cry. Her life wasn't a failure. She'd just had some bad breaks, was all. But Trevor hadn't been a bad break. He'd been the best thing that'd ever happened to her and by God, she wasn't going to give him up without a fight.

She grabbed her purse and dug her keys out of it. She was going to go over to Bryan's right now and explain this to him. Make him see reason. Hear what she had to say.

Except… she didn't know where he lived.

Jenna sank down on the chair, the irony of having made love with a man, could possibly be carrying his child, was raising his other one, yet had no idea where he lived—*just like Mindy*—was not lost on her in so sad a way. Was she so hard up for a man to love her, to want her, to stay with her that she would resort to this?

That's what her mother would want her to believe.

…

Jenna sat up.

Wait. That *was* what her mother would want her to believe. Her bitter, lonely mother whose husband had left.

He'd *left*.

He'd left Ellen and, yes, he'd left *her*. Jenna. His

daughter.

He'd chosen someone else over her.

As a mother, Jenna couldn't understand it, and as a child, she obviously hadn't been able to either. And even if she had, she hadn't been able to do anything about it.

But *now* she could. *Now*, she could fight to keep both Bryan and Trevor in her life. She didn't have to sit back and let it happen. She had the legal right to see Trevor, and she had the moral right to, as well.

And as for Bryan… She had love to keep Bryan from leaving her. Hers for him. Yes, he was angry—rightfully so, perhaps—but she'd been planning to tell him the truth—the *whole* truth. That she loved him and about Trevor. She'd been planning to tell him tonight, actually, and if it hadn't been for him finding that video, she would have in her own way.

Which still could have gotten you to this point.

She shoved her conscience aside. She wasn't listening to that annoying voice anymore. She owed it to Trevor to fix this and she owed it to herself. She owed Bryan, too. For so much, but especially for the excitement and love she'd seen in his eyes when she'd said yes to him. They could get through this. He just had to listen.

***

"I'm sure she had her reasons, Bryan." His mother wrapped him in a hug.

It was times like these when he was so thankful to have her.

No, that wasn't true. He'd been thankful every day of his life that she'd taken him in when his own mother hadn't wanted him.

Just like Trevor's…

Where was Mindy? Why was Jenna raising his son? What was wrong with his gene pool that the mothers left their children—and, dear God, if he and Jenna *had* created a baby the other night would the same thing happen to that child?

Bryan held his mom tighter, the one rock in his stormy sea of self-doubt. "Why, Mom? Why would Mindy just walk out of his life? Why wouldn't she have found me?"

His mom pulled back and cupped his face in her small, strong hands, the gleam in her eye fierce, like a mother bear defending her cub. "Maybe she looked, Bryan. Jenna might not have been lying about all of it. Maybe there are extenuating circumstances."

"There's no excuse for walking away—"

"Bryan, that's not true and you know it. I know you've felt the loss of your birth mother, but you don't know *her* circumstances. We may never know. But she could have been a scared teenager who was all alone. She could have been thinking of what was best for you. There are a hundred different scenarios about why she gave you up, but the fact is, she did and Henry and I adopted you. We chose you, Bryan. Don't you remember me telling you that? We could have said no, we could have waited for another one, but we didn't. We saw you and we fell in love with you and knew you would make our family complete. I wish it were enough for you."

"It is, Mom." And it was. Suddenly, just like that, Bryan realized it was enough. It was *more* than enough. In a world where divorce was almost fifty percent, his parents had stayed together until the 'til-death-do-us-part part had come true, and he and Kyle had always known they were loved and wanted. Their parents had told them time and again about how they'd chosen them because they'd fallen in love with them on first sight and Bryan had grown up never doubting that love.

No, it was his birth mother's love he'd doubted, but he finally realized that he couldn't live his life on that. The truth of it was, Jenna loved Trevor as fiercely and as much as Tabitha Lassiter loved *him*, and before he'd known the truth about Trevor's parentage, Bryan had been both thankful and envious of how much Jenna loved Trevor.

That hadn't changed because she hadn't carried him. If anything, it only made his admiration for her stronger. His appreciation of her love for his son greater.

She'd come find him. Bryan knew that. As soon as she recovered from him finding out the truth and her devastation over him taking Trevor, Jenna would track him down. This wasn't over between them.

And, hell, he didn't want it to be.

He turned away from his mom and shoved his hands into his pockets. He wanted Jenna. He'd fallen in love with her—with who he thought she was.

But she had to be that person somewhere. He'd connected with her. Their lovemaking hadn't just been physical. It'd moved the heavens and the earth just like all the poets spouted. He'd felt it. He'd known it, had believed in it. It couldn't be a lie.

"Listen to her, Bryan. Give her a chance to tell you the truth. Then judge her. You might have done the same thing in her position."

"I'd never deny a child his birthright."

"You don't know what you'd do in those circumstances. And you owe it to Trevor to find out the truth. Remember that. At the bottom of all of this is a little boy who has just been removed from the only mother he's ever known. Think what that would have done to you at his age, Bryan."

Ouch. Mom didn't use guilt often, but when she did, it was effective.

He drew in a ragged breath and pulled his hands from his pockets. "You're right, Mom. I overreacted."

"No, you *re*acted. And just like you don't know what you would have done in Jenna and Mindy's positions, no one knows what they'd do in yours. So cut yourself some slack and do the same to Jenna. Hear her out."

"You're assuming she's going to want to talk to me."

"Oh, I'm not assuming. I know. Because she just pulled up in the driveway."

Chapter Forty

Bryan met her halfway. The symbolism wasn't lost on Jenna, but she wasn't sure he'd done it on purpose.

"I don't think Trevor should hear this," he said, proving her point. "Let's go somewhere."

He held out his hand for her keys since she'd parked him in, and Jenna gave them to him. It wasn't worth fighting over.

He backed out of the driveway. "I took Bobby home and my mom's with Trevor."

She nodded, knowing Bryan would have made some provision before leaving. He loved Trevor.

She had to remember that. And *he* had to remember it. "Where are we going?"

His fingers that had been thrumming on the steering wheel stopped. "I don't know… Somewhere we won't be interrupted." He glanced at the dashboard clock. "Shit. I have to open the club. Let's go there, and then we can talk in the apartment."

The apartment where they'd made love. The club where they'd made love…

Jenna wasn't sure she could handle the memories if this didn't work out.

***

Backstage was a hustle of activity like the night she'd

danced, though, luckily this time, no one was getting sick and Bryan was able to do his register and inventory functions quickly, then handed the reins over to a big guy named Tanner who was half undressed—or actually half-dressed since those clothes would be coming off in a little bit—as a construction worker, and led her up to the apartment.

What a difference a few hours and a giant lie made.

"Why did you lie to me?"

Bryan hadn't even let her step two feet into the apartment before he tossed the opening volley.

"I didn't know you, Bryan. I didn't know how you'd react."

"What gave you the right to care how I'd react? Why do you get to be the gatekeeper for this information? Where's Mindy to own up to all of this? You two looked pretty chummy on the tape; you can't tell me you haven't heard from her since she just upped and left. Does the woman even care about her child?"

Tears threatened to choke her, but Jenna swallowed them She owed it to all of them to get this story out in its entirety. "Let's sit, Bryan."

"I prefer to stand."

"You're going to want to sit for this. It's not at all how you're imagining it."

Bryan sat. On the recliner. Away from her.

So Jenna got off the sofa and sat on the floor beside him. She needed to be beside him because when he learned the truth… Bryan wasn't callous. He was hurting. And this would make him hurt more.

"Mindy had cancer. She found out while she was pregnant and she elected to go through with the pregnancy without any treatment so she could give Trevor his best shot at life."

"What?" Bryan's voice was harsh, ragged. As full of emotion as hers.

She nodded. "That's why she's not here. That's why she couldn't find you. She looked, oh, yes, she looked, but the diagnosis was awful and then her only focus was on making it to the end. Making it to the birth so her life wouldn't have been in vain." She went on to tell him just who Mindy was to her, about the guilt that Mindy had shared with her on her deathbed of taking her father from her. Jenna had, of course, absolved her—Mindy was as much a victim of the whole mess as she had been, and Jenna had never blamed her.

"So she signed Trevor over to me. We went to a lawyer and had it all done properly so that I'm his legal guardian. And because her mother had died and she had no one, she wanted me to tell everyone that Trevor was my son. She didn't want him to be the kid whose mom got pregnant at a bachelor party and didn't know his father. I'd had a boyfriend and my mom was still around. Plus, I, well, the other baby… People wouldn't have been surprised when I showed up with a child."

"You allowed her to use your pain?"

"It didn't matter, Bryan. I wanted—*we* wanted—to do what was best for Trevor. And that was knowing he was loved and wanted and his life was stable. We'd actually hoped my fiancé at the time, Carl, would be willing to adopt him as well, so Trevor would grow up in a two-parent home, loved and cared for and secure in his life."

"What happened?"

"Carl didn't want someone else's child. He wanted his or none at all."

Bryan's face got hard. "*Someone else's child*? That's how he referred to Trevor?"

She left out the bastard part. No need to make it worse than it already was. She'd spare him that. "Yes. I know. Awful isn't it? I tried to tell him that Trevor would be *our* child, but Carl couldn't get beyond biology. So we broke it off and I've raised Trevor ever since."

"But why didn't you tell me? When you knew who I was to him, when you saw that I wanted to be in his life—when I proposed to you—why didn't you tell me then?"

This was the hard part, though remembering Mindy's death had been hard, too. But this… this could shape their future and if she messed it up…

"I was scared, Bryan. Just like I am now. So scared that you would do something to take him away from me. We knew the adoption could be questioned because the father hadn't signed away his parental rights. It was always there, hanging over my head, that Trevor's father could come back into the picture and want him. Might even be able to win a case for custody and I'd have to share him, or worse, lose him.

"So when I saw you on my porch, when I saw your eyes, and I knew who you had to be… I panicked. I'd been living with this half-truth for so long, I just kept it going. I couldn't tell you. Even after you proposed… I figured it was to make us a family. And I was okay with that. It might have been different if you were in love with me, but you aren't and I couldn't risk anything because of Trevor.

"He loves you. And you love him. And us being together makes so much sense that I was thrilled to continue the lie for him. Or so I thought. But then…" She gulped. "Then things changed and I had to tell you the truth. I *was* going to tell you the truth. I was. I'd decided tonight in the grocery store that I had to. I'd planned to come clean after we put him to bed tonight, and ironically, I was going to show you the video." Her voice cracked and the tears she'd worked so hard to keep from letting loose wouldn't be denied any longer. "I wasn't trying to keep you from finding out, Bryan; I was just trying to make sure I wouldn't lose him."

The club's music thudded mutedly from below them, while Jenna held her breath, waiting for Bryan to say or do something. Anything. This unknowing was almost worse than if he told her get the best attorney in town because he was going to fight her for full custody.

"What changed, Jenna?"

"What?"

"You said that things changed. What things?"

Jenna looked at him. Here it was. Her moment of truth. Did she have the courage to go for it? What if she did and lost?

What if you don't and still *lose?*

Damn her conscience.

"I…" She licked her lips. "I fell in love with you."

The music marked the time it took Bryan to answer, every beat drumming into her soul.

Bryan leaned over and reached for her hands. "You're not going to lose him, Jenna."

"What?" She hadn't expected those words.

He drew her to her feet and stood beside her, so close beside her, and brought their joined hands to his heart. "You're not going to lose Trevor. Or me either if you can forgive me for thinking the worst of you. For not being there for you when you and Mindy were going through something so unbelievably awful that it amazes me you're not bitter and angry. That you can still love Trevor so fully and completely as if you had given birth to him yourself. That you've changed your life for him and given up the man you'd planned to marry for him. There's no greater love in this world and you've proven it beyond a doubt—even when you didn't *have* to prove it. You did it because you wanted to. Any child would be lucky to have you for his mother."

He kissed her fingers, lingering on the one where he'd put his mother's ring. "Just like any man would be lucky to have you as the mother of his children, whether genetic or adopted."

He cupped her cheek, not letting go of her hands with his other one. "I want to be that lucky guy, Jenna. I don't want to throw away what could be because I made a mistake. I understand your fear, and, frankly, I love that you went to such lengths to protect him. I couldn't ask for a better mother for my children, and more importantly, if you love me even half as much as you love him, it'd be more than enough for me."

"But I don't, Bryan."

He stiffened and the light I his eyes disappeared. "You don't?"

She licked her lips and shook her head. "No."

"Oh."

And then he dropped her hands and stepped back. Away from her.

She reached for him. "Where are you going?"

He winced and swiped the hand that had, moments ago, been holding her face so tenderly, across his jaw, the rasp of his stubble grating through the silence.

"I don't want to force myself on you. We can come to some amicable arrangement with Trevor, I'm sure. I mean, we both love him and wants what's best for him and—"

It was her turn to cup his cheek. "You're doing it again."

"Again?"

She nodded. "Making another mistake." She took another step closer. "I said I didn't love you half as much as I love Trevor. I love you *just* as much. In a completely different way. One that will take me a lifetime to prove to you."

"A lifetime?"

She nodded again, liking this unsure side to him. "*Our* lifetime. If you still want it, that is."

Then Bryan's arms swept around her and he crushed her to him, hiking her up so her lips were even with his, and Jenna had to say that she liked this side of him even more.

"Oh, I want a lifetime with you, lady. Most

definitely." He lowered his lips and just before they met hers he stopped. "And for the record? I'm *in love* with you, too. Just so there's no mistake about that."

And there never was.

The End

Read on for Gage and Lara's romance,
Book 1 in the *BeefCake, Inc series,*
Beefcake & Cupcakes

The Morning After

This wasn't her hotel room.

The suit jacket tossed on the chair was Lara's first clue.

The discarded matching pants on the floor in front of it was her second.

The dip in the mattress as someone got off the bed behind her was her third.

Oh my God. What had she done?

Well, it was pretty obvious what she'd done, but, oh God...

Lara clamped her eyes shut as that someone came around the foot of the bed, peeking only when she heard the bathroom door slide open.

Oh my. The guy's bare naked ass looked really good. Probably better out of those pants than in them—too bad she didn't remember what it'd looked like in them.

Too bad she didn't remember him.

The door clicked closed and Lara shot to her feet—to the second shock of the morning.

She was wearing only a t-shirt. And it wasn't hers.

She didn't want to think about whose it was or how she came to be in said t-shirt; she just wanted to grab her dress, shoes, and purse, and get the hell out before her one-and-only one-night stand finished doing whatever it was a one-night stand did the morning after.

She scooped the dress off the dresser—no, she wasn't

going to think about how it'd gotten there—tore his shirt up over her head then the dress down over it, and bagged looking for her bra. She just wanted out.

Her shoes were next to the chair—one was under it—and her purse, thank God, was hanging on the hotel room door.

Twenty-five seconds. That's all it took her to escape from the most un-Lara-like thing she'd ever done in her life.

It took thirty-five more seconds for the damn elevator to make its way to the—she squinted at the floor marker above the "Down" arrow—the tenth floor.

Thank God there was no one in the elevator. She didn't need witnesses to her walk of shame.

God, wouldn't Jeff be shocked to see her now? "Sexually boring and uninspiring" was what he'd said to explain the affair—among others—but this walk of shame negated those.

She couldn't believe it. Thirty-years-old with her own up-and-coming bakery, yet one too many shots at her college roommate's bachelorette party had her picking up some random guy for a night of uninhibited monkey sex to soothe her smashed-to-smithereens ego from an ex who didn't deserve the time of day let alone this kind of prove-him-wrong strategy.

It *had* been uninhibited monkey sex, right?

She closed her eyes and tried to conjure up an image, but the last thing she could remember was jitterbugging on the dance floor.

She didn't know how to jitterbug. But, apparently, that hadn't stopped her.

Oh, God, her head. And her stomach. And that cotton mouth thing…

The bell dinged as the elevator arrived at the second floor. She fumbled for her room key and stumbled out into a blessedly empty hallway. Her room was down a few doors, and thankfully she'd decided to forego a roommate on this trip.

Well, a regular roommate.

Who was the guy? She didn't even remember what he looked like, let alone his name.

She groaned as she made it into her hotel room. How bad was it that the only recallable part of him was his bare naked ass and *that* she only remembered because she'd seen it on her way out the door?

She peeled the dress off her body—it'd been on backwards—and headed into the bathroom. Shower, breakfast, and a big glass of orange juice, then she could grab her car and get the hell out of Dodge so she wouldn't have to risk running into her biggest regret anytime soon.

But the question was: what was her regret for? That she'd picked him up in the first place, or that she couldn't remember a damn thing about what had come after?

***

Gage ran the towel through his hair, then wrapped it around his hips. Didn't want to shock Sleeping Beauty out there with nudity upon opening her gorgeous eyes.

He caught his smile in the mirror. Yeah, it was wolfish, but why shouldn't it be? He'd ended up with the most gorgeous woman at the party, and that included the bride-to-be.

Of course, he'd broken his own rules to do so—no partying with the patrons—but she'd walked in and knocked him sideways.

It'd be funny, really, if it weren't so, well, not. He never went for short, dark, and curvy. Model-thin bombshells were more his type. At least, they had been. But then she'd walked in, her curves making his palms sweat, her curls begging for his fingers to dive in and hold on, and those chocolate brown eyes... They'd screamed *bedroom* so loudly they'd almost drowned out the music, and he'd had a hard time keeping his mind on the show.

Thank God the guys knew their shit. Markus had known it a little too well; he'd been focused on Lara from the first bump-and-grind number.

Luckily, no one had questioned the quick change-up in routines he'd made so that Markus was off stage until the middle of the second act.

By then, the shots that'd been flowing around that table had insured Lara's interest had no longer been solely on Markus.

That's when he'd made his move.

Made his move. Gage groaned. What was he—twenty? He never had to make moves; women flocked to him.

But she'd been wedged in the corner of her booth, surrounded by friends, staring at the stage, and hadn't looked like she was going to get out anytime soon.

He grabbed his toothbrush. He should have moved sooner. Then maybe she wouldn't have done those last two shots. The woman was a lightweight. She'd made it to the hotel elevator and had literally passed out in his arms. It'd put a damper on his evening, but not his libido.

He just hoped she was more awake this morning.

He finished brushing his teeth and poured a glass of water. She was going to need it and it'd give him the excuse to sit beside her.

And hopefully do much more.

He opened the door softly. He wanted to be the one to wake her, not the noise or the light from the bathroom.

Except… she was gone.

He slumped against the doorframe. Served him right. He played to the fantasies of hundreds of women every weekend, but the one whose fantasy he'd personally wanted to grant apparently had no interest in letting him.

And here's the first in the *Once-Upon-A-Time Romance* series,
Beauty and The Best

Once upon a time...

a long time ago,
there lived a beast of a man,
locked within a castle
with no one to love him.

This is not his story.

This is the story of another man,
locked within himself,
and the Beauty
who sets him free.

Chapter One

There's a naked man in my kitchen.

The thought registered just as the terse, "Who the hell are you?" had Jolie Gardener spinning around faster than a figure skater on speed.

He had the nerve to ask this? He of the broad shoulders, six-pack abs, and other, nice, um, parts...

Really. A naked man. In her kitchen.

Well, *technically*, she was in a naked man's kitchen. Even more technically, she was in a naked Todd Best's kitchen—and there wasn't one hint of self-consciousness or embarrassment on his part. Of course with that body, there shouldn't be. The guy *should* flaunt his nudity for the world to see. Which, at present, consisted of one single, solitary person: Jolie Gardener, aspiring writer and personal chef extraordinaire.

"Well?" His hands slammed to his hips.

"You're naked," she squeaked, which, really, was the only way to state that kind of obvious.

"I'm what?" Mr. Six-Pack Abs glanced down.

Jolie tried not to—so unsuccessfully it was pitiful.

"Shit," he muttered. "I am. I, uh, fell asleep last night…"

As butter sizzled in the new super-slick omelet pan on the top-of-the-line range, Jolie's gaze alternated between some rock-hard abs and a scruffy eight a.m. shadow while her fingers danced along the speckled granite countertop in search of a napkin, placemat, oven mitt… something.

Mercifully, they scooped up a thick dishtowel that, in her world, would constitute a very plush, very luxurious hand towel from The Ritz or The Four Seasons, but which, here, apparently, was used to soak up water from designer flatware. She dangled it in the direction of Mr. *Au Naturel*. "Here."

He placed an empty bottle of Jim Beam on the island countertop with a *clink*, then took the towel with a grunt. "So, who are you, what are you doing in my kitchen, and would you mind turning around?"

She turned. "I'm the new girl the agency sent over."

"Hell. There better be some aspirin left," he muttered beside her, his bare (of course) feet making no sound on the limestone floor.

She peeked over at him.

His eyebrow soared skyward.

Right.

She turned back to the sizzling butter. Which had started to burn. Sigh.

He rummaged around in one of the drawers as she carried the pan to the sink. Trying to impress the new boss on her first day with his favorite omelet ranchero and she burned the butter. Not good, but then, it wasn't exactly her fault because nowhere in those papers she'd signed with her employment agency, Domestic Gods & Goddesses, was mention made of an optional dress code. And she didn't care how much they were paying her, nudity did tend to throw one off. As for the alcohol-before-breakfast debacle, she wasn't even going to address that. His rudeness said it all.

And here, *she'd* been worried about making a good impression on *him*.

A click of plastic bottle cap followed by a shake of the bottle, the fridge opening, a gulp, then Naked Guy sighing punctuated the silence before she turned on the faucet. She cleaned out the pan, all the while the Naughty Girl side of her brain screaming, "Turn around!" with the other, Jolie side, going, "You *want* to keep this job?"

Self-preservation being the backbone of her existence since being dumped into the foster care system, she decided to listen to the Jolie side—no matter how much groaning Naughty Girl did.

Naughty Girl, however, couldn't resist a peek, and was rewarded with a swish of his longish golden hair, a flex of his well-defined arm, and an accompanying sizzle to her own nerve endings.

So not good. Jolie had known he was a hunk before she accepted this position. Had had quite the crush on him, too. How could she not? The guy had been plastered all over every magazine in the country for years, most especially here in his hometown.

Todd Best. *The* Best, as the media had dubbed him. And rightfully so. The man's landscape paintings were hanging in every high-end hotel, public library, and courtroom in the country. Even the White House, for Pete's sake. Not that she had an eye for art, but when a painting looked like the scene down the road and made her think she was standing there, feeling leaves rustling, smelling fresh cut grass, hearing birds singing in the trees and ducks quacking on the pond, the whole set-up, that, to her, was talent.

And, of course, there'd been his fairytale marriage. But then, sadly, his wife had died suddenly and he'd moved out of their home, turned the reins of his company over to his brother, and put down his paint brushes.

Yes, Jolie had known *exactly* who she'd be working for. That'd been half the incentive.

"So, new girl, do you have a name? And what are you doing here today?"

Since he was talking, she assumed it was safe to turn around.

The old adage about making an "ASS out of U and ME" proved true.

Although he was the one with the A-S-S. And what a

nice one it was. As was the muscled shoulder leaning against the stainless steel of the microwave above the stove, and the ninety-degree jut of his jaw line, the sculpted cheekbones, a perfectly proportioned brow, the fall of hair over his forehead…

She tore her gaze away from the visual smorgasbord and, traitors that they were, her eyes headed south.

Thank goodness he had the dish towel spread across his nether regions like a loincloth. But a hot guy in a loincloth was just as distracting as a naked hot guy. And she'd seen him in both. Or not in both. Whatever.

She ordered her eyes back on the pan. "Um yes, I do have a name, and as to what I'm doing here, I think that's obvious—burning the butter for your morning omelet." She raised the pan to illustrate and managed a quick push with her hip to get him to back away from the stove so she could start cooking again, praying all the while she wasn't hitting something vital.

Luckily, the guy had quick reflexes—or a good hunch—'cause he stepped out of the way before her hip came anywhere close to anything important, saving them the extreme embarrassment of *that*.

"How'd you get in?" Mr. Clothing-Optional asked.

Okay, what was the protocol here? How long did one actually have to converse with a buck-naked human being before someone said something about it? Or did a strategically placed dishtowel negate all observances of nudity?

"Look, um, *Mister*." What did one call their bare boss? Todd? Sir? *Big guy*? "How 'bout you go freshen up a bit and I'll make breakfast. We can have our chat when we're both, um, well, prepared for the day. 'Kay?"

"Fine. I'll get dressed. Then we'll talk."

"You do that."

As he sauntered—okay, maybe that was her overactive imagination, because could one *really* saunter with a Jim Beam-sized hangover?—from the fourteen-foot-ceiling kitchen with its state-of-the-art appliances that looked as if they'd come out of their packing boxes yesterday, so stainless steel shiny she could have used them as a mirror to fix her lipstick—if she'd worn lipstick—and she inhaled enough oxygen to jump-start primordial ooze.

Which posed a whole new set of problems for this job. How was she supposed to focus if she kept getting sidetracked by the physical?

But she would.

She could.

Heck, if she could outwit social workers and manage to keep her teenaged self out of the gutter, not to mention, actually *make* something of her life, she could certainly keep her own libido in check.

She had to. Her job, her livelihood, and all her dreams depended on it.

***

Each step up the goddamned grandiose stairway reverberated through Todd's skull, setting his teeth on edge and his stomach roiling. Why the hell hadn't the builder put carpet on these stairs?

Todd grabbed his head with one hand, keeping the other one hovering above his groin with the damned kitchen towel. It'd be funny if it weren't so ungodly pitiful.

He, a grown man, hiding his modesty behind a piece of eight-by-twelve cotton because he didn't have enough sense to pass out in his own bed.

He kicked open the bedroom door and grimaced. Bare, tan walls, minimal furniture, and the fucking king-sized bed mocked him.

He knew exactly why he'd chosen the couch.

And he wasn't about to dwell on it. He'd done enough dwelling last night. More than enough, apparently.

He barreled through to the bathroom, his refusal to dwell on the reason just one more part of the person he'd become in the past two years.

And the poor woman downstairs who'd had to witness the person he'd become last night… God, wasn't it just *perfect* she'd shown up this morning?

Todd grabbed the shower handle and turned the water full force to hot. He'd burn the alcohol out of his system if he had to. No one deserved that greeting her first day on the job. Even if it was his house.

Todd sucked in a breath as he stepped beneath the pelting liquid fire and realized he wasn't as tough as he pretended. He turned the spigot back to warm and leaned his forehead against the cool ivory tile, and listened to the phone ring in his bedroom. Let the machine get the fucking thing. He couldn't deal with the calls and the goddamned hounding.

Not today.

The water ran into his eyes and he wiped it away with the heels of his hands. Why *today*? Why'd she have to start *today*?

Why'd she have to start at all?

Why wouldn't they all just leave him alone?

***

"You see what you're up against, Jonathan?" The archangel, Raphael, waved his hand in front of the computer monitor in the executive office of Domestic Gods & Goddesses and the split-screen images of Todd and Jolie faded to a serene, heavenly blue screen saver. "Todd doesn't think he's ready to let go of his wife's memory and Jolie is still a work in progress. Getting these two together could be difficult."

Jonathan Griff took a seat on one of the burgundy chairs opposite the mahogany desk and sipped the lemonade Raphael had given him. Well, perhaps he gulped it. This was a big assignment. Todd was front-page news. Still. After two years out of the public eye, the man could have media coverage in an instant. He was high profile. He was hot.

What if Jonathan failed? Not only would Todd and Jolie, his Charges, suffer, but it'd be public. Then he'd never earn his wings.

Of course, personal aggrandizement was not what a Guardian should worry about. His Charges' happiness should be his sole focus.

He'd had some success in the past, but there always seemed to be *something* he never got quite right. Could he take that risk with such a prominent case?

"You can do this, Jonathan."

The archangel's words reverberated inside his mind—another talent Jonathan hadn't yet mastered. Why was Raphael offering him this assignment? The archangel had no malice in him so he couldn't want to see him fail. Perhaps he had an overabundance of Hope?

Jonathan, left eye twitching, touched the keypad and the close-up of Todd's face reappeared. The poor man was in so much pain and, while The Boss had a Plan for Todd, Jonathan couldn't bear to see someone hurting.

And then there was Jolie. No one should have to endure what she had as a child. She was trying so hard to be all right that she'd almost convinced herself she was.

But she wasn't. Not really. She played a good game, but she craved acceptance so much that she'd do anything to get it.

Well, almost anything.

Jonathan smiled, the twitch subsiding. He'd read her dossier. The girl had a fine moral character, as did Todd.

Character and a run of bad luck; that's what the two of them shared. Not to mention the wellspring of love in their souls. That's why the request for their happiness had been selected for fulfillment.

Now it was up to him to help them along.

Jonathan set the lemonade on an antique walnut-inlay table beside him and hopped off the chair to stand before the archangel. If Raphael thought he was capable of this job, then he owed it to his Charges to be the best Guardian possible.

"Yes, sir. I believe I can help them."

About the Author

Judi Fennell has had her nose in a book and her head in some celestial realm all her life, including those early years when her mom would exhort her to "get outside!" instead of watching *Bewitched* or *I Dream of Jeannie* on television. So she did—right into Dad's hammock with her Nancy Drew books.

These days she's more likely to have her nose in her laptop and her head (and the rest of her) at a favorite writing spot, but she's still reading either her latest manuscript or friends' books.

A PRISM Award and Golden Leaf Award winner, Judi loves to hear from her readers. Connect with her at:

www.JudiFennell.com
www.facebook.com/#!/JudiFennell
www.facebook.com/#!/JudiFennell.Author
twitter.com/JudiFennell

Books by Judi Fennell

The Tritone Trilogy

In Over Her Head
Wild Blue Under
Catch of a Lifetime

Bottled Magic series

I Dream of Genies
Genie Knows Best
Magic Gone Wild

Once-Upon-A-Time Romance series

Beauty and The Best
If The Shoe Fits (coming soon)
Fairest of Them All (coming soon)

BeefCake, Inc. series

Beefcake & Cupcakes
Beefcake & Mistakes
Beefcake & Retakes (coming soon)